How to Tame a Willful Wife

a Willful Wife

CHRISTY ENGLISH

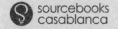

sourcebooks
casablanca

Published by Sourcebooks Casablanca, an imprint of Sourcebooks, Inc.
P.O. Box 4410, Naperville, Illinois 60567-4410
(630) 961-3900
Fax: (630) 961-2168
www.sourcebooks.com

Printed and bound in Canada.
WC 10 9 8 7 6 5 4 3 2 1

For
my mother, Karen English,
and
my father, Carl English

ACT I

"Thou must be married to no man but me."

The Taming of the Shrew
Act 2, Scene 1

Chapter 1

Montague Estates, Yorkshire
September 1816

EVERYTHING DEPENDED ON THIS ONE SHOT.

Caroline Montague pulled back on her bow, the bite of the string sharp against her fingers. She closed one eye, sighted down the slender shaft of myrtle, and let her arrow fly.

There was a moment of stunned silence, followed by polite applause led by the man beside her. She had scored a perfect hit in the center of the target, besting every man present. Her parents would be furious.

"A lucky shot, though impressive, Miss Montague," remarked Victor Winthrop, Viscount Carlyle. Since she was not an official competitor, he had still won the day, but Caroline was pleased to wipe the smug look off his face.

"Luck had nothing to do with it, my lord." She curtsied to the company gathered on her father's lawn and tried to smile demurely—a feat more challenging than any archery contest.

These men were here with one purpose: to win her hand in marriage. She was on sale to the highest bidder to cover her father's mounting debts. But damn them all if they thought she would be an easy prize.

Caroline handed her bow to a nearby footman and took up the trophy Carlyle had won, a golden bowl inscribed with the image of Venus rising from the waves, an object of art her father had liberated during the Italian campaign against Napoleon.

"Forgive my impudence, gentlemen. I can never resist a target when it presents itself." The men around her chuckled.

"To the man of the hour, Lord Carlyle. May his arrow always fly swift and far, and may his aim improve," Caroline said.

She grinned, meeting the earl's blue eyes as she handed him the golden bowl. His gaze shifted from the curve of her breasts to her face, and he gave her a rueful smile. All the men had spent that morning eyeing her curves. Carlyle was the first man to stare so openly, and to laugh at himself afterward. She laughed with him, not knowing that the eyes of her husband-to-be lingered on her even then, and on the man who stood beside her.

❧

Anthony Carrington, the Earl of Ravensbrook, his face as forbidding as stone, stared at the man who would become his father-in-law. Only his great respect for Baron Montague on the field of battle kept him in the room at all. "I have never seen such blatant disregard for a woman's place in the world. To take up arms among men, to best a suitor with a bow, even a man like Carlyle, is unseemly."

Even his own mistress, Angelique, an experienced woman of the world, would never be so brazen.

"Ravensbrook, consider," Lord Montague said. "My daughter is very young."

"All the more reason she should smile and obey, not humiliate the men around her."

Lord Montague sighed. "I am the first to admit she is spoiled. And headstrong. After my last son died, she has been the light of my life."

Anthony heard the sorrow in his old friend's voice and left the rest of his protest unspoken. He fingered the marriage contract that lay on the mahogany table in front of him. He had ridden for four days straight with a special license from London, so the banns would not have to be read. He could marry Caroline within the week and return to Shropshire to beget an heir, and his old friend's debts would be paid with honor. Every detail of his marriage to Montague's daughter was in order. Everything but the girl.

"Her mother warned me of this, time and time again, but I did not listen," Montague said. "I have been so long on the Continent that Caroline has grown up beyond my reach, without a father's hand to guide her. You must teach her, my lord. I have seen you take a battlefield in less than an hour. Surely you can tame one woman in less than a fortnight."

Anthony did not soften. His sister had paid the price of a family's indulgence and would continue to pay it for the rest of her life.

"She must be pure," Anthony said. "I cannot present

a woman to society as my wife without a guarantee of virtue, both in the past and in the future."

Frederick Montague rose slowly to his feet. "I have been your friend as well as your commander. I love you, Anthony, as if you were my own son. But if such words pass your lips again, I will not be able to answer for myself."

Anthony swallowed his ire and tried not to dwell on the mistakes his sister, Anne, had made. Frederick's daughter had to be more sensible than his sister had been. He was allowing his fears and his pain from the past to color his view of the present. And now, in his fear, he had begun to insult his host and his friend. Frederick needed a way out of the mire of his finances. He needed to see his daughter married and settled before the year was out. Anthony would do a great deal more than marry a beautiful, penniless girl to help the man who had twice saved his life.

"Forgive me, Frederick, if I spoke harshly. But she has too much freedom, and you have been away for so many years. How can you be sure?"

"She would never betray me by tossing aside her virtue under a country haystack. Caroline has known her duty all of her life. She has always known that her marriage would be arranged as soon as I came home from the war. The war is over, and I am here. It is time."

Anthony bowed once. His friend was an honorable man, but like all honorable men, he could not conceive of dishonor in those he loved. If Anne could fall victim to a seducer's lures, then any woman could.

"Of course, any daughter of yours would be virtuous, Frederick. I never should have said otherwise. But I would speak with her alone."

Montague met Anthony's eyes, and for a moment, it was as if the baron could read his thoughts. Anthony wondered if even the protection of the Prince Regent had not been enough to squelch all rumors. Perhaps his sister's seduction was common knowledge, in spite of all that had been sacrificed to conceal it. Anthony stared into the face of his friend but could see no evidence of pity or contempt. Frederick knew nothing of Anne, then. Anthony wished he could be certain of it.

"You may speak with Caroline," Frederick said. "If you find that she is not virtuous, you may cast the marriage contract into the fire."

Caroline strode into her sitting room, slamming the door behind her. The sound gave her a small measure of satisfaction. The long evening, with its endless dinner and its games of charades felt interminable. Her suitors had not come alone but had brought their sisters and mothers with them. All London women wanted to talk about was fashion and one another. She hoped her father chose a match for her soon so she could get a moment's peace.

After years of living in a society of fewer than twenty families, the influx of London nobility into her world was more exhausting than she would have believed possible. Southerners, with their superior ways and nasal accents, grated on her nerves.

How could they talk so much without really saying anything? And yet she was honor bound to marry one of them. Why her father could not find her a decent man from Yorkshire, she could not imagine.

She stopped fuming then, for in the shadows of her bedroom, she found a man sitting in her favorite armchair.

"Good evening, Caroline."

She opened her mouth to scream, but reminded herself she was not a fool, nor was she a swooning female like those in the novels she read. She closed her mouth again, the voice of her mother rising from her memory, telling her that open mouths catch only flies.

"Who are you?" she asked, working to keep her voice even and calm.

"A friend of your father's."

"I've never met you before. If you were Papa's friend, he would have presented you along with the rest of my suitors."

The man laughed, his chestnut eyes running over her body. His black hair brushed his collar and was tossed back from his face to reveal a strong jaw. Dressed in a linen shirt and dark trousers, he had cast off his coat, and it lay beside him on the arm of the chair. His green-and-gold waistcoat gleamed in the candlelight, his cravat loosely tied.

His large body was too big for her delicate Louis XVI furniture, but he sat with one ankle casually crossed over the other knee, as comfortable as he might have been in his own drawing room.

"I am your friend, too, Caroline."

"You are no friend of mine."

He was the most beautiful man she had ever seen.

She thought it foolish to call a man beautiful, but she could not deny it. And clearly, he agreed with her.

In spite of his arrogance, this man was worth ten of every fool she had spoken to that day. There was no doubt in her mind that if he had entered the archery contest that morning, she would not have beaten him.

There was a latent power in his gaze, in the stillness of his posture that made her think of a lion set to devour her. Instead of frightening her, the thought gave her a moment's pleasure. She had never before met a man who seemed to be as strong-willed as she was. She wondered for the first time in her life if this dark-eyed man might be her equal.

She dismissed that thought as folly. No matter how beautiful, whether he was her equal or not, a man alone in her room could be there for no good reason. The heat in his eyes warmed her skin, but she forced herself to ignore that, too. She would be ruined if anyone even suspected she had spoken with a man alone in her room. He might be there to kidnap her for the ransom her father would pay...or worse.

As if to echo her thoughts, the stranger spoke. His words were like cold water on her skin, waking her from the madness of her attraction for him.

"I've come to claim you, Caroline."

She did not look at him again but reached into her reticule. No man would claim her. She would be damned if her father's work, and her own, would come to nothing. Not this man, or any other, would touch her that night.

She took a deep, calming breath. Her father's men had trained her for just such a moment, when she would be alone and threatened. Now that the moment had come, she was ready.

"You'll 'claim' me only when you pull the last weapon from my cold, dead hand."

She drew her knife from her reticule and threw it at him.

Her aim was ill-timed, for the man moved with sudden grace and speed, slipping like an eel out of the way of her missile. Her dagger was sharp, and its tip embedded deep in the cushion of her favorite chair. Caroline swore and turned to flee.

She did not get far, for he caught her arm before she reached the door. She moved to strike him, but he dodged her blow with ease. He caught her wrist in one hand, wrapping his other arm around her waist. "Settle, Caroline, settle. I mean you no harm."

"Then let me go."

"I will release you if you promise to stay and speak with me."

His scent surrounded her, spicy and sweet together. She took in the smell of leather, the scent that made her think of freedom, and of her stallion, Hercules. The stranger held her but not too close, his hands gentle now that she had stopped trying to kill him.

"I have nothing to say to you," she said.

"I have something to say to you. Give me just five minutes, and then I will go."

She nodded once. He released her, stepping away carefully as if she were a wild mare he hoped to tame. She stood suspended in the center of his gaze, his unswerving regard surrounding her like a soft trap.

There was something in the way he moved, in the heat of his hand on her arm that was distracting.

She forced herself to forget his touch and the sweet scent of him. She kept a careful distance between them, moving with unstudied grace to light the lamp on the table by the door. As her match caught, the lamp cast a buttery light, bringing the room out of shadow. She infused her voice with a confidence she did not feel.

"Speak your piece, then go."

"You are used to giving orders, it seems, Miss Montague. You will find I am not accustomed to taking them."

She drew her breath up from the depths of her stomach and used all the power her father had taught her, giving added strength to her voice. This man claimed he wanted to talk, though he did nothing but plague her. Caroline stared him down, as she had been taught to stare down unruly servants until they bent to her will.

"Give me your name or get out."

The man laughed. He stepped back toward her favorite chair, drawing her blade from the cushion, leaving a few downy feathers to trail the air in its wake. Those bits of down settled on the carpet, and Caroline cursed again. Her mother was always telling her not to throw daggers in the house, that they ruined the furniture.

"My name is for my friends," he said.

His fingers caressed the edge of the blade as he contemplated her, a half smile on his face. Her eyes narrowed. She could not begin to guess why he was so familiar with her. She had met many men that day, but he was not one of them. She would have remembered him.

She kept her voice even, in spite of her rising temper, in spite of her nerves. She did not move to the bellpull to ring for assistance. She could not allow word of his presence in her room to get out to the guests at large. Her reputation would be lost, along with her father's plans to pay his debts from the profit of her marriage.

"My friendship must be earned," she said.

"And yet, I seem to have your enmity, though I have not earned it."

"You're here, aren't you? After I have asked you repeatedly to go? I say again, leave this room, or next time my blade will not miss you."

Caroline kept her eyes on the man who stood holding the weapon he had claimed. His dark gaze drifted from her face to her breasts nestled against the soft silk of her gown. Her breath quickened. She had been ogled a great deal in the past twenty-four hours, but her body responded as if it knew him already.

"I would not attack again, if I were you," he said. His eyes moved over her breasts where they swelled above the high waist of her gown, and over her hips where they curved beneath her skirts, returning once more to her face. "Whatever you choose to do, I am going nowhere yet."

There was a promise in the way he looked at her. Though he was half a room away, she fancied she could feel the heat rising off his body through the thin silk of her gown. Unable to look away from him, like a snake with its charmer, Caroline wondered what it would cost her to stand in that man's heat even for a moment.

"If you will not go, then I will."

"And leave me in possession of the field? I am surprised to find you such a coward."

The fury in her belly rose like a flash fire, lodging itself in her throat so she choked on it. Her anxiety was burned away as she sputtered with ire.

"I would never be afraid of the likes of you."

"No?" He raised her knife to the light before laying it down gently on the mahogany table. "You seemed quite frightened when you first saw me, frightened enough to cast this dagger." He sat in her favorite chair once more and smiled at her. "It seems you missed. Perhaps you need more practice."

"It is dark in here," she said, the excuse paltry in her own ears.

He laughed. "Myself, I prefer a more biddable woman who does not carry knives."

"Then by all means, you have my permission to go to her."

"You will find, Miss Montague, that I do not need your permission for anything."

He did not move to leave but stared at her, taking in the contours of her face as if he were trying to read her soul. She forced her body to relax as she always did before a fight. She thought of the second knife hidden beneath the mahogany table beside him. If she could not get her dagger back, she could always take up the second knife and kill him with it.

The thought was not as comforting as it would have been five minutes before. He watched her, still smiling, as if he knew all her secrets, as if he wished to teach her one or two more.

She shook off the stupor she had fallen into. She dismissed the thought of the hidden knife and turned her mind to escape. Whether or not she lost her reputation, whether or not he thought her a coward, she had to get out of that room.

The man rose to his feet and closed the distance between them so swiftly she did not see him move. She felt only the warm pressure of his hand as he drew her against him. His body was hot on hers where his chest pressed into the softness of her breasts. He breathed in her scent, as if she were a loaf of newly baked bread or some morsel he meant to devour in one bite. He did not keep her standing but sank down once more in her favorite chair, bringing her onto his lap in one smooth motion.

After a day of men ogling her, all eager to paw her if they could, Caroline had had enough. She struggled to free herself from his grip and managed to get at the knife on the table. Her father's training came back to her without thought, without fear. She drew the blade up to his throat but found she could not drive it home. "I could run you through right now, sir. But first, tell me who you are."

"I am impressed, Caroline. You have defended your honor well. But you do not need to defend yourself against me."

"Who are you?" she asked.

"I am Anthony Carrington, the Earl of Ravensbrook. The man you are going marry," he said.

Caroline barely registered the stranger pushing her

arm away from his throat as he claimed her dagger. She blinked at the shock of the news that she was betrothed to this man, and then wondered if he might be lying.

Caroline found herself distracted once more by his touch. He kept one of her arms pinned between his weight and the arm of the chair. He held her other wrist so she could not move against him again. His free arm wrapped around her waist, drawing her close, keeping her safe from falling. They sat together, her skirts foaming around them as she perched on his lap. His thighs were hard beneath her, unyielding. His chest was warm against her breasts.

Their breaths mingled as they looked at each other, his dark eyes holding her prisoner just as his hands did. Caroline forgot about decorum, reveling in the scent of him and in the new-discovered flame he stoked deep in her belly, one that burned even as she touched him. She was still pressed against him, her breath coming short, her mind lost to all but what she felt, when his hand touched her breast.

She leaped like a scalded cat, moving so quickly he lost his grip on her. Freed from his embrace, Caroline was on her feet in an instant. She raised her hand to him, intent on causing him what harm she could.

The man stood and caught her wrist before she struck his face. Her aim was true, and he had to move fast to stop her. They were both breathing hard, as if they had been engaged in mortal combat. They faced each other like enemies, measuring each other with their eyes.

"Never touch me again. Get out of my room," she said. "Get out of my father's house."

His chestnut eyes lost their intensity. The fire in them was banked slowly as he breathed. She watched the effort he made and what it cost him to let her go. She snatched her hand away, rubbing her wrist where his grip had bruised her.

"I had to know if you'd ever been touched before, Caroline."

"I was not, until you sullied me. Now get out."

He straightened, donning his coat with the air of a man pleased with himself and with what he had discovered in her room. Caroline felt the overwhelming need to curse him, but she swallowed the words. She would not give him the satisfaction.

"Good evening, Miss Montague. Until tomorrow."

"If I never see you again, it will be too soon."

Anthony smiled, his dark eyes gleaming as he walked away. "I think you'll change your mind."

"You are wrong, my lord."

"I am never wrong."

Her fingers closed on the dagger he had left on her mahogany table. She threw the knife without thinking, embedding it in the frame of the servants' door, just inches from his head. She heard his mocking laughter as he closed the door behind him.

Chapter 2

CAROLINE STOOD STARING AT THE CLOSED DOOR. SHE strode across the room and drew her dagger from the door frame. A flake of white paint fell from the wound in the wood, and she cursed under her breath.

Marriage to a stranger was bad enough. Marriage to Lord Ravensbrook would be a nightmare.

Her interminable day had gotten even longer. She sank onto her favorite chair, still warm from Anthony Carrington's body. She could not stand to be reminded of his touch. She stood up and tossed the cushions on the floor. Another feather escaped from the tear her dagger had made.

She sighed, placing the knife on the table beside her. Her mother was going to kill her.

She stared with longing at her bed covered with dark green velvet brought from France before the Terror. The softness of that haven beckoned her. She wanted to bury her head under those pillows and forget the man she had just had the misfortune to meet.

Lady Montague walked into the sitting room beyond, the door thrown open before her as if by a great wind. Caroline plastered on a smile and went to meet her. Lady Montague's dark blond hair was streaked with silver, tucked away beneath a cap of lace.

Caroline forced herself to meet her mother's eyes. She knew the baroness saw everything, even things Caroline so often wanted to hide. She could not bear the thought that her mother would look at her and somehow know Lord Ravensbrook had just been there. As long as no one knew of his visit, she could pretend she had never met the insufferable man. Desperate to distract her mother, Caroline curtsied.

No doubt it was the spectacle of her daughter showing obedience that made Lady Montague stop in her tracks, the sound of her lightly tapping feet suddenly silenced on the hard mahogany floor. Caroline realized then she had gone too far with her curtsy, but she braved it out, summoning a sweet smile.

"I have news, Caroline. News that would not wait."

"Will you sit, *Maman*? Shall I call for tea?"

"No, Daughter, I have just drunk pots of tea with the ladies downstairs. Southerners do not know when to go to bed. I am exhausted from all this to-do."

"I am sorry, *Maman*. It is all because of me."

"No, *ma petite*, it is all because you must marry. And marry you will. Your father has made his decision."

She wanted to ask her mother if her betrothed was a tall, beautiful man with black hair, chestnut eyes, and insufferable arrogance but for once in her life, she held her tongue.

Lady Montague was French by birth, and very tiny,

the top of her head coming only to Caroline's sternum. She put her hands on her daughter's arms, drawing her down to kiss her cheek.

"In two days you will have the honor of becoming the wife of Anthony Carrington, the Earl of Ravensbrook.

Two days. The words rang like a death knell over her head. It was bad enough that she would have to spend the rest of her life with that arrogant man. But the thought that her new life would commence in two days was absurd. She would speak with her father. Surely they could extend what was left of her freedom into weeks, not days.

Her mother continued, never acknowledging that her daughter could barely stand upright. "You will live in his country house in Shropshire most of the year. You will be an obedient wife to him, and you will bear him fine sons."

The word *obedient* filled her ears like poison. "But I don't even know him."

"He is rich and titled. You will be a countess. That is what you know of him, and all you need to know."

Caroline swallowed hard. She knew her duty, though it chafed her like an ill-fitting harness on her best horse.

"We could not afford to give you a Season in London," her mother reminded her. "This marriage is the best path for you, for all of us. Your father has chosen the best man he knows."

Lady Montague did not speak of her husband's mounting debts. Protecting and feeding the veterans of his regiment, giving even the wounded men a place in the world, was the honorable thing to do. And as her mother was fond of saying: honor cost money. Caroline would marry an earl, and the earl would pay her father's debts.

Her parents had not bred a coward. It was one thing to learn knife play from trusted men who had served under her father in war, or to ride to hunt on an unruly stallion. Now it was time for her to show true courage. Women were married off to strangers to make advantageous matches for their families every day. Caroline knew this truth. She had been raised on it. She would prove her courage now, by facing her future unafraid. She straightened her back and raised her gaze from the floor.

"I will do my duty, *Maman*."

Lady Montague gave a Gallic shrug, as if the matter had never been open for discussion, but her eyes softened. "Of course you will. When all is said and done, you are your father's daughter."

Caroline was startled when her mother raised herself on the tips of her toes and kissed her lips in blessing. As she took in the scent of her mother's light perfume, she realized she would miss her deeply when she was gone to live in her husband's house.

Lady Montague's voice did not waver. The warmth in her eyes was not betrayed in her tone as she gave her daughter the last instructions of the day. "His lordship will send a dressmaker to attend you tomorrow, to fit you for the wedding gown of his family."

Caroline held her tongue. She could not believe her fiancé had already chosen her wedding dress. It boded ill for their future that his need for control extended to her wardrobe. She did not voice these concerns to her mother, who she knew did not want to hear them. "I will be ready."

Lady Montague's pride shone in her eyes, along with moisture that might have been tears. "Daughter, I have no doubt of that."

Her mother closed and locked the outer door to her rooms behind her. By now, the men downstairs would have heard of her father's choice. No doubt, her husband-to-be sat among them. Numb from the sudden onslaught of her future, she turned back to her bedroom, reaching for the bell to ring for Tabby, her lady's maid.

Caroline would marry Lord Ravensbrook, the most insufferable man she had ever met. What did kind of future was that?

Chapter 3

ANTHONY FOUND AN IMPROMPTU PARTY CELEBRATING his engagement in full swing two floors below. Footmen offered him Madeira and brandy, but he wanted only to go to his own rooms and be alone.

He moved through the almost empty hallway, out a back door into the garden beyond the house. Ornamental shrubs stood guard in the moonlight, and lamps lit the terrace. Anthony took refuge in the shadows, gazing up at the window of his betrothed's bedroom.

Caroline Montague was the most beautiful woman he had ever seen. He had sampled lovely women and their charms from Italy to Spain, but no other woman had caught his eye and held it as this slip of a girl did. The moment she had walked into the room, he had wanted her as he had wanted little else in his life, and he was a man known for his appetites as well as for his ability to control them.

His control had almost slipped with her as she challenged him, not once, but over and over again. She had sparred with him, not caring who he was. He was sure if the Prince Regent had met her alone in her rooms, she would have been just as ill-tempered. Never in his life had anyone spoken to Anthony with such blatant disrespect. He had not been offended as he should have been, as any other man of his acquaintance would have been. Instead, he felt the rising need to tame her temper, to make her his.

He remembered the soft skin of her arm beneath his fingertips, the swell of her breasts rising beneath the scalloped neckline of her gown. She had been warm and willing in his arms until he touched her breast. In that moment, he truly felt she might do him harm. The threat in her eyes, the certain power behind the maple brown of her gaze, had lit a fire in him that still had not gone out. He had left the room almost at once for fear that he might forget the honorable agreement he had made with her father and have her then and there.

Anthony stared up at her window, thinking of the days to come, wondering how he would stop himself from touching her. Even now, she was changing into her night rail, her long blond hair curling across the peaks of her breasts. He thought of how her nipples would harden at his touch, the warmth of his palms covering them, his mouth closing over them.

His thoughts did not continue down that pleasant path for long. He was thrown from his reverie abruptly, as if an icy sluice of water had been tossed over his head. All desire died when he heard the voice of his enemy.

"So, Anthony, how did you fare with your lady love? She seems more of a man than you are."

Carlyle lounged against the railing of the marble terrace, gloating as if he were the winner of Caroline's hand. Anthony wanted to reach for the knife in his boot, but he had given his word to the Prince Regent the year before that he would never spill a drop of this man's blood.

Anthony held on to his control. He knew that to show emotion was to let the bastard win. "Why did you come here?"

Carlyle laughed. "To marry the fair Miss Montague, of course. She is the beauty of her generation. She would have taken London by storm, if her father had wit and money enough to give her a Season. I had hoped to marry the girl without much fuss, and get an heir on her. When I was done, I would have sent her to the country and gone on with my life."

Anthony felt his hatred of this man rise like bile in his throat, and he swallowed it down.

"But as so often happens abroad and at sea, Anthony, I find you are here before me. Her father tells me the marriage contract was signed this morning."

"That is not your affair."

As always, the sight of his smile was like acid on Anthony's skin. He held himself still under that smile. He thought of poor Anne, living quietly now in Richmond, where she would no doubt live out the rest of her life.

"I leave for home tomorrow. And you will stay and marry the girl and find bliss in her arms, no doubt." Victor's voice dripped with contempt.

Anthony moved so quickly Victor had no time to draw a weapon if he even had the sense to wear one.

His blade caressed Victor's throat. Though fury had prompted him, his anger crystallized into a deadly calm. His hand was steady as it held the knife. Anthony sounded almost as if they spoke of the weather or the state of the roads as he gave his final warning. "You will not speak of her again."

Victor did not flinch. He did not look down at where the knife's point threatened to slice into his jugular. He only smiled. He seemed to fear nothing, not even death.

"As you say, Ravensbrook. I will obey you in this, as in all things."

Carlyle's mocking tone brought him back to reason. Anthony lowered his weapon, his fury draining away as wine from a broken bottle. Carlyle turned from him and strode up the marble steps toward the house, not caring that Anthony had a knife at his back.

Carlyle stopped at the door that led into the warm light of the front hall. "Until we meet again. Much wedded bliss to you. I hope she is as good to you as your sister was to me."

Anthony threw his knife. It left his palm before he stopped to think of his oaths or of the dishonor such an act might bring. But the blade was not made for throwing, only for close combat. His knife fell short and struck the marble of the terrace. It bounced harmlessly, its hollow ring the only sound in the courtyard. As Anthony strode up the terrace steps and picked up his knife by its thick leather hilt, he heard Carlyle's laughter echoing back to him from somewhere within the house.

Anthony did not sleep in his room that night.

Instead, he hid himself in an unused bedroom across the corridor from his betrothed's chambers and kept vigil, watching over Caroline's door. He would not put it past Carlyle to take the girl from her father's house to spite him. As the light of day began to rise from beyond the walls of the great house, Anthony found himself thinking not of his enemy, but of the girl who would be his wife. For all her defiance, he could not deny her courage. She had faced him down alone in her rooms, when any other woman might have fainted from the shock or screamed like a fool.

The memory of Caroline beckoned to him, the way she had looked as she stood before him, her breasts rising with her breath beneath the warm silk of her gown. Her golden hair had been bound with pins, but he wondered what it would look like when he took it down to fall along her shoulders, down her back, and over the peaks of her naked breasts.

He thought of drawing her beneath him on their wedding night, even as she insulted and baited him. He thought of how sweet it would be to tame her with his body as he would one day tame her mind, to silence her with his mouth and hands until all words had fled and all she could do was gasp and moan beneath him. Her inner fire would no doubt scorch his bed with undiluted heat. No doubt that even in the heat of passion, she would defy him.

Anthony smiled. He had always loved a challenge.

Chapter 4

CAROLINE WOKE LATE THE NEXT MORNING AND BLINKED in the warm sunlight that fell across her bed. The curtains of her bed were drawn back to reveal Tabby standing over her, offering a cup of tea on a tray. The girl did not wait for her mistress to greet her but began to speak before Caroline could even draw breath.

"Miss Caroline, what a fuss! There are people all over the breakfast room, eating us out of house and home. My mam's been cooking since dawn, and there's no end to the guests and their morning appetites."

Caroline smiled in spite of herself. "I'm sure your mother could handle Caesar's army, much less a horde of my father's guests."

Tabby looked frightened. "Caesar's army? Did he fight with Lord Montague? Will he be coming here too?"

Caroline laughed, and sipped the hot tea. The cream and sugar had blended perfectly. Tabby might lose Caroline's dressing gown for days at a time, but her cups of tea were always perfect.

"We're safe from Caesar, Tabby."

The young maid crossed herself against invaders and

their armies, looking over her shoulder to the sitting room beyond. "The seamstress is here with your wedding gown," she whispered.

Caroline felt a rising need to flee but forced herself to hold her ground. Her marriage contract was signed; her future was sealed. Since her husband-to-be had chosen her gown, she would allow herself to be fitted. In an hour she would escape for her fencing lesson. She needed to be outdoors almost as much as she needed her next breath.

The madness of marrying so soon was daunting in the light of day. Since she had met her fiancé, Caroline knew she could not agree to it. Such impatience was folly at best, a disaster at worst. She would speak to her father before the morning was out. He would have to see reason and give her more time before the wedding.

Mrs. Muller, the seamstress from the village, entered her rooms then, bearing a long, trailing gown of silk and lace.

"Miss Montague, this is an auspicious day. The earl is a lucky man indeed."

Caroline stood to greet her with a forced smile. "Thank you, Mrs. Muller. I hope he knows it."

The older woman laughed, her bright blue eyes merry in her round face. "Of course he does, miss. What man would not cherish such a bride? He has sent this gown for your inspection. I'm to make it fit you as if it were your own, as if it had been made for you."

Mrs. Muller helped Caroline don the skirt and the bodice, both a faded dark blue that complemented Caroline's blond hair. The style was from the last century, with long, sweeping skirts that called for panniers to hold them up. Its silk was smooth, its design simple, with long sleeves that trailed from its bodice lace. As outdated as it was, as soon as she put the dress on, Caroline felt beautiful in it.

Mrs. Muller pinned the gown, making deft stitches where she could, leaving most of the changes to be made in her shop later that afternoon. Caroline stood as still as she could, her frustration mounting as each moment passed. The sun had come out, and its warm light pooled on the floorboards by the windows. She longed to be outdoors in her breeches, riding Hercules over her father's fallow fields, and on out into the moors. She longed with every breath she took to be free.

Caroline sighed as the seamstress moved about her in silence. She wanted to shout, to break the quiet that was becoming almost brittle. Tension mounted her, closing her throat until she was close to shivering with it. It was all Caroline could do to stay still while Mrs. Muller stitched, for each flash of her needle and each new tuck of lace made her realize her life was now like this dress, ordered and fashioned by someone else.

When Mrs. Muller finished her work, she helped Caroline out of the dress. Tabby stayed with her and wrapped the old silk in tissue paper for its journey back to the village. With her maid distracted, Caroline said a quick good-bye to the seamstress. She did not waste a moment, but dove into her dressing room, pulling on the breeches and linen shirt she wore for fencing and riding. She buttoned a man's vest over the shirt to hide the fact that she was not wearing stays.

As she slipped from the room out the servants'

hidden door, she heard Mrs. Muller tell Tabby that the veil that went with the gown was too long to fit her. The old lace could not be trimmed but came as one long piece. Caroline was not as tall as the last Countess of Ravensbrook had been.

Hearing that she was too short, Caroline bit her tongue and swallowed a scathing remark. It was all she could do not to slam the door behind her.

Caroline moved silently through the servants' corridor, down their staircase, and out behind the main house. She made her way through the kitchen garden, careful to keep to the path. She did not stop to talk as she normally would have done, but she waved to the people she saw as she slipped by silently. They all raised a hand to her in greeting, and the men took off their caps.

When she made it to the stable yard without being seen by her mother or her fiancé or by any of her father's guests, she released her breath in one long sigh. Paul would be waiting for her in one of the back riding rings, hidden from the main house behind the stables and a copse of myrtle trees.

"Well, young miss, it looks like you forgot your boots," Martin said.

The old groom's brown eyes held Caroline's. He smiled down at her, his cheeks reddened by the sun and wind. She knew he saw beyond her bravado to her fears about her wedding day. He had run her father's stables since before she was born and had set her on her first pony at the age of three. Tears rose in her eyes when she saw his sympathetic face and heard the familiar kindness in his voice. She ducked and hid when a new horse walked past, a mount being taken out of the stable for one of her father's many guests.

"It's a ride you need," Martin said.

Caroline could not mask her desperation. "Yes."

"Well now, miss, it's not as bad as all that. All women marry, and your father has chosen well. Besides, you'll still have Hercules here." He patted the stallion's neck fondly. The horse snorted and tossed his head, unwilling to be coddled by anyone but Caroline.

She ignored his well-intentioned comments. She almost wished she could be as dispassionate about the changes in her life as everyone else seemed to be. "I'll ride in half an hour, Martin. I'm off to my fencing lesson first."

"Paul's waiting for you in the riding ring around back. Look lively now, miss. We wouldn't want any of your father's guests to see you in breeches."

Caroline glowered. "God forbid they should see that a woman had two legs and two arms and knows how to use both."

Martin laughed and waved as she left the stables for the riding ring beyond.

Paul bowed as she closed the gate behind her, and she smiled. "No need to be so formal just because I'm betrothed," she said.

"You will be a countess, miss."

"I still plan to trounce you. You won't find me putting on ladylike airs."

"But you are a lady," Paul said.

"A lady who likes to fence."

She moved in then, raising her rapier. Paul was ready for her and parried her first thrust. She worked against his skill while he led her into each move. As her muscles warmed in the heat of the sun, her mind unclenched and her fears of the future began to fade. She would get a reprieve from her wedding. No man in his right mind would ask her to wed him after knowing him for only two days.

She had gotten the upper hand with Paul, a difficult feat, for he never gave an inch. She held the blunt-tipped blade at his throat, not an acceptable move in fencing but one of her favorites.

Paul smiled appreciatively. "I yield, miss."

"You're a brave man to stand against me," she said.

"I'd rather face you than the French," Paul answered, and Caroline laughed.

"You need to work on the way you hold a blade," Lord Ravensbrook said.

Caroline turned to find Anthony just beyond the riding ring. He stood with one polished boot raised on the lower rung of the fence. His obsidian hair fell to his collar in rich waves. His dark eyes held her as if she belonged to him already.

"I have been told I have a great deal of skill with a blade, my lord, both with a rapier and a dagger."

"Then you've been lied to. I think we discovered your prowess is lacking when we met last night."

She felt a frisson of irritation at that gibe, but she swallowed it down.

"Do you fence, my lord?"

"Not with women or youths who do not know enough to hold the proper form."

"And which am I? A woman, or a youth?"

"Dressed as you are, I cannot tell."

Caroline laughed, her eyes gleaming with mischief. She knew she had scored a point. In spite of his words, she saw his eyes roaming over the curves of her hips and thighs, the softness of her breasts beneath her vest. He might call her boyish, but he was lying.

"Perhaps you will spar with me here."

"I do not tutor amateurs."

"Is that so?"

"Not in fencing, at any rate."

She wondered what else he might seek to tutor her in. From the desire in his eyes, she could begin to guess.

Caroline did not look away from him, and his dark gaze did not leave her. She did not move to safety but stood just a few feet from him, drawn to him by the heat in his eyes. She knew better than to come any closer. Like a fire in winter, he warmed her from a distance, but that heat would burn if she came too near.

Anthony stepped into the riding ring. He did not stop until he stood close enough that his waistcoat brushed the front of her vest. Caroline did not back away, though all her instincts sounded a warning that she was out of her depth. She held her ground, taking in the scent of leather and spice on his skin, the same scent that had almost been her undoing last night.

Her rapier was still in her hand. Anthony took it from her, his hand caressing hers. She let him take the blade, curious to see what he might do with it.

He tested the rapier for weight, then tossed it to Paul, who waited to be dismissed. Anthony nodded to him, and her teacher withdrew. Caroline did not look at Paul or speak but kept her eye on the man she was destined to marry.

"I have disarmed you," Anthony said.

Caroline smiled. "You have taken one blade, my lord. I wear many others."

"Perhaps I should search you for them and see where they lie."

Caroline shivered with pleasure at the thought of his hands on her body. She could feel the heat of him through his clothes and hers. She wondered for a moment if she had completely lost her mind.

"I think I will keep my blades where they are for now."

Anthony stared down at her, his gaze hot with desire. She wondered where the superior man from the night before had gone, the man who had driven her to such heights of fury. She did not have long to wonder, for his eyes grew cool once more, and his tone look on an air of command. The warmth between them faded, almost as if it had never been. But Caroline remembered it.

"Go inside and change into a gown. And put your knives away."

Disappointment rose in her breast. She wondered which man was real, the warm man full of desire or the commanding, arrogant bastard who lived to rule her life. Caroline shrugged, feigning indifference, as if his superior tone did not affect her.

She stepped away from him, giving herself room to breathe. His eyes narrowed, but he did not move to follow her. She raised her chin to look him in the eye.

"My lord, you have an unfortunate tendency to

give orders when none are needed. I am behind the stables of my father's house. I am free to come and go here as I please, with no interference from you."

"No wife of mine will wear breeches. No Countess of Ravensbrook will fight at hand-to-hand combat with a servant. Go change into a proper gown."

Caroline stared at the man who would be her husband, the man who would control her for the rest of her life, if she let him. His chestnut eyes gleamed with fury, his beautiful face dark with ire. Her anger rose to meet his, and she did nothing to tamp it down.

"I am not your wife yet."

She did not open the gate of the riding ring but climbed over the fence, springing easily to land safely on the other side. Before Anthony could follow her, she moved to Hercules, where he waited for her in the stable. She did not look for the mounting block but slid her boot into the stirrup, raising herself into the saddle with no other thought than to escape. Caroline wheeled the great horse from the shadow of the stable yard and into the sunlight. She set Hercules's head for the road that led away from the house, toward freedom. Moving as one, she and her horse cleared the ornamental gate that contained her mother's flower garden.

Caroline heard Anthony shout behind her, but she did not pause. She loosened her grip on the reins, and Hercules thundered away from the house. She did not stay on the road long but turned Hercules toward her father's fallow fields and the moors that lay beyond. Her escape from her fiancé and his strictures filled her heart with sudden joy and overflowed into laughter. Exhilaration filled her as the wind lifted her long golden braid from her shoulders. Perhaps she would be free in truth. After that display, Lord Ravensbrook might take himself back to London. She could marry some other man.

Caroline brought Hercules to their favorite spot on the moor, close by the river where a willow tree grew. Her grandmother had planted that tree years ago, and it still stood out of place in the wilds of Yorkshire. As she drew up to her haven of peace, the cold light of reason began to dawn on her. Anthony had signed a marriage contract with her father, and her father needed Ravensbrook's money. She would not be able to turn the man away. She would have to marry him, for she had given her mother her word that she would.

She climbed down and stroked her horse, noticing he was the same color as Anthony's eyes. Caroline felt her future following her, coming to seal her in like a great fist. She was trapped, and she knew it.

She leaned her cheek against Hercules's satiny neck. "I forgot your treat," she said, her voice hoarse. "I'm sorry."

The great horse tossed his head, dismissing any need for treats. Still, Caroline clung to him, so he lowered his head again and breathed gently into her hair. She sniffled and rubbed his forelock.

"You're right," she whispered to him. "It is too fine a day for self-pity."

She took Hercules's bridle and turned him loose on the tall grasses that grew at the river's edge. She did not tether him, for she knew he would not leave her. She sank down next to the river and watched the water flow beside her, making its slow, inevitable way to the sea.

Chapter 5

ANTHONY WATCHED AS CAROLINE RODE AWAY LIKE A fury. Just as she showed surprising skill with a blade, she rode her stallion as if she had been born in the saddle. For the hundredth time in the last twenty-four hours, Anthony questioned why Lord Montague had let her grow so wild. It was time to rein her in.

Once his stallion, Achilles, was saddled, Anthony pounded after her. He found his fiancée seated by the river under a willow tree. He had spotted her from a long way off, but she did not look up at him until he was almost standing over her on the riverbank. She did not rise to greet him but watched him from where she sat on a mossy stone. Anthony dismounted and took in the sight of her. Her golden hair was coming down from its braid, slipping in loose curls around her face.

He thought of the list of grievances he had to rail against her: leaving her parents' house without a word to anyone; fighting a servant while wearing breeches for all to see; defying him openly and in public, only to run from him on horseback, leaping over fences and hedges to escape him. Never mind the fact that she had ridden out of her father's stables without a groom. Anything could happen to a lone girl on the moors. And now that she was betrothed to him, Carlyle and his people would always be watching her.

Anthony tried to reprimand her, for he must take her in hand for her own good as well as his, but his voice caught in his throat. He swallowed hard before he could speak. "You ride well."

She smiled at him then, and he felt as if he had earned a reward. He savored the brief moment of peace, for he knew it could not last.

"I am even better at fencing."

Anthony opened his mouth to tell her again that no wife of his would fight with a blade when he noticed her stallion walked loose without his bridle. The great beast did not look at him but only at his horse. Achilles, the horse Anthony had ridden in the war, stood watching the other stallion, as still as death. Neither approached the other to test for dominance, and neither struck out with his hooves. The two stallions blew at each other, each silently taking the other's measure. Anthony waited by his stallion's head, careful not to let go of the bridle. But the moment of danger passed. There seemed to be no rivalry between them.

Anthony moved to sit beside Caroline on the riverbank.

"Let's hope they stay so easy with one another," he said.

"As long as your horse minds his manners and doesn't get in Hercules's way, I am sure they will get along splendidly."

"Is that so?" he asked.

"Most decidedly. After all, Hercules barely knows this interloper."

"I assure you, Achilles is quite friendly—as long as he is shown the proper respect."

"Respect must be earned, my lord."

They did not speak for a long moment but sat together and watched the river slide by in companionable silence. Anthony decided to try again.

"I was told you understood your duty and were willing to do it."

Caroline cast a sharp look at him. "I am willing to do my duty, my lord. I am not willing to become someone I am not."

"Are you willing to be my wife?"

"I am willing to take a husband. I gave my father my word."

"You will like having me for a husband, Caroline. I will see to that."

Caroline sighed and stood. He felt their moment of truce end as abruptly as it had begun.

"I can't marry you after knowing you for only two days, my lord. Surely you can see the sense in that."

"I know this is unusual, Caroline. I would prefer to have met you at assemblies, to have courted you with flowers, to have taken you for drives in the park. But I do not have the time for such pleasantries, and neither does your father."

Caroline stared into the river at her feet. "I hate balls and assemblies. And flowers wilt and die."

He smiled. "So perhaps our lack of courting is less of a hardship than I supposed."

"It's not flowers I want, my lord. I want to know who you are before I become your wife."

Anthony sighed. "Caroline, my parents were married

for twenty years and never knew each other. Time and familiarity does not make an alliance."

"What does?"

Anthony stared into the water as it passed. "Chance," he answered honestly. "Perhaps luck."

"I have always been lucky," she said.

"As have I."

Anthony relaxed for the first time since he had sat down beside her. Perhaps she had begun to follow his lead. Perhaps like a good horse, she balked at first until she felt the guidance of her master's hand.

"I have important business with the Prince Regent in London in two weeks' time that cannot wait."

"More important than getting to know the partner of your future life?"

"You will not be my partner, Caroline. You will be my wife."

"I thought they were one and the same."

"You thought wrong."

She did not answer him but stared out over the riverbed, her shoulders hunched. Her beautiful golden braid lay tangled on her shoulders, and he longed to run his hand through it, to smooth it down as he wished to smooth her feelings.

"You will be my wife, Caroline. We will have the rest of our lives to know each other."

He shivered at the thought of knowing her, of drawing her beneath him on the soft sheets of his feather bed. He shook his head to clear it, ordering himself to focus on the matter at hand. She was angry, and he was sorry for it. He did not want her to loathe her new life but to embrace it.

"I will speak to my father," she said. "Perhaps he can make you see reason."

Anthony's hard work was beginning to slip away. He watched as she moved past him to place the bridle on her horse. She also had to pass Achilles, and she greeted his stallion warily, offering him the heel of her hand. Anthony's warhorse, a mount that had slain men in battle with his hooves, was conquered by that woman in the space of a breath. The horse took in her scent, just as Anthony had the night before, and accepted her as his own.

Caroline smiled at the great beast, rubbing the streak of black that ran between his eyes and down his nose. Achilles tossed his head, but he was not affronted. The stallion pressed closer to her, that she might pet him again.

Caroline patted him absently as if he were her lapdog. She moved to her own horse then, her back to Anthony.

If he let her go now, she would think she could do whatever she wanted for the rest of their lives. She *would* learn to afford him the proper respect. She must. He was no milksop to be led around by a young wife.

He rose to his feet and caught her arm, drawing her toward him. Caroline dropped the bridle, her body pressed against his. Anthony almost lost his train of thought at the feel of her soft curves beneath the hideous breeches and vest. Holding her close, he realized she was not wearing stays. Achilles snorted, displeased that his master had taken away his new prize. Hercules looked up to watch the scene in front of him, still munching grass.

"I will woo you after we are married, if you wish," Anthony said. "But you must believe me when I tell you that you are mine. I have chosen you. You will be my wife. You must learn to obey me."

Fury filled the eyes of the woman in his arms. "I must obey you? Like your horse? Like your dogs?"

Anthony's anger faded at the touch of her body on his. His lust for her was rising, taking his breath. He had never yet met a woman he could not have, if he applied his skills and wooed her.

He had never before met a woman who could spit and fume at him while he held her in his arms. Perversely, he found he liked it.

"Like all wives, you will promise to obey me when we marry. But obedience will not be as terrible as you suppose."

He lightly pressed his lips against her temple. She tensed, resisting him, but he did not let her go. His hand slid down to her waist; the other cupped the back of her head. She let him cradle her hair, but she still glared at him.

"You seek to distract me, my lord, but I will not be moved."

"No?" His lips came to her temple again, and this time, he felt her catch her breath. "What of this then? If I touch you here?" He ran his hand up her spine, and she shivered.

"What if I kiss your cheek?"

"I will be unmoved, my lord. I would speak to you like a reasonable person, not a plaything."

"You are no plaything, Caroline. Believe me when I say I know that already."

His lips slid over the softness of her cheek, even as his hand smoothed her hair.

"I do not seek to play with you, Caroline. I am in deadly earnest. I am going to have you for my wife. Now, in two days' time, in two weeks' time, the outcome will be the same. You are mine."

His lips were on hers then, tasting her, drinking her in. The heels of her hands pressed against his chest, but he would not release her. He lingered over her sweetness, even as she seemed to fight the pleasure he offered her. He did not press her hard but kept her in his arms as his lips courted hers. Her mouth did not open beneath his, but she shivered again as his hand ran down her back.

Anthony did not want to push her too far. She was a virgin, and pure. Clearly, she did not yet know how to kiss him back. He drew away, pleasure surging through him, along with proprietary triumph. He would teach her all she needed to know. The heat between them would do the rest.

She was breathless when he pulled away. She did not try to escape his embrace but leaned back in his arms far enough to meet his eyes. Her maple-brown gaze stared at him, perplexed by what he had shown her. Her innocence was almost his undoing.

"I will make a good husband, Caroline."

Caroline held his gaze. With all the power he would soon be granted over her life, he saw in her eyes that she was not afraid of him, or of anything. "So you say, my lord. Time will tell."

She stepped away from him. This time, he let her go. Anthony watched as she set the bridle on her horse's head, taking the great stallion's mouth between her hands as if he were a newborn foal with no teeth to bite her. The horse did not object but nuzzled her hand when she was done.

She rose into the saddle with grace and power, an unarmed Amazon. He thought she might ride away without another word between them. Like an addled boy, he had lost his tongue and could only watch her, any words he might have spoken, lost.

She did not leave him in silence. Caroline wheeled her horse in a half circle, smiling at Anthony over one shoulder.

"Your kisses are charming, my lord. But the facts remain unchanged. I will not marry you yet."

"I beg to differ, Caroline."

"That is all you seem to do, my lord. But this time, I will win."

"Time will tell."

If she was annoyed to hear her words thrown back at her, he could not see it.

"Indeed it will, my lord."

Anthony watched her ride away, the thunder of her horse's hooves the only sound on the moors. He stood staring after her, the taste of her sweetness still on his lips. He thought for a moment to ride her to ground again, but he stayed where he was. He would give her time to think and to speak with her father. He would see her tonight. In spite of all she said, he would try to woo her. Perhaps a few soft words and a waltz in the candlelight would move her where reason and good sense would not.

Either way, she would be his.

Chapter 6

CAROLINE GUIDED HER STALLION BACK ONTO THE ROAD
that led to the stables. She rode past a party of
gentlemen out to hunt. They raised their hats to her,
and she bowed from the saddle, her public smile
curving her lips, a smile that did not reach her eyes.

They stared at her breeches and hose, at the curve
of her calves and at her breasts beneath the shapeless
vest. They said nothing, but she felt the heat of their
censure as well as their shock. She had spent so long
on her father's estates that she had forgotten how
unconventional it was for a woman to go about in
men's attire, even for riding. She realized she should
have brought a riding habit to wear over her breeches,
but it was too late now. She squared her shoulders and
rode into the stable yard. She was greeted by Martin,
who helped her down from Hercules's back.

"Your father calls for you, miss," he said as one
of the younger grooms warily led her stallion away
to be stripped of his saddle and rubbed down. She
preferred to care for Hercules herself, but when she
saw the unsettled look in Martin's eyes, she nodded

and accepted her fate. She could no longer ride about the countryside willy-nilly as she had always done. She would soon be a married woman. God help her.

Caroline did not sneak in through the kitchen garden as she had escaped that morning but took the formal path through her mother's roses up to the main drive. She mounted the steps to the front door, and her father's butler, Jenkins, swung the door wide. She took the marble steps two at a time, thinking of her father and of how to face him with a smile, though her heart was hurting. She was thinking these things when she ran directly into a man coming down the stairs.

"Miss Montague."

She blinked, the sunlight in her eyes. She moved away, a polite apology on her lips, but the man held her arm to keep her from falling. "My lord. I beg you pardon me."

"No pardon is necessary. What man would not want such a woman in his arms, even for a moment?"

"Lord Carlyle, you are too forward."

Caroline said this to chastise him, and though Carlyle bowed in apology, he did not look in the least contrite, nor did he seem scandalized by her attire. He perused her calves briefly but returned his gaze to her face almost at once. His blond hair fell across his forehead and over one eye, giving him a rakish look.

"Victor, please, Miss Montague. Or should I say Lady Ravensbrook?"

"I am not married yet, my lord."

"But you soon will be."

"Indeed. So it seems." Caroline could not keep the irritation out of her voice.

Carlyle's smile widened. He gestured to the white gravel drive where his carriage and footmen waited. "Best wishes on your forthcoming nuptials. I am for London, and home. But as soon as your new husband brings you to town, I hope to see you there."

"I have longed to see the city."

"I am sure you will get your wish. Until we meet again."

Carlyle made an elegant bow before he continued his descent. A man with such warm wit and easy ways might have made a pleasant husband. She wondered why her father had not chosen him.

Jenkins closed the door behind Carlyle with an emphatic slam and glowered at her. He did not approve of her speaking freely with strange men, and loathed her boy's attire.

She found her father in his library tucked away on the first floor toward the back of the house. Lord Montague stood ramrod straight, his hands clasped behind his back as he stared out at the moors beyond the window. The archery range was still on the lawn from the contest the day before.

He turned to face Caroline as she closed the door to the hallway quietly behind her.

She thought perhaps she might sketch a bow, as she still wore breeches, but such a gesture might show too much cheek. She had spent all her life wishing she had been born the son he longed for, the son he needed. Though she was only a girl, he loved her beyond reason, just as she loved him. She knew her wild ways displeased him, though he had never spoken of them

to her. Only her mother had chastised her. Caroline
curtsied instead.

"I see you have lost your gown," was all he said.

"No, Papa. My gowns are in my room. I was out
riding, and fencing with Paul."

"I suppose it is too much to ask that Lord
Ravensbrook did not see you dressed this way."

"It is," she said. "He did see me, I mean."

Her father got a pained look on his face as if his
trusted spaniel had bitten him on the leg. For the first
time, she was ashamed of herself. Perhaps she should
have shown more caution.

She braced herself for a set down, for no doubt she
deserved one, but her father did not censure her. He
simply took her in his arms.

He was not a man given to tender gestures,
but that day he held her close to his heart. Lord
Montague kissed her and drew back so he could look
into her eyes.

"Caroline," he said. "You have saved the family
with this marriage. I hope you know it."

"It is my honor to make the alliance you need,
Papa," she said, her voice unwavering, her eyes calm.
"I only hope we might put it off for a while. Long
enough for me to know him better. A week or two
is all I ask."

He sighed, and she knew he would not grant her
request. She realized he could not, for left to his own
devices, he would have at least considered her needs.
Her anger rose at her fiancé. No doubt Ravensbrook
had the wedding date stipulated in the marriage contract.

"Your betrothed is a good man," her father said.

"He is the best man I could find, both in wealth and character. Whether you marry him tomorrow or in two weeks, I think you will come to love him."

Caroline did not flinch or look away, even then. She did not believe in Anthony's goodness, nor did she share her father's confidence in the man's character, but she knew her duty. "God willing, Papa. But I will be a good wife, whether I love him or not."

"If I had to be cursed with the death of every child but one, I thank God I was left with you."

Caroline's eyes filled with tears so quickly she could not blink them away. She stayed in her father's arms, hiding her face against the shoulder of his coat. He held her until she had control of herself. When she drew back, she saw tears on his cheeks, but she knew better than to remark on them. She kissed her father once more, then let him go.

Chapter 7

CAROLINE WIPED HER EYES WITH HER FINGERTIPS AS SHE climbed the staircase to her room.

As she came to her sitting room door, she half-expected her mother to appear and chastise her for riding alone in breeches while the house was filled with guests. But Caroline saw only one of the upstairs maids, a girl named Mary, who curtsied as she passed, carrying a heavy bin of coal.

Caroline looked down at her breeches and vest, which smelled distinctly of horse. She had missed tea already. Though she may have gotten away with neglecting her duties as hostess for the day, she could not be late to the evening meal. She would have to bathe again.

She thought of her husband-to-be, of his fine dark eyes, and of his black hair caressing his cheek in the breeze at the river. He was the most infuriating man she had ever met, but she could not forget his touch. She was clearly losing her mind.

The door opened of its own accord, and Tabby immediately took her hand and drew her in, slamming the door closed behind her.

"Miss Caroline," Tabby gasped. "I am going to London with you, Mam told me today. I pleaded with her to let me go, and she made a special trip to Lady Montague's rooms to get her permission. When I came back, you were gone and no one knew where, until Martin at the stables sent word."

Tabby had to breathe then, and Caroline could get a word in. "Thank you, Tabby. Please call for some bathwater. I smell of horse."

"Of course, miss, but you don't smell bad to me. My mother said that there is nothing to be ashamed of in the stink of a good day's work. Not that you would ever work…"

Caroline held up one hand, grateful to be surrounded by the buoyant talk of her maid but already needing a moment of silence. "Tabby, the bath…"

"Yes, Miss Caroline."

Caroline looked at the trailing blue gown now carefully laid out for the morrow. Mrs. Muller had done fine work. Caroline could see where the dress had been taken in and taken up so it would fit her on her wedding day. The long veil of lace lay beside it, slightly yellowed with age. Caroline swallowed hard and turned away. She could not think of wearing that gown and of all that came after. She resolved to think only of today.

Her sitting room door flew open then, and Tabby froze in place, hoping to avoid the eagle eye of Olivia Montague.

"Leave us," Olivia said, her voice imperious, her French accent distinct in the midst of her ire.

Tabby escaped into the bedroom, closing the door behind her.

"You are still in breeches, I see." Lady Montague paced, her tiny feet tapping on the mahogany floor. "By God, I never thought I'd live to see the day when I would say I have raised a fool."

The insult stung. "You did not."

"Is that so? Then please explain to me what you are doing running about in breeches like some savage from the Americas. Do you think you are a Scot from the Highlands? This is a civilized house."

"Scots wear kilts," Caroline said.

"I half expect you to come down to dinner in one."

Lady Montague paced in silence for a moment, anger radiating off her small body in waves. Caroline held her tongue in the vain hope that the storm might have passed.

"I know you have spoken with your father, and I know he has not chastised you as he ought. He never does. You hung the moon for him, and there is an end to it. But you are a woman, and you must see the world as it is."

"I do, *Maman.*"

"No, Caroline, you do not." Lady Montague stopped her pacing and stared at her only daughter. "Marriage is a business arrangement, Caroline, yours as much as anyone's. Your beauty and purity buy Lord Ravensbrook's regard. If one of those is called into question, you lose your value."

"Like a lame horse that must be shot."

"Like a ruined woman who cannot be married."

"Am I ruined then? Has he cried off for the capital offense of my wearing breeches in public?"

"He has not. Not yet. But he could, which is the salient point you seem unable to grasp."

Lady Montague took a measured breath, trying to calm herself, and Caroline did the same.

"You must be unimpeachable, your virtue untouched, or this marriage will not take. If this marriage does not take, not just your reputation but this family will be in ruins. Have I made myself clear? You must behave like the lady I raised you to be."

Caroline remembered the feel of his lips on hers, the possessive way he had held her beside the river. "He will not let me go."

"Pray God he does not. If all goes as it should, tomorrow morning he will take you as his bride and keep you in style for the rest of your life."

"Keep me like a mistress? Like a whore?"

Lady Montague moved with lightning speed and slapped Caroline's cheek before the words were barely out of her mouth. The blow stung, but her pride stung more. She had overstepped badly with her mother, and she knew it.

"Never speak of yourself that way again, not even in jest."

Caroline rubbed the sting from her cheek. She felt a measure of guilt for driving her mother to such a display. "I am sorry, *Maman*."

Olivia Montague frowned, guilt written on her face. "And I am sorry I hit you. But I will never stand by and allow you to speak of yourself in that manner."

The two women stood together in silence for a moment, neither certain how to bridge the gap that had opened between them.

"I understand you have been throwing knives indoors again," her mother said.

"Who told you?"

"I have eyes in my head, Caroline. I saw the ruined cushion when I came looking for you in your bedroom earlier."

"I will mend it."

"Please do not." Lady Montague held up one hand. "You have no hand with a needle. You will botch it. Leave it to Tabby."

"As you wish. I won't throw a knife in the house again."

"I should hope not. What you mean to do in your own home is your own affair, but please respect the peace of mine."

Caroline smiled. "As you say, *Maman.*"

Lady Montague moved to the door. "I expect you to be bathed and dressed and downstairs in an hour. You have guests to attend to, not just his lordship."

"I will be there." Caroline went so far as to curtsy in her contrition, and Lady Montague's lips quirked in a rueful smile, a smile that fled just as quickly.

"You are so beautiful, Caroline, and headstrong. You are the work of my life. But that work will lie in ruins if you do not comprehend the simple truth that you cannot do as you please. You must live in the world."

Caroline did not answer. Her mother left her alone with her thoughts.

The sun had set when Caroline came downstairs to greet her guests. She kept her smile sweet and her eyes cast down. Though she knew she could never retain that façade for long, if she began the evening in the guise of a demure young woman, her mother would be pleased. The guests who remained to attend the wedding waited for her in the drawing room. She was five minutes late. The heavy gaze of her mother was on her as she stepped in from the hallway.

Her father was present, ready to lead her mother in to dinner, a sure sign that this night was like no other. Her father tolerated guests only when it was absolutely necessary. When Lady Montague insisted on entertaining, he often took his meals in his library. Tonight, he was playing the host, though Caroline supposed that even a battlefield in Belgium would be preferable to being surrounded by so many people from London. She found herself agreeing with him as the women descended upon her like hawks on a dove.

"Miss Caroline, what a wonderful thing! To be engaged, and so suddenly, to the Earl of Ravensbrook! Do you know, he has been the catch of Town this last year? And now you have him! And you will be married tomorrow!"

Lady Heathbury gushed, her words running together in one long stream as she repeatedly stated the obvious at the top of her voice. Caroline blinked under the onslaught but kept her smile firmly in place. The young girl smiled into Caroline's face, her eyes shining, the light blue of her gaze as clear as cool water. Caroline found her smile shifting into a real one. This girl might be loud and uncouth, but there was no harm in her. "Thank you, my lady. It is an honor."

"A singular honor," Lady Westwood said, her face inscrutable save for the soft light of contempt in her eyes. Her mother stiffened on the other side of the room, but Caroline's smile widened.

This lady had arrived that morning, come up from London to witness Anthony's marriage. Her mother had mentioned that Lady Westwood was one of two relatives left to Lord Ravensbrook, and that his elderly aunt was one of his favorite people in the world.

Clearly, Lady Westwood was displeased to find her cherished nephew selecting his bride from the wilds of Yorkshire instead of among the demure misses of the *ton*. Caroline met the old lady's eyes and smiled. Perhaps not all the women of the South were mealy-mouthed liars.

Caroline curtsied to Lady Westwood. "I beg to differ, my lady. Our alliance is commonplace, I would say. I have honored your nephew with my hand, and he has honored us with his money. By all accounts, an even trade."

She felt the sharp gaze of her mother like a dagger on her skin. Young Lady Heathbury gasped and drew back, as if Caroline had suddenly grown two heads.

The old woman looked at her sharply from beneath her green silk turban. But it seemed she was not offended. Her gray eyes began to gleam with amusement. "You are decidedly blunt, Miss Montague. Perhaps my nephew has offered for a harridan."

"Indeed, my lady," Caroline said, her voice deceptively soft, "he has."

Lady Westwood laughed, a short bark that rang on the crystal of the chandelier overhead. Jenkins stepped into the drawing room then like an emissary from God and called for dinner to be served. Caroline renewed her intention to better guard her tongue as she turned to lead the guests into the dining room behind her parents. Before she took another step, her fiancé appeared at her side, offering his arm.

"Good evening, my lord."

"Good evening, Miss Montague."

If he had heard her remarks to his aunt, he had not taken offense. His eyes devoured her as if no one else were present. A blush rose from beneath the lace-edged bodice of her gown. Caroline forced her gloved hand not to shake as she placed it carefully on his arm.

Her silk gown was cast in soft tones of peach and cream. The white roses she wore were from her mother's hothouse garden, and the tiny flowers set off the golden blond of her hair. She wore no jewels, save for pearls at her ears.

"You look lovely this evening," the Earl of Ravensbrook said.

He looked untouched and untouchable, calm and reserved as any man might be in her mother's drawing room. But his eyes were dark with fire. His hand on her arm heated the silk of her glove as if he had placed a brand there. She looked down at his blunt, square nails and the calluses along the edges of his fingertips, and she shivered. Caroline met his eyes and realized that though his touch heated her, his gaze burned.

"Thank you." Her voice was slightly breathless, but her words did not catch in her throat. "You look very well yourself, my lord."

He laughed, and the ladies walking in front of them turned to stare. He nodded to them, but instead of drawing Caroline into step behind them, he held her back alone.

"It is not for you to compliment me, Caroline, though I thank you."

"I do not recall giving you permission to use my given name."

Anthony laughed again. "I do not need your permission for that, Caroline, or for anything else."

"Indeed, my lord, I beg to differ." She tried to pull away from him, to follow the rest of the party in to dine, but he held her where she was with just his hand on her gloved forearm.

"You may indeed beg from time to time, Caroline. And from time to time, I may indulge you."

"It was merely a figure of speech, my lord. I am not in the habit of begging for anything."

His eyes smoldered with desire, and Caroline began to wonder if she had missed a salient point in their exchange. His eyes lingered on her lips until with great effort he drew them back up to her eyes.

"We will see, Caroline. I may have you begging yet."

"I would not take that wager, my lord. I fear you will lose."

"I never lose, Caroline. I will make you beg before the week is out."

It was her turn to laugh at that absurdity. "Please yourself, my lord, but I tell you, you are mistaken."

He must have felt he won that round, for he led her into dinner with a smug air of satisfaction, even of anticipation. Anthony drew her chair from the table, ignoring the footman who stood by. He took his own seat beside her.

Though Caroline and Anthony were seated together, they spoke little throughout the meal. She could feel his eyes on her as he made conversation with the other gentlemen and ladies, polite talk of London during the Season, of hunting, of war.

Her fiancé drew the eye of every woman there, even her mother. Caroline caught other women staring at him openly, some of the older ones, the married ones, casting glances his way in invitation. Invitation to what, Caroline could only guess. Though she had not asked for the wedding that would take place in the morning, he was her fiancé. She felt sudden proprietary ownership of him, and when the beautiful Lady Clarice smiled at him, a spear of jealousy shot through her. She fumed, first at the other woman's smile, then at herself for being a fool.

The conversation sparkled around the table without a word from her. On any other evening, Caroline would have been in the center of it. When her father had guests, she always longed to stay behind and drink port and smoke cigars with the men when the real talk of the evening began, though her father had never allowed it. But that night she stayed silent as everyone conversed over dinner, as if she truly were the demure girl her mother had raised her to be, as if she had never made those impertinent remarks to Lady Westwood at all. She ate sparingly and watched her husband-to-be from the corner of her eye.

Though Anthony answered questions about the final campaign at Waterloo, he spoke only of things the ladies might hear. Caroline hoped to ask him one day what the battle was really like. All anyone would say in her presence was the battle was long and honor had prevailed, the usurper vanquished, and Europe brought once more into peace. Caroline read the papers her father received from London and the Continent. She knew nothing was ever that simple.

But she had never had the courage to ask her father about the war. As she listened to Anthony's deep voice speak pleasantries about the honor of the king's cavalry, she wondered if he might be more forthcoming with her.

She looked up then and found him watching her.

Another man was speaking, some young fop who had never been to war. Caroline did not hear a word the boy said, for Anthony's eyes were on her, dark pools filled with promise. Caroline's desire for his touch burned along her skin where his eyes caressed her, chasing every other thought from her head.

Under the watchful eye of her father and all his guests, Anthony could not even brush her hand. The knowledge that he could not touch her only fed the fire within her. By the time the ladies rose to leave the gentlemen to their port, Caroline longed for his hand on hers, even with the silk of her glove between them.

She heard nothing of the conversation among the ladies, though most of it was about her wedding the next morning. Her mother discussed the flowers in the church and the lace of the veil Anthony had brought for her to wear. All the women, young and old, seemed to think it the height of Arthurian romance that the Earl of Ravensbrook had brought the wedding gown his mother had worn, and his grandmother before her. Caroline listened with half an ear as the young women rhapsodized over the sweetness of the gesture, while their mothers looked on, smiling. Only Lady Clarice's smile did not reach her eyes.

The gentlemen came in then, and the carpet was rolled up so the ladies and gentlemen might dance.

Caroline thought to play for the company, but her mother's hand on her arm kept her from the pianoforte. She frowned at Lady Montague, for playing well was the only ladylike accomplishment she possessed. But then Anthony towered over her, offering his hand, and she knew why her mother had held her back.

They stepped onto the dance floor in the middle of her mother's drawing room, in full view of all her father's guests. As Anthony nodded politely, first to her father, then to her mother, she felt the heat of his hand through the thin silk of her glove. When they began the measured steps, the rest of the world drew back. Caroline was aware of no one but him.

She could feel the heat of his gaze on her skin. She was as sure of his desire as she was of her own. But she could see no evidence of his thoughts behind the shadowed darkness of his eyes.

She moved as if to lead him, and he laughed. "No, Caroline, I will lead. I thank you."

She was used to leading young men in the dances she attended in the village assembly room. It was a little disconcerting to be drawn through the steps, strangely relaxing to relinquish control to another, even for the space of a song.

Her first moment of irritation was absorbed by the warmth of his hand on hers. She focused on the steps of the quadrille and soon found she did not have to pay attention, as she always did with other young men or with her dancing master. Anthony moved with smooth, unconscious grace, and at his touch, she moved with him.

"You dance well, my lord," she said.

His teeth flashed white in a smile. "I must admit I have not had much practice of late." His grip grew firm, his hands heavy on her waist as he led her through a turn. His touch burned through the thin silk of her gown. She swallowed hard, fighting to keep her wits about her. For some reason, her good sense had almost gone begging.

"You appear to be a natural, my lord."

"What one lacks in experience, one may make up with enthusiasm." His eyes took on a heated gleam, and her mouth went dry. "You appear to have a natural talent for many things yourself," he said.

She did not follow where his conversation led, but she was suddenly aware of the warmth of his body in the closeness of the drawing room. Caroline's mind began to wander as she and Anthony moved together smoothly, almost as if they had been born to it. This time, she did not resist, but let her mind go blank, the tension in her shoulders relaxing as she danced with the man she would marry tomorrow.

The quadrille ended as it had begun, with her fiancé standing close beside her. He spoke low, so no one else would hear. His breath was warm on her cheek. He did not lean too close this time, but she felt his nearness anyway, as she would the heat of the sun at midday.

"When you return to your rooms, stop first in your father's library. I will meet you there."

Caroline laughed at him, arranging a clandestine meeting as if they were lovers. She looked into his eyes and saw the warmth there, the same heat in the pit of her stomach as she took in the spicy scent of him.

"My lord, it would not be proper."

Anthony took her hand in his and kissed it. "Your honor is mine. I swear I will do nothing to break it."

For a moment it seemed they were alone, with no one to watch them. It was as if her parents did not stand close by, as if the other dancers had melted away. She could see only him and the light of his smile.

His smiled turned wicked. "I will only bruise it a little."

Anthony brought her back to her mother and bowed to the baroness. Lady Montague smiled at Lord Ravensbrook but frowned at her. Caroline knew she had spent too long in conversation with her fiancé. "*Maman*, I would like permission to withdraw."

"Your guests are still dancing."

"I know. But tomorrow is my wedding day."

Her mother's eyes softened, and she pressed Caroline's hand, hiding the gesture with her body so no one else might see it. "Very well, *ma petite*. I will see you in the morning."

Caroline curtsied to Lady Westwood, whose eyes were always on her. The old lady nodded to her. She had been taking Caroline's measure all evening and now looked satisfied. Most of the other guests were engaged on the dance floor and did not see Caroline go. She slipped into the hallway, but not before she met her father's gaze. She raised one gloved hand, and he smiled a small, tense smile.

Caroline saw for the first time that her father feared for her, that he would miss her once she went to Shropshire. A lump rose in her throat, and she swallowed hard, stepping into the hallway before anyone else might notice she had slipped away.

Chapter 8

CAROLINE STEPPED INTO THE SILENCE OF THE HALL. The moon was high, its light coming in through the windows as she made her way down the carpeted corridor.

In the library, only one candle was lit. The fire had long since gone out, and with the drapes drawn against the moonlight, the room was shrouded in long shadows. Caroline hesitated in the doorway, but when Anthony emerged from those shadows, she closed the door behind her.

Caroline came to the edge of the candlelight.

"You seem to have a habit of lurking in the shadows, my lord."

"Only when I am with you, Caroline. A man cannot help being cast in shadow by the light of your beauty."

Caroline snorted. "Please, my lord. I have already consented to be your bride. You have no need for such false flattery."

Anthony grinned. "I am wounded, Caroline. Is it that you do not believe the truth behind my poetry?"

"I believe you are amusing yourself, my lord, at my expense."

This time, he did not smile, but moved closer. "You are so eager to remind everyone of your strength that I think you forget your beauty. It is intoxicating."

Caroline was breathless, her limbs languid at his nearness. He had not touched her yet, but he stood close, so close the buttons of his waistcoat brushed the bodice of her gown. She forced herself to hold her ground. Indeed, she found she did not want to back away.

"So you were drunk when you set our wedding for tomorrow?" she asked. "Perhaps you've taken leave of your senses."

Anthony drew her toward him with a gentle hand on her arm. He did not take her prisoner as he had down by the river. Instead, he kissed her tenderly, holding her with only the soft touch of his lips on hers.

She pulled back. "We should wait until after your business with the Prince Regent is complete. We have no need to marry tomorrow. People may think we are avoiding scandal."

Anthony laughed, and this time his laughter did not fill her with fury. Instead, the dark sound of it made her shiver.

"But we are avoiding scandal, Caroline. Because I will have you tomorrow night, no matter what the prince decides to do in two weeks' time, whether you and I stand together before the curate tomorrow morning or not. You are mine, and I am going to see that you know it."

"I am not yours," she said, but her voice was faint. She lost her breath as he pressed his lips to hers, this time not as gently.

It was she who leaned into him so she felt the

hard planes of his chest against her breasts. His arms tightened around her, first to catch her in case she fell, then reflexively as she opened her mouth under his.

His hunger overwhelmed her. She felt his strength along the curves of her body, the hard length of him against her belly through the light silk of her gown. She shivered, pressing closer, sure that in this way, at least, they were well matched. It was not enough to base a marriage on, but it was something.

In the end, it was Anthony who drew back, his breathing harsh. Caroline leaned against him, taking in the spicy scent of his hair.

When she raised her head, she could just reach the edge of his jaw with her lips. Her lips were feather light on the stubble of his beard as she reveled in the sweet, salty taste of him.

Anthony groaned and pulled away, holding her at arm's length so he would not kiss her again.

Caroline found her voice. "I must go to bed."

"And I must let you go to your bed alone." Anthony bent over her hand and unfastened her glove at the wrist, slowly, one button at a time. Caroline watched him, transfixed, sure she might never move again. He drew the long sheath from her hand, leaving her arm exposed to the cool night and to his gaze. He raised her hand to his lips and kissed her wrist where her pulse beat in frantic time, his lips lingering on her skin.

"But tomorrow night," he said, "I will be with you."

He pressed his lips to hers once more, very lightly, like a butterfly's wing.

"Say you will marry me tomorrow, Caroline. Say you will be mine."

She was breathless, longing for his touch, wishing he might kiss her properly one more time before she slept. "I will marry you tomorrow, my lord. And we will take what comes."

Anthony let her go. Caroline stumbled and told herself she lost her footing only because of the dark.

She stepped toward the door and opened it, the corridor beyond pitch-black save for the moonlight. When Caroline looked back, Anthony stood where she had left him, still watching her. He did not move except to raise one hand. Caroline smiled and took the memory of his face with her into the dark.

∽

Anthony frowned as he saddled his horse for his morning ride. He had not slept after leaving Caroline. Fantasies of her golden hair falling over his skin, of her soft body laid out beneath his had burned in his mind, leaving him awake and more frustrated than he had ever been. This fascination with Caroline and her golden hair was unwelcome at best, and at worst, a sign of weakness. He was a man in control of himself. He would not be one of those elderly husbands of the *ton* who hung on their wives' every word, those dotards who were led around by wives half their age.

Caroline would learn to be a proper wife, even if she never set foot in London. She would stop her wild ways and hold her tongue when he spoke to her instead of challenging everything he said. Their bargain would be kept on both sides. She would give him his heir, while he paid her father's debts and kept her safe from men like Viscount Carlyle. Caroline would never suffer as Anne had suffered, but would live under the protection of his name. She would live quietly on his family estate in Shropshire, and he would go on with his life.

Anthony felt a pang of remorse even as he entertained this thought, but he dismissed his remorse at once. Some men kept their wives in the country, birthing their children and running their houses, leaving London to their mistresses. Anthony had not come through fire and war to be led around by his wife.

He thought of his mistress, Angelique Beauchamp, the Countess of Devonshire. By now, word of his marriage must have reached her. No doubt there would be a scene when he returned to the city. He would bring her a jewel so her inevitable anger would fade quickly, an offering that might encourage her to accept his marriage, to see the world as it was.

As Anthony rode out of his father-in-law's stables, he could not hold onto thoughts of his mistress. On the morning of his wedding, Anthony could not even remember her face.

All he could see was the curve of Caroline's throat when he bent to kiss her in the library the night before. She had bewitched him with her beauty and her fire. No doubt the spell would break once he had tasted her body, once he had her for his own.

The thought of his wedding night made him lose his breath. He let his horse gallop across fallow fields, so tenants had to scatter before him on their way to market. But no matter how fast he rode, or how far, Caroline rode with him, her maple eyes following him, and the scent of her long golden hair.

ACT II

"If I be waspish, best beware my sting."

The Taming of the Shrew
Act 2, Scene 1

Chapter 9

CAROLINE WOKE ON HER LAST DAY OF FREEDOM, BUT she was not free. She was bathed and combed and plucked until she thought she would go mad. She longed to be out riding across the moors, but she knew those days were over. Soon she would be riding on her husband's lands, across the hills of Shropshire that would look nothing like the wild moors of her home.

She did not want to think of her husband's estate or what her new life might bring. Instead, she brought her mind to where she was, taking in the scent of the fresh bread from the kitchen, drinking cool, clear water from the well as Tabby dressed her hair.

That morning, Caroline stood in the gown her husband had brought. The indigo silk was smooth against her skin, its skirts held in a wide circle around her by vast petticoats. The intricate lace of the veil fell behind her, covering her hair to her waist, continuing all the way to the floor.

Tabby had asked her if she would wear the veil draped over her face as the women of Anthony's family had always worn it on their wedding days. But

Caroline had never covered her face in her life, and she did not mean to start now. So the old lace doubled back over her hair, hanging down in cascading folds of white, covering the deep blue of her gown like a layer of snow. She wore jewels from his family vault, sapphires that had been sent from London. The heavy necklace gleamed gold against her skin, and the earrings weighed her down as she turned her head.

Even her slippers had been made for this one day, the soft leather dyed blue to match her gown. Such extravagance was beyond even her mother's indulgence in fashion, and Caroline raised her hem to look at those slippers more than once. She sighed, regretting she had no more interest in clothes. Another woman would like the gown and shoes much better. She smiled to herself, but her smile soon faded. It was time to walk to church.

Her father met her in the entrance hall by the front door. Jenkins had the heavy oak door open and ready. The stern butler managed to nod to her once, no doubt happy to have the hoyden of the house out of what was left of his hair.

Caroline smiled at the familiar sight of Jenkins's disapproval, and her father smiled back. "You look very fine," he said. "Your mother and I are proud of you."

Caroline's hand was steady as she took her father's arm. "Thank you, Papa."

The church was full. Their guests and the villagers were there already, happy to see her married at last. There was a feeling of a festival in the air, even in the chapel. Caroline felt she stood somehow outside of it, as if the festivities indeed had nothing to do with her.

Tabby stood with her mother, the head cook, Mrs. Hill, at the back of the church, a posy of late-blooming heather in her hands. She waved to Caroline as though it were any other day, and Caroline found a smile to give her. Lady Montague sat at the front before the curate and the altar. Caroline also gave her mother a smile, and then she saw him, and the rest of the festival and all the people in it fell away.

Anthony waited for her, quietly, calmly, as if he had all the time in the world. Dressed in dark blue superfine and well-tailored black trousers, he stood patiently as if she were his wife already. When he saw her veil thrown back over her hair instead of covering her face as it was meant to, his lips quirked in a smile, but that soon vanished as her father led her down the aisle.

Anthony took her hand and stood with her in silence before the curate who had baptized her. Caroline did not listen closely to the words of the ceremony, until they came to the vows. When the curate spoke the word "obey," she repeated it, though it caught like a briar in her throat.

Anthony's lips quirked again, but then it was time for his own vows. As he swore to worship her with his body, his eyes lit with a dark flame. Caroline shivered at the sight of it, thinking of how he had kissed her the night before in her father's library.

The moment passed, and the ceremony was over. When Anthony's lips pressed hers at the front of the church, his kiss was cool, remote, a stranger's. A surge of nervousness consumed her now that it was all over, now that the die was cast. She had agreed to her father's choice. Her life had been given into the earl's hands for all to see. But Caroline knew that no matter what vows she uttered that day, she belonged to herself.

After the wedding breakfast, Caroline went to put on her traveling gown as the rest of the guests lingered over their meal. Her mother dismissed Tabby and helped her daughter dress. Caroline sat on the stool in front her dressing table while her mother braided her hair and coiled the long braids beneath a riding hat of blue velvet trimmed with peacock feathers. She stood at last, her trunks already trundling down the road away from the house, her portmanteau gone, whisked to the carriage in which she would soon ride away with her husband.

Her mother turned to her and pulled her close, drawing her down so she could press her lips to Caroline's forehead. "I hope you will be happy with him."

"So do I, *Maman.*"

Caroline clutched her mother close, then took a deep breath of her orchid perfume and pulled away. Lady Montague handed her a bouquet of pink and yellow roses from the hothouse tied with a yellow ribbon, all their thorns shorn away.

Her father stood with Anthony in the entryway. All the guests had gathered outside by the traveling coach to wish the couple well. Her father waited for her in the shadow of the front door. Jenkins had been dismissed so the moment could be a private one.

Her father said nothing but drew Caroline close for the third time in two days. He bent down and kissed her hair. He looked into her eyes, but when he spoke, his words were not for her but for Anthony, who stood beside her. "Care for her well."

"I will."

Anthony took Caroline's hand and led her out into the sunlight. Her mother and father stood in the doorway, each with one hand raised in farewell. Caroline looked back and waved to them. Though all the guests and many of the villagers were cheering her into her new life, all she saw were her mother's tears and her father's unbending back as they bid her good-bye.

Chapter 10

THEY RODE THROUGH THE HOURS OF THAT AFTERNOON in silence. The road south was smooth beneath the carriage wheels, the squabs of the coach soft at his back. Anthony watched his young wife, but she did not look at him. They had another two days on the road ahead of them, for it was a long way to Shropshire. Caroline's eyes never left the window, drinking in the sight of her home county as they passed through it. Finally, after four hours' travel, they reached the city of York.

They came at last to the inn where they would spend their wedding night. Caroline turned to him with the ghost of a smile. "We are here," she said.

Anthony offered his hand and helped her down from the carriage himself. The inn yard was bustling with many travelers, all on the road south to London, as they were. All others stopped to stare at the black-lacquered traveling coach emblazoned with his family crest, a knight's helm flanked on both sides by two silver plumes. The people standing by looked at the matched set of four gray geldings with long black manes and well-combed tails.

Caroline did not notice the people gawping at her but went at once to the horses that still stood in their traces. The footmen and coachman tried to stop her, though they knew they could not touch her and indeed should not even speak to her without being spoken to first. They each cast sideways glances at their lord, then stepped back when he nodded once. Caroline noticed none of this interaction but went to offer the flat of her palm to the lead horse.

"Thank you," she murmured to him, low under her breath. Anthony was close, ready to pull her away if the horses shied. He was the only one who heard her speak.

The great beast cast one dark eye on her, took in her scent, and shook out his mane. Caroline smiled and pressed her hand against his sweaty neck once, very lightly. His wife turned to him then and stopped when she seemed to catch sight of the heat in his eyes. Anthony did his best to bank it down, so as not to frighten her. She did not frighten easily, but she was a maid, and her wedding night had come. Tonight he would have to be cautious and gentle and bring to bear all his hard-won skill to make his wife glad she was in his bed.

Caroline did not seem afraid at all as she looked at him. After a slight hesitation, she stepped forward, placing her hand on his arm. The cart bringing Hercules and Achilles rolled into the yard, and he had to restrain her with one hand to keep her from going to greet them.

"You will see them tomorrow," he said.

His wife looked into his eyes and considered what he said. He thought for a moment she might disregard his words as if he had never spoken, that her usual defiance would come between them. Instead, she nodded and allowed him to lead her into the inn.

Anthony was shocked by her sudden acquiescence, by the silence that had lingered between them all that afternoon. Perhaps the wedding vows had tamed her. Perhaps she was indeed a biddable woman who would do as she had sworn and obey him for the rest of her life.

He had expected to be pleased by this, but a niggling sense of disappointment lingered, an unexpected sour taste like a bite into an unripe berry.

⁕

Caroline came into the sitting room her husband had chosen. A large table was drawn close to the fireplace, and an old wooden settle faced the hearth. She stepped toward the fire and warmed her hands, though they did not need warming.

"Our bedroom is on the right, Caroline."

Her husband had barely spoken three words together since they had been bound as man and wife. She repressed her irritation and forced a smile.

"Indeed. Thank you, my lord."

"They will bring supper up in a moment, some tea and fresh bread, some beef. The fare is plain but very good. You did not eat much at breakfast."

Caroline turned a sharp glance on him, but his face was impassive. She could not tell if he was merely being solicitous of her welfare or chastising her for not eating enough. She chose discretion as the better part of valor and kept her answer bland, her voice mild.

"Thank you, my lord."

Caroline washed her face in the warm water Tabby brought, sparing only a glance for the bed where she would spend her wedding night. She did not change her gown but went back into the sitting room. The food had come, and she could smell the fresh-baked bread and the beef stew. She was hungrier than she had thought.

"I hope you had a pleasant journey," Anthony said.

"Thank you," Caroline answered. "I did."

"We made good time."

Silence descended again. She was not a woman for silence or for polite conversation. Suddenly her future yawned before her in an unbroken line of boredom. The horror of the thought made her shudder even as she ate her beef.

"York came upon us quickly," Caroline said. "You have fine horses, my lord."

A wry smile touched his lips. "Indeed, my lady. I have been told so."

"I tell you so again," Caroline said. "Someone who works for you has a good eye for horseflesh."

"I choose all my own horses."

"Perhaps I might come with you to Tattersall's when we are next in London," she ventured.

"A horse dealer's is no place for a lady."

Caroline swallowed her irritation along with a bite of bread. She gave up on her attempt to converse with him civilly and turned her attention to her dinner.

The silence was broken only by the sound of cutlery scraping against their plates. She finished as her husband did, and a maid from downstairs came in to clear away the remains of the meal.

"I will retire then," Caroline said.

Anthony met her eyes. "I will follow in a few minutes."

He took her hand, and a frisson of heat ran up her arm. She had removed her gloves before beginning the meal, so her hands were bare as he raised her palm and pressed his lips to the center of it. Caroline gasped, all fear of boredom gone. There was only this man and the need she felt for him. Anthony stared into her eyes, and she gazed back, trying to find some answer to the riddle of his soul behind the brown of his eyes. If an answer lay there, it was well hidden.

Caroline did not say another word but went into her bedroom. Tabby threw her arms around her as soon as Caroline closed the door.

"Miss Caroline…I mean, my lady, have you ever seen such a fine inn? The food is not as good as Mam's, but you could never expect that. What a miracle this bed linen is… almost as fine as at home. I've got a little water here for your bath…we'll just sponge you off and take down your hair, my lady. I'll brush it out, but I'll not give it a hundred strokes this night. You've other fish to fry."

Tabby stopped to draw breath then, and Caroline laughed as her friend from childhood helped her strip off her traveling gown. "You'll be wearing a new dress tomorrow, my lady. I'm pressing it now…isn't it grand that they keep a clothes press right here in the room like civilized people? Of course, the farther south we go, the less civilization we'll find, but no matter. We'll make our home among the heathens and say our prayers, as my mam says, God save us."

Tabby paused then to cross herself, and Caroline

followed suit, knowing if she did not, Tabby would not get any sleep at all that night.

Her maid continued to chatter, but as always, Caroline let go of the words and just listened to the lilting sound of her voice. The soft accent sounded like home. Caroline washed her face and dressed in the nightgown her mother had made, a white silk gown with lace on the sleeves and around the low neck of the bodice. The night rail floated around her like a fairy cloak. Caroline saw the silk was very fine and her body could easily be seen through the folds, even as she moved. For some reason, this fact did not make her nervous but made her wonder what her husband's face would look like when he saw her in it.

Tabby placed the roses from Lady Montague's hothouse in a vase of water and set it on the mantel. The yellow ribbon was still tied around their stems. Tabby left Caroline with a quick kiss on her cheek, furtively, as though she could hear her mother scolding her for her familiarity in her strident voice all the way from the kitchen of the Montague house. Tabby was gone then, and Caroline stood by the hearth, staring into the flames. The door opened quietly behind her, and the silence changed. It became charged with heat that did not come from the fire.

Caroline turned and faced her husband. He stood just inside the doorway, his hand on the latch. He seemed to have stopped in midmotion, caught by the sight of her in her thin silk gown.

"Hello, Caroline."

His voice was rough, as though he had swallowed something harsh and might soon choke on it.

"Hello, my lord."

"I think here, within these walls, you might call me Anthony."

"I might."

He smiled and stepped toward her, the sound of his boots muffled on the heavy carpet. He reached for her, and she did not move away. He did not draw her to him or toward the bed, but took her hand gently in his own. "I think another glass of wine might be in order."

"If you wish," she said.

"I do."

Caroline took in her husband's beauty as he moved across their bedroom to the champagne that lay cooling in a wooden bucket. How he had found champagne was a mystery, for more often in York the favored drink was mead. No doubt he had brought it with him, as he had brought her wedding gown.

She watched him pour the wine, taking in the unconscious grace of his motion, reveling in the fact that he now belonged to her. She knew this was not really true. Her mother had taught her that the wife became the husband's property on their wedding night and not the other way around. But as she looked at him, Caroline found such pleasure in his rugged strength that she smiled. He may have dallied with many women in the past, but he would have no other wife.

Anthony poured wine into only one glass and brought it back to her without taking a sip. When he stood beside her, he drank from it first, out of old courtesy. She had read many times of the old customs, wishing they might somehow come back again. There had been a time when poison was slipped into wine cups. During those dark times, the man had drunk first to take the poison on himself.

Caroline was touched by the simple romance of the gesture, though she knew there was no poison in that inn. She felt like a princess in a fairy tale, as if she were living someone else's life. She accepted the wine and drank deeply to show her trust before handing the cup back to him.

He finished the glass, tossing his head back to take in the last of the wine. In that moment, it seemed to Caroline that they had truly entered another world. He had taken another oath with her there in that borrowed room, a silent one. That one gesture was a second oath to protect her for the rest of his life.

Anthony set the wineglass on the mantel next to her mother's roses and took her hand. He led her to the bed, but he did not draw her down on it or take her beneath him. As they stood together next to the high mattress, he leaned over and kissed her once, very sweetly, careful not to touch her in any other way, save for his hand on hers. When he drew back, his brown eyes stared into her own, and she saw the fire banked there, waiting for her. She knew, as she had known the night before, as she had known since the night she met him, that she wanted to step into that fire and be consumed.

"Sit down on the bed, Caroline."

Though she was rarely one to obey an order, she did as he said. It was as if she were under an enchantment, distant from this moment and this night, as though they were not truly happening to her. Then he stripped away his white cravat and tossed it on a chair. He drew off his fine coat of midnight blue and tossed it after his cravat. When she saw the dark hair on his chest beneath the open collar of his shirt, her breath caught in her throat, and she knew this night was real.

Anthony stripped down in front of her, one layer of clothing at a time. He did not douse the candles but stood where she could see him. Instead of closing her eyes or turning away, Caroline watched as he removed first his waistcoat, his shirt, and then his breeches, never taking her eyes from him. He was like a Greek statue she had seen in the books in her father's library, but larger, more beautiful, more real.

She raised her head to meet his gaze and found him smiling. He quirked a brow at her so she laughed. "So, Countess. What do you think of your husband?"

Caroline drew her knees onto the bed, moving back into the center of the snowy linens and the down-filled coverlet. She knelt with one arm outstretched so he might take her hand. Her throat was dry, but she managed to find her voice. "You know you are beautiful, my lord. As I am sure you have been told before."

Anthony stepped forward and took her hand in his. The heat of his palm was like a brand, and she felt his body through the thin silk of her nightgown. She took in the heady scent of him, the mix of spice and sweet together. Though she had never seen a naked man before, she did not turn away.

"What I have been told before does not matter. There is no one here between us."

He joined her on the bed, his heavy weight pressing

down into the feather mattress so that she rolled to him. She laughed again, and he caught her and kissed her. Caroline pushed away all thought of the days to come, all thought of her past, of her family, of her home, now left behind. She kept her mind on the here and now, leaning into him, her breasts pressing against his chest. Caroline reached behind him and drew him closer, her arms around his neck, her hands in his hair. She met his eyes before he could draw her down onto the bed.

"Then I say it, Anthony. You are beautiful, and I am a fortunate woman."

Caroline saw her husband's face soften as she spoke. There was tenderness in his eyes she had not seen before, warmth that had nothing to do with lust, nothing to do with the bargain they had struck. In the face of that tenderness, the world as she once knew it slipped away.

There was fire in his touch as he drew his open palm slowly over her back, down her waist, until his large hand cupped her bottom, pressing her tight against the hard length of him. His hands were hot as his grip tightened around her, bringing her close, drawing her deep into the flames of his desire. She could taste the passion on his lips as he kissed her. This time he held nothing back. Caroline thought he might devour her, the way paper was consumed and turned to ash. She welcomed it, reveling in the feel of his hard body against her softness. She pressed herself against him, her arms twined around his neck, her mouth open under his. And still, no matter how close she got, it was not enough.

Anthony pulled her down onto the bed. The cool sheets warmed beneath them as his hands moved over her body, stripping away her night rail. She shivered, the night air caressing her skin.

In the light of the candles, she watched his face as Anthony drank in the contours and hollows of her body, the rise of her breasts, the curve of her stomach, and the blond curls between her legs. Inch by precious inch, his eyes feasted on her, and then his hands followed the path his eyes had taken, his mouth not far behind.

Caroline cried out as he took one of her nipples into his mouth, drawing on her with lips and tongue and teeth until she writhed under him, the heat between her legs growing with every passing moment, with every touch on her body. After he had feasted on both breasts, he raised his head and met her eyes, his smile wicked. His gaze slid down to the curve of her thighs. She wriggled beneath him, and he rolled a little away from her and shifted down the bed. She murmured in protest, thinking he meant to leave her, but then he parted her thighs so he might lie between them.

Caroline gasped when she felt his mouth close over her. He kissed her there as he had kissed her mouth, with the same care, taking pleasure in her even as he gave it. She lost her breath as his tongue tempted her. She thrashed, trying to escape him, but he held her fast and would not let her go.

Her heart was pounding in her ears, and she could not see his face. She saw only his dark head between her thighs, and when she lay back against the bolster, she saw only the wooden canopy over the bed. She closed her eyes and reveled in the pleasure coursing through her, the race her body ran without her consent.

His tongue beckoned, and her body followed as over a cliff. A great tightening and then a wash of pleasure began to build like a flood behind a dam until it swamped her, making her cry out his name.

Caroline came back to herself as the ecstasy receded like an outgoing tide. Her mother had never mentioned a wife's satisfaction when she told her what her duties would be on her wedding night.

Anthony rose to lie beside her. He held her, stroking her hair. Her breathing began to even out, and her heart began to slow its frantic pace.

He did not speak, nor did she. The gulf between them seemed wider for the pleasure he had given her. She did not understand how such pleasure could be possible between strangers who were often at daggers drawn. She did not know what to do next, but she felt something surely needed to be said.

"Thank you."

He drew back and met her gaze. "There is no need for thanks between us. I give to you freely, and I will teach you to give to me."

"So," she said, forcing a lightness into her voice she did not feel, "how will you teach me these things?"

As he smiled, she was struck once more by the contours of his face, the strong line of his jaw, the soft curve of his lips.

"Slowly," he said as he bent down to press his lips to hers.

Chapter 11

CAROLINE LET GO OFF ALL MISGIVINGS, ALL THOUGHTS of the future, and allowed herself to enjoy her husband's lips on hers. She would savor her wedding night, just as she savored the taste of champagne on Anthony's lips. Her mouth opened under his, and his tongue found hers, tempting her, drawing her forward to lie against him. He relaxed against the bedclothes and let her drink her fill. Caroline pressed herself to him, forgetting he was supposed to be teaching her.

She took in his beauty in the candlelight, his strong thighs and tapered hips. His chest was hard under her hand, lightly dusted with dark hair. When his eyes met hers, she lost her breath, his desire was so clear. But he did not touch her.

Caroline ran her hands over his chest and shoulders. She reveled in his strength, the smooth planes and hard muscle, the satin of his nipples under her fingertips. Anthony's breath came short when she touched him there, and she smiled, watching his eyes darken.

She bent down and laid her lips against his skin just over his left breast, where she could feel the beating of his heart. Still he did not move but watched her hungrily, until she raised her lips and took his nipple into her mouth.

His hand moved into her hair, and he groaned before drawing her up to meet his lips. His mouth opened over hers, and this time, he held nothing back. Anthony rolled across the bed so she was beneath him, and covered her mouth as if he would devour her. His lips and tongue ran over hers until she thought she might lose her breath completely. Caroline did not want to breathe. She would rather taste his tongue on hers.

Anthony drew back. When she moved to cover his mouth with hers as he had taught her, he only smiled. He kissed her lightly before trailing his lips along her throat, over her collarbone, and down between her breasts. She froze, holding her breath as his lips closed over one nipple. She moaned as he laved the peak with his tongue. He did not linger but soon feasted on the other, until she was writhing under him. As good as his mouth felt on her skin, she wanted more.

Only then did he raise himself over her, pressing between her legs until her thighs fell open, gates that would not hold against him. He kissed her deeply as his hand moved between them to caress the nubbin of flesh at the apex of her thighs.

Caroline gasped, but he did not linger long. As soon as he found her wet and ready, he met her eyes, all traces of his smile gone.

"I would have you now, Caroline, if you will let me."

This was when he would take her. Her mother had instructed her to lie still and quiet in obedience.

But this heat, the feeling of his body covering hers, was something her mother had not told her of. The warmth of his flesh and the melting heat between her thighs made her desperate for something she could not name. Caroline found she could not speak, so she drew him close to her and pressed her lips against his. She took strength from his kiss, as if he had given back to her the power of speech.

"I am yours," she said, "if you will have me."

Anthony thought he might lose control then and there with her soft voice in his ears, low and throaty like the caress of a more experienced woman. When Caroline met his eyes, he saw the unfettered depths of his lust mirrored back to him. For all her youth and innocence, in this, she was his equal.

He meant to tell her it would hurt at first, but he would take her slowly, that he would be gentle and as careful as he could be. But all such thoughts fled as he looked at her and she writhed beneath him.

He kissed her, taking her breath from her lips as he slid into her, finding his home in the cradle of her thighs.

Anthony felt her tense at the pain of his entry, but as he moved slowly and steadily over her, careful to keep his full weight from her, she relaxed, her eyes widening with wonder. He had thought to take his fill at last, to lose himself in her selfishly, since he had earned it. The deflowering of a virgin was not supposed to be easy, and he had done so with courtesy and care. Anthony knew he could possess her as he had wanted to since the moment he saw her. She would enjoy his touch, for he was a skilled lover, but she would not feel the pleasure again. As he looked down into the maple brown of her eyes, he found he wanted to give her that bliss a second time.

So he raised himself higher, still joined with her but withdrawing a little, so she whimpered at the loss. Her soft moan almost drove him over the edge. As it was, it was all he could do to hold onto his strength and keep his climax at bay. He raised her hips from the bed and angled his entry to give her the most pleasure.

Anthony moved over her, lifting her hips to meet his thrusts, watching as her eyes lost their focus, looking inward toward the ecstasy he promised her as he moved against her.

He found the spot he sought, for he heard her sharp intake of breath. Anthony smiled, triumphant, as she began to thrash under him, as if she would escape the pleasure he was giving her. He held her under him and kept up the steady motion of his hips so she was trapped beneath him, able only to let the pleasure come.

She cried out, calling his name. He fell against her and gave himself over to sensation, driving into her as a man possessed. When his pleasure took him, it was the most intense of his life. Anthony wondered at that, when he could think again. How could a girl from deep in the country, a girl of family and breeding, with no experience and nothing but her beauty to recommend her, how could such a girl give him the most intense orgasm of his life? He wondered if he had begun to lose his reason, if the wedding vows had worked some magic on him, if her soft sweetness, her acquiescence to all his demands had seduced him as much as he had seduced her. But he soon let these thoughts go, for Caroline was warm against him, her soft breasts and thighs cushioning him, her long golden hair spread out upon his pillow, just as he had imagined it would be.

Anthony wondered if he had hurt her at the last, when he lost control of himself, but as he raised his eyes to look at her, he found her smiling.

"Husband," Caroline said, her voice throaty from the pleasure he had given her. "When can we do that again?"

Anthony laughed, drawing her close against him, rolling onto his side so he was no longer crushing her. She laughed with him from sheer joy, for she did not understand that even the strongest of men needed time between bouts of love. That this was yet another thing he would teach her filled him with a sense of peace he had rarely, if ever, felt. In that moment, the world as he had always known it fell away. There was only this bed, an island in an uncharted sea, and only this woman, soft beside him.

Gone was the wild woman who had defied him at every turn since he had met her, the woman who had leaped over hedges on horseback to escape him. He had tamed her, and the taming was as sweet as he might have wished for.

In the relaxation of the moment, a niggling sense of disappointment filled his breast to mingle with his bliss. He thought of the woman he had seen besting all comers on the archery range, the woman who had thrown a knife at him not once, but twice. That woman was strong enough to bear fine sons. He hoped that strength still lived in her, though her wedding vows seemed to have made her as docile and warm in bed as he might have wished.

Her breath was warm on his skin where she lay against his chest. Caroline slept, safe and at peace. Anthony knew that, whatever came, he would do what he could to protect this woman for the rest of his life. But he found he would miss the woman he had met in her father's house. He wondered where that woman had gone, and when, if ever, she might come back again.

Chapter 12

CAROLINE WOKE IN THAT STRANGE BED ALONE. SHE lay still for a long moment after she reached for her husband and found him gone. Cocooned in the soft feather bed, the down comforter covering all but her eyes and her hair, keeping her warm, the cold of morning touched her heart. He had left her.

She heard her mother's voice in her head, warning her against folly, reminding her of what marriage meant to the men of the South, to the people of the London *ton*. Marriage was business with them, a bargain made for the exchange of wealth, for the birthing of children. Caroline had known this. Her mother had instructed her of this as soon as her father came home from the war, their finances in ruins and their estate entailed away to a cousin she had never met. Caroline's sons would inherit from Anthony. Her children would be well cared for all their lives. In exchange, she would keep his house, both in the country and in town, smile at his guests, and teach herself to be content.

Her mother had been content all the years her

father had been away at war. Though their own marriage had been a love match, Caroline had known since she was eleven years old that her family was all but ruined by debt, that she would not be able to choose her own husband for love, as some girls did. She had always known she would have to marry to save her family from disgrace.

Now that her marriage had been made, the reality of that choice was her only bedfellow. She feared she and Anthony would be partners in nothing but the act of love, strangers who greeted each other at the breakfast table on the few mornings he deigned to come home at all. She had heard of that kind of marriage all her life. And now it seemed she had one. She shook her head to clear it. Their lovemaking had left her hopeful for better things. And who knew what might come in the years ahead. They might learn to like each other beyond the sheets of their marriage bed. They might even learn to laugh together.

There was a pain over her heart, and she swallowed it down. She was no weak woman to pine for what she could not have. The tenderness she had seen in her husband's gaze the night before had been more than she had hoped for, but as her mother was fond of saying, she was a woman grown. She must live in the world and accept its realities. The fact that Anthony had made love to her with such sweetness, that he had initiated her into their marriage bed with abandoned sensuality, had nothing to do with the bargain they had struck.

Caroline got out of the bed in one swift move, tossing the covers back. The blood of her innocence marred the sheet. She left it in full view in case he might come back to look at the proof that she was pure, that she had kept her part of their agreement.

She did not think she would be able to stand Tabby's idle chatter, so she did not call for her to help her dress. Alone, she drew on her traveling gown from the day before and a cloak to go over it, for as cold as it was in her room with the fire lit, it would be much colder outside this early in the morning.

Her husband had left her alone on their wedding night. But Hercules was down in the stables. Though she could not ride out on him, she could go and see him.

Caroline slipped her hand into her portmanteau and found the apple she had hidden in its depths. There were two more tucked away in the same side pocket. Caroline drew on her hood, leaving her golden hair to fall past her shoulders and down her back beneath the cloak. If she was quick and quiet, perhaps no one would see her.

She opened the door to the sitting room where she and her husband had taken their dinner the night before. Anthony was not there. God alone knew where he had gone when he had left her bed. Caroline pushed that thought from her mind. She slipped out of her husband's rented rooms, leaving the door unlatched behind her. She did not trust herself to find the back stairs, so she went down into the taproom.

A few men slept still by the fire, wrapped in their cloaks. The woman who ran the inn was busy in the kitchen, giving orders to her cook. One girl knelt by the fire, building it up. Caroline moved quickly past when the girl's back was turned and escaped into the inn yard.

The morning light was gray; the last indigo of the night sky had faded. A glimmer of orange rose from the east, and Caroline smiled to see it. They would be in Shropshire in a few days. Once on her husband's estate, she would go riding, far from him and the life she was now forced to lead. She would have time to herself in that new place. Nothing brought her as much joy as riding on Hercules across the moors. Shropshire had no moors, but surely there was some wild country there she might enjoy. She might even learn to love her new home with Hercules and Tabby there with her.

Caroline stepped into the stables. Two grooms mucking out the stalls paused to lift their hats before they continued their work. She nodded to them and passed on until she found Hercules. Her great horse was menacing Anthony's coachman, rolling his eyes and stomping his front hooves in warning.

"Now then, you great bully. Are you frightening my husband's man?"

At the sight of her, at the sound of her voice, Hercules calmed at once, lowering his head so she might rub the splash of white along his nose. "You must be polite to those who serve you, Hercules. This behavior is ungentlemanly and beneath you."

She offered the apple then, and her stallion's lips closed around it, bringing it into his mouth without putting his teeth too near her tender flesh.

Her husband's coachman stood by, not too close. He seemed to fear her almost as much as he feared her horse.

Caroline smiled at him. "I am Caroline Montague."

She corrected herself. "Lady Ravensbrook now. What is your name?"

"John, my lady." He had taken off his hat as soon as he had seen her, and now he bowed low to her.

"No need for bowing, John. I am sorry Hercules has given you trouble. He does not like new people or new places."

"No, my lady, no trouble at all. He is a fine horse."

She saw John's hand was wrapped in dirty linen. Hercules had nipped him already.

"We'll have to see to that bite. I don't want it turning putrid."

"No, my lady. I mean, as you say, my lady."

Caroline turned to Hercules, who had eaten his apple in one bite and was now nuzzling her hair. He had knocked her hood back already.

"You must not bite our John, Hercules. He is my husband's man, which makes him my man, which makes him yours. Do you understand me?"

Hercules shook himself all over, then pressed close to her again, seeking in her cloak to see if she might have brought him something else.

"I will take that for a yes." She laid her hand against his neck. She stayed and watched as both Hercules and Achilles were led into the cart in which they would continue their ride south. Achilles was as gentle with John as a lamb, and Hercules, while surly, did not try to bite the coachman again. Caroline petted both horses to reward them for their quiet obedience before she turned back to John. "Come with me into the inn," she said. "I'll need to wash your wound."

"It's nothing, my lady."

"I will be the judge of that."

With one last pat on Hercules's neck, Caroline led her husband's coachman out of the stables and into the taproom at the inn. She called for warm water to clean the bite and honey to fight against infection, and dressed his wound herself. "You must keep this dry and clean, John. Have you a wife?"

"Yes, my lady. Marjorie, who cooks for his lordship at Ravensbrook in Shropshire."

"Very well, then. Have Marjorie apply honey to it twice a day once you are home. And a clean dressing, John. Do you understand me?"

He smiled, his dark brown eyes twinkling. "And you a wife of only one day. You have the way of it already, my lady."

Caroline laughed at his polite way of calling her a nag as she turned to the stairs. She came back to her sitting room to find breakfast laid out for her, soft bread with butter, fresh cheese and stewed apples, fried eggs and bacon. She sat down and ate, surprised to find herself hungry after all she had supped on the night before. Then she remembered what came after that supper and the color in her cheeks rose. Anthony was still nowhere to be seen.

Tabby stood over her chair, worried as she brought jam and warm toast, kidneys and stewed tomatoes. "My lady, you were gone when I came upstairs," Tabby said.

"I was in the stables."

Tabby stood close, misery written on her pretty face. Caroline took her hand. "I'm sorry to cause you concern. Next time, I'll leave a note."

"But I can't read, my lady," Tabby wailed.

"I will find a tutor for you once we reach Shropshire."

The girl's face lit up as with a sunrise.

"Oh, that would be wonderful! May I learn, my lady?"

"Of course, Tabby. You don't need my permission for that."

"But you need mine, Wife."

Anthony stood in the doorway to the outer hall, glowering at her. "Do I?" She tried to keep her voice even, but when his back stiffened, she knew he heard the insolence in her tone her mother had often chided her for. Caroline held his gaze, drinking the last of her tea. Tabby had prepared it just as she liked, with cream and two lumps of sugar.

"Leave us," Anthony said.

Tabby withdrew, with the teapot in one hand and the toast in the other. Caroline sighed to see her go. She was hoping for one more slice of toast with jam and one more cup before they took to the road. She turned to her husband and saw the anger in his eyes. Her ire rose to match his, but she bit down on it. She would keep her dignity and her temper, no matter what he said.

"Do not be rude to my maid, if you please, my lord. We are adjusting to our new life, and I would rather not have you interfere."

"Interfere?" Anthony slammed the door behind him so the room shook. "I think you will find that, as your husband, I will interfere with you about a great many things."

Caroline almost spat out a curse. She swallowed the foul words. "So I see, my lord. I would have thought you might have better things to do than to concern yourself with my household staff."

"Perhaps once you prove yourself capable of running a household, I will be able to attend to other matters."

"Why you—"

"After all, what proper wife—a countess, no less— disappears from my bed before dawn to go to the stables alone in her nightgown to see to her horse? Or flirts with my coachman in the taproom of a public inn, or any place else?"

Caroline jumped to her feet, her eyes blazing. She pressed her hands onto the table in front of her, trying to hold her temper. She had never known anyone to provoke her as this man did. And she was married to him. If she was not careful, he would do nothing but infuriate her for the rest of her life.

"My lord," she said. "I did not step out in my nightgown, but in this dress and a cloak. I went to the stables, as any free Englishwoman should be allowed to do. And I did not flirt with your man in a public house but tended his wound that would no doubt have festered, a wound he got taking care of my horse."

"You are the Countess of Ravensbrook, Caroline. You cannot traipse about in public inn yards, caring for servants."

"I can, and I will."

"You will not. You are not free to do as you please. You are my wife."

"Do you think I need reminding of that fact, my lord?"

"Yes, damn it, you do!"

Caroline stood her ground, her eyes never leaving his. The woman clearly had no intention of changing her ways at all.

Anthony crossed the room in two strides and held her upper arms, drawing her close. She did not flinch or look away. He saw a flash of pain on her face and her need to hide it.

He cursed himself silently for a fool. He should not have left her alone that morning. If he had stayed and played out a pleasant fiction of a romantic morning after, there would be no gossip about his countess in an inn yard at York.

When he thought of how any rogue might have come upon her in the stables, his heart almost stopped. The day Anne had run away with Carlyle, she had disappeared while going out to saddle her horse for a sedate ride into the village. She had not come back until a week had passed, her honor in ruins. Their mother, horrified to see the family so disgraced, had died a month later from a failing heart weakened by shame.

Anthony still remembered the days he had spent scouring the countryside, looking for Anne. He had not found her until Carlyle dropped her off at the gate at Ravensbrook House. The bounder had not even bothered to drive her to the door but made her walk the mile up to the house, alone and friendless, not knowing if her family would even take her back again. Anne would never recover, no matter what care the Prince Regent took to preserve her reputation. She was unsullied in the eyes of Society but blamed herself for everything.

Anthony had salvaged Anne's reputation and tucked

her safely away on a small estate in Richmond. He had sworn no woman under his protection, especially not his wife, would ever be indulged so foolishly again. Gently bred women had no idea of what the world was truly like. It did not take a man like Carlyle to ruin a woman's life. Just one unguarded moment might lead to a kidnapping for ransom, a throat cut, or worse.

As Anthony looked down at his wife, he knew if such evil were to befall her, he would not be able to bear it.

Slowly, he took in the soft brown of her eyes tinged with green, the alabaster of her skin, smooth where it met the silk of her rumpled traveling dress. As angry as he was with her, he wanted her with a desire so strong he could not catch his breath. But he would not indulge that desire. He would tame her with the force of his will. He was not a man to be thwarted, not by a woman who had sworn to obey him.

"Caroline, in London, among civilized people, ladies do not go out in public unless they are fully clothed."

"You hope to instruct me on manners, my lord?"

"Clearly someone must."

Caroline did not falter under the heat of his gaze. His hands held her too roughly, and he knew it. But he would begin as he meant to go on. She could not run about with no thought for her safety or for his honor. He would see to that.

She spoke finally after a long silence, contempt for him in her eyes. "I understand that in London things are done differently than they are in Yorkshire. It must be a hardship for you, to be tied to such a wife. But it

Chapter 13

CAROLINE TENSED UNDER THE ONSLAUGHT OF HIS mouth and almost flinched away, but her pride would not let her. She would not give in to his unreasonable demands. She was his wife, but she was no man's servant.

She met his lips with coldness, not opening her mouth under his. His teeth pressed into her lips, as though he would bite her. Anthony did not release her. He kept his mouth over hers as if to punish her, as if by the strength of his will he would force her to do his bidding.

But Caroline did not yield. His lips became gentle, his hands on her arms softening into a caress.

Only then did Caroline try to move away from him. His hands were like steel on her arms, his lips like iron. He would not let her turn away.

Instead, Anthony drew her back into the bedroom, steering her toward the bed where they had spent the night before in so much bliss. She knew then he meant to conquer her another way.

Caroline twisted in his grasp. The suddenness of

her movement seemed to catch him off-guard, for Anthony loosened his grip, and she slipped out of his hands. She ran into the sitting room, moving fast toward the door to the corridor beyond, but he was faster, catching the door just as she opened it. He slammed it shut, his arm above her head, trapping her between his body and the dark wood.

"Wife, I will not let you leave me."

Caroline was breathless, as much from his nearness as from her anger at him. "I fear you forget yourself, my lord."

"I forget nothing."

Anthony's arms rested on either side of her head as he leaned down to whisper into her ear. The heat of his breath touched her temple and cheek, making her tremble even as her belly started to heat with desire.

"I remember every kiss you gave me last night, Caroline. I remember every sound you made as you writhed beneath me. I remember how you called my name. I will never be able to forget."

He ran his lips down her temple to her jaw, his hands still holding the door closed behind her. She leaned back against the heavy walnut, her knees liquid. His mouth moved over hers as he kissed her again, holding her still with nothing but his body on hers, and his lips on her skin. Caroline almost lost herself in his kiss that time but was brought back to her senses by the sound of the bolt sliding home.

She ordered herself to push him away, to free herself, but he held her with just his lips on hers. Her knees were as weak as they had been a moment before, and she made a small sound of acquiescence in the back of her throat, a little moan of pleasure as his hands rose to cup her breasts. She leaned into his touch, following the warmth of his hands. The hard planes of his body pressed her against the door, so she felt the smooth wood on her back.

Anthony's lips were on her throat then, teasing her as he unfastened his breeches. Caroline lowered her hands to help him, but he brushed her fingertips away. His lips and free hand were everywhere at once, on her cheek, on her throat, on her hair, on her breast. He raised the skirt of her gown, and heat coursed between her legs as it had the night before. He held her immobile, his lips on hers, plying her with kisses even as he readied himself to enter her.

"Anthony," she gasped.

"I must have you, Caroline. Let me have you."

His voice shook with need, and her throat closed with her own desire. She had not known that love-making could be like this, so hard and fast. But she found, as his lips traveled over her throat, as he waited for her answer, that she liked it.

"Yes," she said, her voice so soft she almost could not hear it. He did, though, and he did not hesitate.

Anthony drew her up, his hands spanning her waist. He lifted her, and she leaned back against the door, her arms around him, her legs around his hips. He raised her up with both hands on her bottom and entered her wet warmth without a word, a deep groan torn from his throat.

He held her high so she did not have to bear the brunt of his assault. He was a careful lover, even as he had her against the door of the inn. He lost himself in her, the motion of his body slapping hers against the wooden door, faster and faster as he sought his release.

Something about his desperation drew her in, and she felt her own desire rise. He had been so careful with her the night before in their borrowed bed, but now he had lost all control. Now it was he who murmured her name against her hot skin as if it were a prayer. She had a measure of power yet.

As his thrusts increased in intensity, a streak of pleasure shot from the core of her being. The spike turned into a wave of ecstasy, until she was clutching his hair and moaning his name as he called her own.

His satisfaction took him, and he groaned against her throat, his hands on her bottom still supporting her weight.

Anthony lowered her carefully to the floor even as he caught his breath. Her skirt slid down, covering her legs. He did not release her, for he seemed to know she had no strength to stand. They stood together, one of his hands cupped behind her head, the other on the curve of her hip.

Caroline came to herself slowly. Her body ached as if she had been caught in a thresher, as when the chaff is drawn from the barley. She leaned against her husband, the warm velvet of his coat soft against her cheek.

She realized he was dressed for the road, and she remembered they were to have left at first light. He had meant to let her sleep longer than he should have, and all the rest of the morning's business had come from that kindness.

Caroline looked at him and found his eyes on her,

watching her already. She laughed, a low and throaty sound she almost did not recognize. Her anger had burned away in the heat between them, heat that had already begun to dissipate. Anthony quirked an eyebrow at her.

"So we both have a temper," he said.

Caroline heard a polite cough behind the door they leaned on and realized the entire inn likely had been listening to their antics.

"Perhaps we should begin again. Good morning, Wife."

Caroline met his eyes, laughter still on her lips. "Good morning, Husband."

"We ride out soon, if you are willing."

Caroline pressed her body against his in a way that never would have occurred to her the day before. She watched his eyes darken with desire as she moved against him. She leaned up to whisper to him. "I am indeed willing, my lord. There is other riding I would prefer. But if we must leave here, we must."

Drawing back from him, she saw the hunger on his face. But he was a man used to restraint. As soon as Anthony knew she could stand without his help, he stepped away from her, fastening his breeches tight.

"We will have to leave off the other riding until tonight, my lady. We have many miles to travel before then."

Caroline's eyes took him in, reflecting on the memory of what he looked like under his clothes. She raised her gaze to his, but he did not accept her challenge. Anthony simply stood and looked at her, his desire betrayed only by the unevenness of his breath.

She accepted his harsh breathing as a concession, proof he still wanted her, that she still held power over him. She stepped past him, brushing against him before she walked away.

"As you say, my lord."

Caroline turned back to take one last look at him before she walked into the bedroom. Anthony was already gone, the door to the hallway closing behind him. Tabby came in the next moment, her face a blank mask. For once, she did not say a word. Caroline did not speak of what had passed but kept her voice even, her tone light. She could still feel his hands on her body and taste him on her tongue.

"You'd better pack before you dress my hair, Tabby," she said. "I think his lordship means to leave within the half hour."

Caroline stripped off the soiled traveling gown from the day before and dressed in a new gown and shift, this one of emerald green trimmed in harvest gold. She went alone behind the wooden screen in the corner of the room and washed while Tabby packed her portmanteau, dropping a hairbrush and comb in her haste.

"Tabby," Caroline said as the girl bound her hair in braids. "Don't be troubled. Lord Ravensbrook is a good man."

"So they say, my lady. But his temper is fierce," Tabby whispered.

Caroline smiled. "Indeed. So is mine."

Chapter 14

CAROLINE AND ANTHONY RODE ONCE MORE IN SILENCE, though on the second day of their marriage, his wife did not spend as much time staring out of windows as napping. Her bright emerald dress hurt his eyes, and he reminded himself to take her to a modiste in London and make certain she was fashionably dressed. Of course, as he looked at her, he knew he would love her body in any dress she wore, and better in none.

Her breasts rose and fell with her gentle breathing beneath her green spencer. Her soft blond hair was beginning to come free from its pins beneath the monstrosity of the bonnet she wore, this one trimmed in ostrich plumes. Anthony saw her mother's hand in that. He wondered how beautiful Caroline might look in the finest London fashions, in the softer shades of mint and pink, light blue silks and sprigged muslin frocks. He would dress her in gold and silver for her first ball, with nothing in her hair but diamonds.

Anthony spent a joyous, tortured afternoon thinking

of his wife in diamonds and nothing else. She woke, raising her head from his shoulder as they approached his friend's house in Derbyshire. Raymond Olivier, the Earl of Pembroke, back from the war, lived now at Pembroke House almost full time.

The old castle, its interior converted to a modern dwelling, was still dominated by the shades of the past. Pembroke House sat on a bluff surrounded by a well-kept park of oaks and hawthorns. Ivy clung to the old walls, and in spring, the wisteria climbed the stone to bloom white and purple in the sunlight. Anthony had spent many happy days of his childhood at Pembroke House whenever Raymond's father was away. Now that the old earl was dead, a man his friend still hated, Raymond, the new earl, had finally come home.

The traveling coach drew up before the great house, and the door opened before the footmen could come down from their perch. As soon as Anthony stepped down from the carriage, Pembroke's great hand took hold of his shoulder and brought him into his embrace.

"Anthony," he said. "It has been too long."

While Anthony had returned home at once after resigning his commission, Pembroke had stayed on the Continent to indulge in fine wine and women. His friend's dark blond hair still fell rakishly over one eye, and his blue gaze was bloodshot, though it was only four o'clock in the afternoon. But Pembroke's smile was as warm as it had ever been. Behind the depths of Pembroke's hidden pain, Anthony could see the boy he once had known smiling back at him.

"It has been three months since I saw you last," Anthony said.

"Too long," Pembroke repeated. "Where is your wife?"

"Here, my lord."

Caroline did not wait for one of the gentlemen to help her but climbed down from the traveling coach in one leap, her white leather boots crunching on the gravel driveway. "Good day, Lord Pembroke. I thank you for welcoming us to your home."

"You have had a long journey. You must be tired."

"I am well enough, my lord. I slept most of the day away. There is little else to do in a rocking carriage."

Pembroke did not raise a brow or offer a knowing smile to Anthony. Indeed, there was a great deal more to be done in a rocking carriage, as they both knew well. There was no reason for a man to ride in a closed carriage other than to indulge himself with his chosen woman. Pembroke did not look at Anthony at all but only at Caroline.

"I am happy to find you well. Anything I have is yours, for as long as you are here." He bowed over her hand, and she covered his hand with both of hers. "I see my friend's taste in women has only improved with time," Pembroke said.

As Anthony knew she would be, Caroline was quick with a pert answer. "Indeed, my lord. I am glad to hear it. I wonder if his temper has improved as well?"

Pembroke's great booming laugh filled the courtyard, and he clapped his hand on her shoulder as if she were a companion-in-arms. She winced but did not flinch away.

"If it has, I haven't noticed, my lady." Pembroke led them into his house as he spoke, and Caroline fell into step beside him, letting her husband follow as he would.

"If I lose my temper, I have good reason," Anthony said.

Caroline raised her eyebrows, and Pembroke laughed again. "You always think you have cause, at any rate," he said.

He turned to Anthony as they stepped into the entrance hall. "I must warn you, Anthony. I think you have forgotten the date. Gentlemen of our acquaintance have arrived for our monthly meeting."

"The Hellfire Club," Anthony said, frowning like thunder.

"Yes," Pembroke answered. His friend kept his voice scrupulously empty of all emotion. "Viscount Carlyle is among them."

Anthony felt the blood drain from his face. Caroline must have noticed his sudden pallor because she reached for him. Her hand lay on his arm, but he did not acknowledge it or look at her. It was all he could do to hold himself in check.

"Should I turn them all out?"

Caroline's eyes rested on his face, so Anthony was careful to keep his expression blank. She, like all decent wives, need know nothing of the Hellfire Club and its proclivities.

"I think we can share space with them for one night. Pembroke House is large enough."

"I should say so," Caroline interjected. "I look forward to meeting the members of your club, my lord. The company sounds bracing after so long a journey."

It was Pembroke who answered, for Anthony's throat had closed with ire. "Forgive me, Lady Ravensbrook, but we are not fit to accommodate a lady this evening. This is my fault entirely. I hope you will indulge me and take your dinner upstairs."

"Will my lord be dining with you?" Caroline asked.

Pembroke looked distinctly uncomfortable and did not speak.

"Yes, I will, Caroline. And you will eat in your rooms."

"Like a petulant child? I think not."

Anthony's voice sounded strangled in his own ears. "Caroline, please indulge me in this."

She stared at him mutinously for a moment before her face transformed into a gracious smile. "Do not trouble yourself, my lord," she said to Pembroke, turning from Anthony altogether. "All will be well."

Pembroke's smile showed his relief, but Anthony knew better. Caroline had not agreed to stay away. She had only smiled prettily, which meant she was up to mischief.

He would lock her in her rooms if need be. He needed all his energy to prepare to meet Carlyle in company for the second time in the same week. The man dogged his steps like a plague. Caroline would simply have to stay away.

&

Caroline was shown upstairs into a suite of rooms clearly meant for a lady, beautifully appointed with maple furniture and a soft blue rug. There was none of her mother's dark burgundies and emerald velvet here. All was light and airy, the satin bedclothes embroidered in tones of ice blue and cream. For a fanciful moment, Caroline wondered if Pembroke had matched the room to some lady's eyes.

She gave herself over to the ministrations of her maid as Tabby brushed her hair out, making it gleam gold in the firelight. Caroline listened with half an ear as Tabby recounted all the details of her journey in the baggage cart as if Caroline had not ridden the same road.

Caroline's mind wandered to Anthony and how well he had looked in his fine green coat, which had encased the muscles of his arms almost like a second skin. She had spent the entire coach ride thinking about him, and of their lovemaking the night before.

Whatever Anthony said, she would go down for dinner soon and see him again. Her body hummed at the thought of her husband's nearness, even in the midst of other guests. She wanted to feel the warmth of his presence and make sure he knew he was hers for the night to come.

"My lady, why are you smiling? Did I say something funny?"

"No, Tabby. I find I am in a pleasant mood."

"Will you stay in your dressing gown after your bath?"

"That would be quite scandalous, as I intend to sup with my husband in the dining room."

"But Lord Ravensbrook gave orders that we are to eat here, to rest for the journey tomorrow."

"And now I am giving you different orders. Tabby, did we pack the white gown I had made last month, the one with the light pink trim?"

"Yes, miss...I mean, my lady. I'll press it for you."

❧

Just as Caroline was dressed to go down to dinner, with her hair swept up in a sophisticated twist that no woman in Yorkshire would have worn, a maid came to her room, bearing a huge tray filled with more food than Caroline could have eaten in a week. The maid bobbed a curtsy and set the tray down on the polished table beside the fireplace.

"Your dinner, my lady."

"Indeed. How kind. And where might my husband be?"

"In the dining room, my lady. With the gentlemen, and the…ummm…"

"Other ladies." Caroline spoke for her.

She watched as the girl blushed and stammered, and Caroline's suspicions were confirmed. The gentlemen's club might well be meeting after dinner, but she was certain the men had brought their wives, as well. She thought she had heard a hint of feminine laughter as she walked up the stairs to her room. Seeing the girl's embarrassment, she was now certain of it.

"Yes, my lady."

So there would be other ladies dining that evening. Anthony wanted to keep her from his friends for some idiotic reason of his own. Caroline squared her shoulders. "Thank you. That will be all."

She walked alone down to the dining room. She had no trouble finding it and did not have to ask one of the many footmen in the household to escort her. She heard raucous laughter, the booming voices of men, and the sinuous, hissing laughter of women. Caroline pushed aside her anger at not being invited to dine.

Perhaps Lord Pembroke was simply concerned that she was overtired. And perhaps pigs would soon take flight over the city of London.

She saw as she entered that the first course had already been served. The dining room was full of laughing people. The gentlemen were dressed in coats of black and midnight blue, their waistcoats in tones of gold and silver, white cravats at their throats. The women wore their hair in curls around their shoulders and flowing down their backs. Their gowns were cut so low that Caroline blinked. This was why she had received no invitation to dinner, why a tray had been sent to her room. Pembroke had filled his house with courtesans.

She saw her husband seated among them. On his left side sat a woman, her dark hair spilling over the globes of her breasts, which she seemed intent on pressing against Anthony's arm. To his right was a blonde with golden hair that had red roses nestled in it.

No place had been left for her. But when she entered, half a dozen men stood and offered their chairs. She recognized one of them from her father's house party, searching her mind for his name. Victor Winthrop, Viscount Carlyle, the man who had won the golden bowl at archery. The man she had beaten. He smiled at her. It seemed that he remembered her, as well.

She straightened her back, ignoring the other women present, acting as if courtesans simply did not exist in that room or anywhere else. She smiled graciously first at Viscount Carlyle, then at Pembroke, who welcomed her with a smile, but who looked horrified to see her.

Ignoring Anthony completely, she seated herself between Victor and a second gentleman who immediately introduced himself as Admiral Washburn of the Royal Navy. The doxy who had occupied that chair only a moment before was escorted farther down the table.

Anthony's glare heated her skin even from the distance between them. She could feel his anger from across the room.

She clung to her own anger, trying desperately to ignore the niggling pain in her heart. Caroline knew very well that, in spite of the heat between them, Anthony did not love her. And what better proof of this did she need than to see him seated among courtesans at his friend's table, making no move to cross the room to greet her.

Caroline was shocked to feel tears pressing behind her eyes and jealousy gnawing at her innards like a jackal. She breathed deeply and tried hard to set her husband from her mind. She could not banish Anthony from her thoughts completely, but she managed to supersede him by focusing on the rest of the room. A lady should never sit with doxies. Indeed, a lady should pretend she does not know such creatures exist. Caroline could hear her mother's voice in her ears as clearly as if Lady Montague sat beside her.

Caroline reminded herself she was a married woman. She was bound for life to a man she barely knew, but she was also her own mistress. She no longer had to fear what her mother would say if she walked her own path as she pleased. Her marriage at least had bought her that.

All the gentlemen treated her with strict courtesy, while Anthony continued to stare at her from down the table. The women ignored her completely.

After offering her a glass of wine and inquiring after her mother's health, Carlyle turned back to the discussion that had begun before Caroline arrived, positioning himself so Caroline might hear every word of it.

She joined the talk of what was going on in Parliament now that the troops were coming home. The Prince Regent was at war with the Commons, as he so often was since he had taken the reign from his father. Caroline had heard a little of this even in Yorkshire. She read the papers brought up from London, though they were often a few weeks late.

When the talk turned to the theater, she listened closely, for she had never seen a play.

"Titania, Prinny's favorite actress, will produce *The Taming of the Shrew* this winter," Lord Bathurst said.

"I have always hated that play," Caroline said. She felt the weight of Anthony's censure as heavy as a stone, but she ignored him.

"Hate Shakespeare? How can that be, my lady? A woman of your wit and sensibility must love the Bard." Carlyle smiled at her, also ignoring her husband as he refilled her glass of Madeira.

"Indeed, my lord, I am fond of Shakespeare in general, but that play is an anathema to women everywhere. Forced into marriage against her will, Katherine is taken from her home and starved into submission. What thinking person in this day of enlightenment could embrace such a theme?"

She looked at Anthony then. His color had risen beneath his tan. His dark eyes rested on her so intently his doxies turned away to hunt better prey on either side. She smiled to see her husband abandoned by his whores.

"But Lady Ravensbrook, Katherine instructs the other wives in the end to serve their husbands with sweetness and obedience."

"As well she might, after having been starved and endlessly berated. One hopes that even Bonaparte would treat prisoners of war better. All I say, gentlemen, is that play is not one of Shakespeare's finer works."

"And which plays do you prefer, my lady?" Admiral Washburn asked.

"*Hamlet* and *Macbeth*. Both are full of intrigue, and both are quite bloody."

The company laughed, save for the doxies, who glared at her for taking so much of the gentlemen's time. Her husband stared at her as if she had grown a second head.

She ate the last bite of her dessert, lingering over the fine chocolate and sweet cream. Clearly Lord Pembroke selected his cook with more care than he did his guests.

There were no ladies present, save herself in her virginal white gown trimmed in pink, so the gentlemen did not hang back for cigars and port but led their chosen companions into the drawing room. Caroline hesitated before she rose from her chair, but Anthony did not come to escort her.

Viscount Carlyle was kind enough to lead her into the drawing room when her husband did not seek her out. The carpets had been taken up, and as Caroline watched, gentlemen and their escorts began to waltz.

No doubt, Carlyle planned to ask her to dance, for he smiled down at her, his eyes gleaming as he offered his hand.

Just as she was about to accept, Anthony was upon her, his eyes darkened with fury to an almost deadly shade of black. He did not speak to Viscount Carlyle at all, but something passed between the two men that made Caroline wonder how well they knew each other.

Without a word, Victor bowed to her and withdrew, taking a buxom redhead onto the dance floor.

Anthony wasted no time in niceties. "Caroline, come away from here."

"I am enjoying myself, my lord. Your friends are quite charming."

"I will not allow you to spend another moment among these whores." His voice was a hiss in her ear, and her eyes narrowed as she gazed up at him.

"Indeed, my lord? You seem to spend a great deal of time among them."

Anthony stopped speaking altogether and dragged her out of the room. He moved so quickly she could not even say good night to any of the gentlemen present. Caroline did not look at her husband as he led her away like a child, his grip hard on her arm.

As they left, Caroline caught the eye of their host. Pembroke smiled at her from where he sat, a woman hanging on each arm and a third perched on his knee. He raised his glass to Anthony and Caroline in salute as they passed. She shook her head. Pembroke was incorrigible, but she found she was not offended by the idiocy of the evening. There was a sorrow in Pembroke's eyes, some shadow of loss hidden behind his mindless pursuit of pleasure. Caroline was sorry to see his pain.

She forgot all about Pembroke and his sorrow at the foot of the stairs when her husband lifted her into his arms like a sack of meal.

"Put me down this instant. Have you gone mad?"

Fury burned in his eyes. Gone was the calm, collected man who had sat silent at dinner. She felt a moment of elation that his iron control had begun to crack.

"If I am mad, you have driven me to it."

He swept her up the stairs, his hands hard on her body. He carried her easily, as if she weighed nothing, while Lord Pembroke's footmen watched from below without saying a word.

Chapter 15

ANTHONY KICKED OPEN THE DOOR TO HER BORROWED bedroom. He set her on her feet on the plush carpet and bolted the door behind them

"Caroline, you cannot do as you wish every moment of the day. You cannot sit and eat among courtesans. I will not allow it."

She drew off her gown, pulling the pins out of her hair and laying them down for Tabby to find the next day.

"I am sick of hearing what you will and will not allow. I follow where you lead me, Anthony. If you sit among ladies of the evening, then I will sit among them with you."

She turned her back on him and slipped on her nightgown. Anthony stood by the door, staring at her.

"When you defy me, you make me a laughing-stock, Caroline."

A maid had left a carafe of wine and two glasses for them. Caroline poured herself a glass and sipped at it. She filled the second glass, as well, thinking to offer it to Anthony, but he still glowered at her.

"Anthony, I did not defy you. I took a meal in company and was going to dance with a man I met for the first time in my father's house. If this passes for defiance in London, I know not what to tell you."

He crossed the room to her with a slow, stalking stride, his face in shadow from the firelight behind him.

"You came among courtesans," he said. "You dined among the most debauched men in England. The man with whom you took your dinner, who gave you your first glass of wine this evening, is someone I would not have you acquainted with."

"Why ever not? For heaven's sake, my father knows him. Viscount Carlyle is a perfect gentleman."

"I am your husband. Never speak to him or to any strange man without my express permission."

The idiotic high-handedness of that statement brought Caroline up short.

"That's rich, my lord. You had two doxies courting you, and you take me to task for drinking wine with a friend of my father?"

"Carlyle is not fit company for you."

"Nor was anyone else there, it seems. But I ate among the people you brought me to," she said.

"You must never speak to a man unless I have introduced you first. There are men in the world who would behave in ways you simply cannot imagine."

"And Viscount Carlyle, a man who was once a guest in my father's home, is one of them?"

"Yes."

Caroline turned her back on him. She was too angry to speak.

Anthony's hands were on her then, bringing her

to face him, the strength of his touch sudden and unyielding. She dropped her glass, and the red wine poured out across the cream carpet, the thick burgundy splattering the hem of her fine linen nightgown. She would have sworn under her breath, but she could not take her eyes from her husband's face.

"Caroline, I would care for you as best I can. If I ask you to stay above stairs, you must trust that I have good reason."

His voice was gentle for the first time that day. For some reason, his gentleness hurt her as his anger did not. All she could see in that moment were those women in Pembroke's dining room, pressing their heavy breasts against him.

"I do not trust you, my lord. And I have reason of my own."

"You can trust me, Caroline. You can trust me to care for you as best I can, to protect you from folly and danger every day for the rest of my life."

"From whose folly, my lord? Yours or my own?"

Anthony sighed then, and she felt the last of his anger drain from him as the burgundy had drained across the carpet at their feet.

Anthony lifted her in his arms. He carried her to the bed without another word between them and set her down on the silken coverlet.

She thought he would leave her, but he stripped instead, his nakedness beautiful in the candlelight. The hard planes of his body called to her, even though she knew nothing had been settled between them. She began to wonder if anything ever would.

Anthony turned to her, and she saw his eyes had

begun to gleam with desire. The pain of his insult began to heal a little as he looked at her as if he would worship her body with his own, just as he had sworn on their wedding day.

He reached out and ran his hand over the soft lawn of her thin nightgown, exploring her curves as if for the first time. Caroline lay back and let him touch her as he would, reveling in the heat of his hands as he drew her wine-stained gown over her head and tossed it away.

He lay on top of her, his hands in her hair, pulling her head back so her mouth was trapped under his. His kiss was hard against her lips, conveying his desire and his frustration together. She kissed him back, her own frustration evident in her touch.

His hands gentled once more, and his lips lingered over hers. "You will never come among such people again," he said.

"I will come where you lead me, Anthony."

"Then come with me now," he said.

He lowered his lips to her throat and suckled there as at her breast. She felt the bite of his teeth, a little nip of pain, a sharp sauce in a larger meal. Her lust flared as his teeth grazed her throat, trailing down; his lips closed over her breast. She moaned as he tasted her, hoping he might once again follow the line of her body down between her thighs. He might kiss her there as he had the night before. Caroline wondered what it would feel like if he used his teeth sparingly, as he had along her throat.

The thought made her moan again, and he met her eyes as he mounted her, one hand between them, coaxing her damp flesh to open to him and to the heavy pulse of his manhood. Caroline opened her legs for him, and she could see he was surprised at her boldness. But whatever she knew of lust and of pleasure, he had taught her.

For a moment, it was as if Anthony could see fearlessness in her eyes and liked what he saw. As he loomed over her, he kissed her, his lips sweet on hers with no trace of anger behind them.

Even as she took his tongue into her mouth, he entered her in one smooth stroke. She gasped, her mouth under his. He moved within her as he had the night before, raising her hips so his access to her was complete. Pleasure gripped her, harder than it had before. Her lungs were crushed with it. The pleasure mounted her even as he did until she cried out, calling his name. This time the pleasure did not stop but went on a second time, and when the tide of it finally receded, she could not speak at all.

Her name was on his lips when he shuddered with his release. She drank in the sound of it like wine.

When they were done, their passion spent, he kissed her once, then rolled away. Anthony found his clothes so casually, she feared whatever emotion she thought she had heard in his voice a moment before was a lie or a passing thing that came and went with his pleasure.

Caroline lay back against her pillows, feeling suddenly bereft. She watched as her husband dressed slowly in the firelight, the hard planes of his body beckoning to her, though she was already spent.

"Will you go to your whores then?" she asked as he drained the glass of wine she had poured for him.

Anthony turned to look at her, and she saw yet again his surprise at her boldness before he masked it.

"No," he said. "I go to sleep in my own room. I suggest you do the same."

"Sleep in your room?" she asked, her voice calm, her eyes never leaving his face.

Anthony came to the bed but did not even rest his weight on it. He leaned over and kissed her once, very lightly, before he drew away.

"I will get no sleep if you lie beside me."

He unlocked the door. Caroline forced herself to lie as he had left her, the soft bedclothes spread beneath her. She forced herself to stillness through pride and strength of will.

She thought he would leave at once, but when he opened the door, Anthony turned back to look at her. She watched the heat of lust cross his face and the shadow of something else in his eyes, a tenderness that might have been only a trick of the feeble light. It was she who moved first, turning her back on him.

She did not move again until she heard the gentle click of the door. She let her tears come silently in case he stood by the door, so he would not hear her weep.

❧

Anthony left his wife while he still had some vestige of self-control.

When he had seen her step into the dining room that night, he thought his heart would stop at the sight of her beauty. Dressed in a simple gown of white, she looked like an angel walking through the gates of Hell.

He had wanted to go to her in that moment, to leave his supper club behind.

He had seen his Hellfire Club with new eyes. What was all in good fun a moment before now seemed sordid and pointless. The men who had seemed witty and rakish suddenly looked lost and alone, even with whores at their sides. The thought of his wife among those people, being seen by those men, even worse, being seen by those courtesans, almost made Anthony leap to his feet and carry her out of there. She should never have been allowed to come among Pembroke's guests. No man present would ever have allowed his wife to know such gatherings existed.

Then Carlyle had claimed her as his dinner partner.

Anthony had felt the eyes of every man in the room on him, weighing his reaction. To keep up appearances, in order to continue the pleasant fiction that the Earl of Ravensbrook and Viscount Carlyle were simply rivals in trade and in Parliament, Anthony had to sit and watch the man speak to his wife, and do nothing.

He reminded himself of Anne, his poor sweet sister, left alone in Richmond. He knew one day he would try to bring her into Society again. He wanted her to have the chance at a happy life, a life with a husband and children, a life in which the haunted darkness in her eyes would finally fade away. It was Anne he kept before him all through that interminable dinner as he watched the slimy bastard sit close beside his wife, offering her wine.

Anthony had resolved to tell Caroline everything once they were alone in her room. But after dinner when she had not returned to his side, when she had moved to dance with Victor without even a glance at him, Anthony's reason had snapped. He had carried her out of the party under the speculative eyes of his club, and even now, he did not give a damn what they thought.

He had not given a damn what Caroline thought, either. He was her husband. It was for him to protect her and what was left of her innocence, whether she wanted him to do so or not.

After he left her alone, Anthony tried to retire to his own bed, but he found the sight of it made him think of Caroline in hers, her long blond hair lying across the pillow in a stream of gold. He turned away from his empty bed and walked the halls of his friend's home.

He faced another sleepless night, and without the scent of battle to keep him sharp, his lack of sleep began to grate on him. He moved toward the library to hide from his friends and their courtesans. No other man would seek the solace of books that night when there was so much else on offer.

He could hear the guests still laughing in the drawing room, with softer sounds coming from the open door to the terrace. Anthony needed silence and to be alone. Instead, in the library he found Pembroke seated among his books, a glass of brandy by his elbow, a cigar lit in his hand.

"Come and sit awhile with me," Pembroke said.

"I thought you would be with your whores."

"The women all look alike to me tonight. After seeing your wife's purity, I found I lost my appetite."

Pembroke's smile did not reach his eyes. Anthony knew his friend well. Pembroke spent the dark hours of each night alone with a bottle beside him. There always came a point in the evening when all the whores and gaming, all the pleasure he had ordered for himself began to sour, and Pembroke would sulk alone.

On the Continent, Anthony had sat up many a sleepless night at his friend's side, neither man speaking. Only once, on the night before a battle from which neither expected to return alive did Pembroke stay sober and speak of what pained him. That night, Anthony's friend spoke for the first and last time of the woman he had lost, the woman he would never see again. Arabella of the ice-blue eyes.

"I am sorry for this evening. I should have thrown them all out."

"You and I both know you could not do that. Carlyle and I have kept up this farce for three years now. No doubt we will have to keep it up for many years to come."

"Until your sister marries," Pembroke says.

"And beyond," Anthony answered. "So her husband will not cry foul."

"I hope she finds a better man than that."

"So do I. Do you think it likely?"

Pembroke did not answer but poured Anthony a glass of brandy. Anthony took a sip of the burning liquid but quickly set the glass back down. He began to pace the room as if searching for a book, but he could not focus on the printed word. He simply felt the need to move. He wanted to go for a ride on Achilles, but it was still too dark, and he would need to leave with his wife early that morning, for they had far to travel.

His mind returned to the sight of Caroline's golden hair falling across her pillows. The memory of her gasps filled his ears as his pleasure rose slowly to consume him. Anthony could not escape these thoughts of his wife. He had left her less than an hour before, but already she haunted him as no other woman ever had. Anthony had always prided himself on his control and on the fact that no woman could hold him. As he walked the carpet in front of his friend, sleeplessness riding him as he rode Achilles, Anthony wondered if he had truly begun to lose his mind.

"So you love her," Pembroke said.

"I cannot love her after only two days," Anthony answered. "I do not even know what love is."

Pembroke laughed at that, drawing the cigar from his mouth, letting his tobacco smoke circle above his head in sinuous spirals. "You may not know love, but it knows you, my friend. And right now, it has you by the throat."

Anthony made a dismissive gesture with one hand, grimacing, but he stopped pacing. He turned once more to look over the books on a nearby shelf, but he did not truly see them.

He came to sit beside his friend finally, giving up on the race he knew he could not win. He could not run from his wife, but here, in the province of men, he could hide.

"She will give you fine sons," Pembroke said.

"If she does not kill me first."

Pembroke nodded. "There is that."

"Do you have another cigar? I will not sleep tonight."

Pembroke offered the cigar box, mahogany inlaid with mother-of-pearl. It had once belonged to his father, one of the few objects of the old man's his friend had kept.

"You need to sleep sometime," Pembroke said. "Wife or no wife, the prince's supporters will meet next week. There will be Victor to face again."

Anthony's eyes darkened. "Yes. There will be that."

The two men smoked in silence. They sat together until the sun began to rise, turning the sky from indigo to the lightest gray. That was when Pembroke took his leave. He said he had two women waiting for him, and he would have to pay for another day if he did not have them before dawn.

Anthony laughed when he heard this, as his friend no doubt intended. As he sat alone in the empty library, the fire in the grate began to go out.

Anthony was tempted to go back upstairs and crawl into his wife's bed. He wanted to make love to her until she breathed his name in the soft way she had, clinging to him in her passion and her innocence.

But he did not go to her. Instead, he watched the sunrise from the window of the library while the last of his cigar burned down. He waited until the sky took on the same golden color as his wife's hair. Only then did he turn and go to his own room alone.

Chapter 16

CAROLINE DID NOT SEE HER HUSBAND THE NEXT morning until she stood in front of Pembroke House, waiting to be handed into the traveling chaise. Hercules and Achilles had both left already, but not before she gave them the last of the contraband apples from her portmanteau.

Anthony was nowhere to be seen, but Pembroke appeared, bowing low to her before taking her gloved hand. "I apologize if my guests made you at all uncomfortable last night, Lady Ravensbrook. I would never have invited them here had I known you and your husband were coming."

"Does Anthony often keep such company?" Caroline turned to look at the horses, as if she was not interested in the answer Pembroke might give.

"He visits my club on occasion, my lady. But…"

She looked up at him past the rim of her bonnet. "I did not mind the dinner or the dancing. I would not choose such companionship for myself or for my husband, but there was no harm done."

Pembroke laughed. "Only to your husband's peace of mind."

Caroline's smile faded. "Perhaps. No doubt he will regain that once we have reached his home."

She met her husband's eyes as he strode down from the house. Anthony was dressed that morning in midnight blue with a black waistcoat, his dark hair still damp from his bath. His beauty made her shiver.

Caroline thought of how he had touched her the night before, of the pleasure she had received at his hands. Warmth began to rise in her cheeks as she thought of the hours she would spend enclosed with him in the traveling carriage. But her pleasure was dampened by the memory of how Anthony had made love to her and then left her like a common whore. At least he had not left gold on her table. She might have drawn her dagger from its hiding place in her reticule and killed him for that.

"My lady." Pembroke's eyes sparkled with mirth and a touch of the devil as he leaned down and placed a lingering kiss on her hand.

She raised one eyebrow but said nothing. She could feel her husband's gaze on her like a red-hot brand.

"Forgive me, my lady," Pembroke said. "I do not mean to take liberties."

"I do not care, if my husband does not."

Anthony came to stand beside them then, glowering but silent. Pembroke's booming laughter filled her ears, bouncing off the stone wall of his old castle. For the first time, Caroline heard a little joy in it. She wondered what had made this man lose himself so he drank to excess and sported with whores. She was certain that with the right woman to guide him, Pembroke might become a man to be reckoned with.

"Indeed, my lady, your husband does care, and plenty. He would run me through if he had not saved my life himself a hundred times already."

Anthony's face remained unreadable but for the muscle twitching in his cheek. Caroline took in the sight of him in one glance and just as quickly turned away. She spoke as if he were not there.

"You are wrong, my lord. What you see in my husband is not jealousy but possession. He would look at you the same way if you were overfamiliar with his horse."

Pembroke laughed again, releasing her hand with a flourish, relinquishing the field of combat to her. "Lady, far be it for me to contradict you. I would, if you would allow it, come to visit you in your new home in a few months' time. I find I have a sporting interest in just how much your husband cares for you and what form that care will take."

Anthony did not smile, nor did he take that bait. Caroline's smile was wide enough for both of them. "I have no objection, my Lord Pembroke, as long as you leave your whores at home."

When Anthony did not step forward to offer his hand, Pembroke lifted Caroline into the coach, allowing his hands to linger on her waist so she frowned at him. He released her, but not before Anthony's fingers flexed as if reaching for a weapon.

Satisfied with the mischief he had wrought, Pembroke turned away from his friend's wife. He extended his hand to Anthony.

"Safe journey, and safe homecoming," Pembroke said.

Anthony clasped his hand in his own. "Safer than Belgium."

"Safer than Italy," Pembroke answered.

Without another word, Anthony climbed into the carriage behind his wife, and the team of four grays drew the coach toward the road, toward Shropshire and Anthony's home.

Caroline stared out the window all that day, except when she was sleeping. She tried to put her handsome husband and his touch from her mind. She was almost successful. Anthony assisted her by not speaking or touching so much as her gloved hand. So she was not distracted as they came into Shropshire, the land of beautiful rolling hills.

There were no moors filled with heather and emptiness, where the winds moaned like specters of the dead. Every neat field was surrounded by copses of trees, lovely maples and birches, as well as oaks and hawthorn. The carriage rolled with the hills as with the swells of the sea. Caroline had never been on a ship, but she hungered for the sight of the ocean, the great swells that would carry her to far, undiscovered countries where the people had never heard a word of English spoken. Or to the wilds of Byzantium, where the great domes and marbled streets led from one delight to another, to Venice, where the very roads were made of water, where the air was filled with spices.

Caroline knew she was foolish to think of such

things. Like all women of her station, she would live out her life in her husband's house, raising his children and keeping his home. She would go to London for the Season, for fittings and for balls. She would walk in the staid park of Regent's Square, and take in the river Thames. London was as close as she was ever likely to get to the places she had read about in her father's library. Caroline cast one surreptitious glance at her husband. She wondered for the first time if he loved books, too.

Anthony stared out his own window and did not turn to her, so she went back to her perusal of the land beyond the coach they rode in, and the lands within her mind's eye. She took in the deep green of the trees that had not yet begun to color with autumn and the golden fields of barley and millet and wheat.

She dreamed of riding Hercules out among those fallow fields once the harvest was brought in. She could ride for days and never be seen again. She could ride as far as London—and beyond, if she chose. The thought of getting Hercules onto a ship and keeping him there for as long as it would take to journey to Venice burst the bubble of her dreaming. She could take her horse nowhere. She was a countess, a wife, and would someday be a mother. She must put away such indulgent longings. She stared out over the green hills of her husband's home county, desire for foreign places burning in her breast. Perhaps Shropshire would be foreign enough. Perhaps she would be happy there.

They turned off the main road through a set of high gates. The walls around the estate had long since crumbled, but the gate remained, a silent testament to the past. The rolling hills continued beyond them, but now instead of tilled fields and blowing wheat, Caroline saw only long swatches of green grass with sheep grazing here and there, a boy following along behind them with a scythe to keep the lawns neat. The road was paved in stones, but they were well laid and did not jounce the carriage as the rutted highway had done. Caroline clutched the strap as the horses picked up speed. Those four matched grays knew their home and that they had come to the end of their long journey.

She took in the sight of her husband's house and almost lost her breath. The high walls were built of gray stone that caught the light of the setting sun and shone with the mica hidden in their depths. Huge picture windows along the walls seemed almost like eyes. Those windows winked as the carriage pulled around to the front door, the sunlight catching their clear panes of glass. Ivy grew along the walls in places. Caroline could see a rose arbor and a folly with wisteria growing over it. Though no flowers bloomed there this late in the year, she knew that come spring, the roses and wisteria would be plentiful enough to fill the air with their heady sweetness.

There was something warm and inviting about the house before she even entered it. For a moment, it was as if her future called to her. She could almost hear the laughter of her children yet to come as they ran along those corridors and out into the sunlight, coming to greet her as she came home. She knew she could be at home there, just as she had once been at home on the moors. She blinked hard as the carriage stopped and the footman opened the door. She could not greet her husband's household with tears in her eyes.

Before she stepped from the carriage, her husband caught her hand. Caroline turned to him and met his gaze. "Welcome home, Caroline."

Anthony climbed out before her. She let him help her down, conscious of the eyes of the household on her. Every servant in that great place seemed to be lined up along the driveway in two neat lines to the front door. Caroline knew her mother would be pleased with such orderliness. It spoke of a house-keeper who knew her trade and took pride in it.

It was the butler who stepped forward and bowed to her. "Billings, my lady. At your service."

Caroline inclined her head, and the man stepped back. He looked to be about sixty but had a military bearing, just as all the men on her father's estate did. His iron-gray hair was cut short, and his shoulders were straight, as if he waited for orders to take the hill beyond or perhaps to capture the rose garden from marauding invaders. Caroline's shoulders relaxed. Her father's household was full of ex-military men. She knew how to get on with them. As she took in the straight lines of the servants, all watching her for some sign of who their new mistress was, she felt even more at home.

"I am the housekeeper, my lady. Mrs. Brown." A tiny woman dressed all in black curtsied to her. She came only up to Caroline's shoulder, her bright button eyes and quick movements reminding Caroline of a wren.

"Thank you, Mrs. Brown, Billings. I am very happy to be home."

The rest of the servants applauded when she said that, and each girl from the household staff came forward to offer her a bouquet. They had been culled from the hedgerows and were full of late-blooming flowers, asters and goldenrod, with sprigs of barley thrown in for a blessing of fertility. Caroline's arms were soon full of flowers, so full she could hold no more. Mrs. Brown had thought of that, too, for a quiet girl came up to stand behind her, gathering all the flowers Caroline could not carry.

Caroline turned to walk into the house when she was stopped by her husband's hand on her waist.

"Allow me."

Anthony picked her up with one fluid sweep of his arm, smiling down at her in the half light of dusk. The sun had set beyond the hills, and the courtyard of Ravensbrook House was bathed in shadow and sweet, buttery light.

Caroline kept her face scrupulously blank and met her husband's eye evenly. But her treacherous heart leapt at his nearness, and she wondered whether he noticed.

"It is Ravensbrook tradition to carry a new bride over the threshold."

"Indeed, my lord. We must not break with tradition."

Anthony carried his wife into his house in three strides. Caroline saw a couple of the girls dab their eyes at the romance of the moment, and even Mrs. Brown smiled. Caroline forced herself to smile, too. She pushed away her fear of her own emotions and leaned against her husband's chest, letting herself imagine he carried her for love and not tradition, that this romantic gesture was real.

The great walnut staircase had a dark blue runner, and Anthony's boots were silent on the thick carpet. A flower dropped from her hands as she looked into his eyes. He quirked a brow at her and smiled. In spite of her misgivings, she smiled back. Anthony bore her all the way up the winding staircase. He carried her into a huge suite of rooms where a fire was already lit. Large windows looked out across the park facing south, gathering in the last of the daylight. The bed was hung with heavy blue damask to match the curtains at the windows. The rich red mahogany of the bedstead reminded her of her own furniture at home in her father's house. The fire burned cheerfully in the grate, and a delicate bathing screen stood at the far side of the room. Already, Caroline could hear women behind it, pouring water into a tub for her bath. Tabby stood holding her lady's dressing gown, watching as Anthony held his wife in his arms. For once, her little maid said not a word.

Her husband gazed down at Caroline, his eyes unreadable. "These rooms were my mother's. Now they are yours."

Only then did Anthony lower her to the floor.

"We will dine here, alone, if you wish," he said.

"Do you wish it?" she asked him.

"I do," he said.

Caroline looked into her husband's face, taking in his beauty. She found that for the first time in her life she had lost her tongue.

Anthony kissed her, his lips lingering on hers. He did not stir up the fire between them. She savored his lips and knew the taste of him would stay with her long after he had left the room.

When Anthony drew back, he spoke low, so only she could hear. "I will return in an hour."

"I will be ready," she said.

With that, Caroline stepped away from him and straightened her shoulders. Anthony raised one hand to touch her cheek before he turned on his heel and walked away.

Tabby was first to break the lingering silence. "Holy Mary, Miss Caroline. I mean, my lady. Your gentleman is a good-looking one, and no mistake. He gives me the shivers."

Caroline laughed, forcing a lightness into her voice she did not feel. "He is easy on the eyes, is he not, Tabby? If only he were as easy on my temper. But a woman can't have everything."

ce

Caroline was nowhere to be seen when Anthony entered her rooms. Her husband found her tucked into the window seat, a thick cashmere shawl wrapped around her shoulders. Her nightgown was of thin lawn and lace and did little to keep out the chill of the evening.

When she turned to him and climbed down from her perch, Caroline saw he had bathed and changed into simple trousers and waistcoat, the kind of clothes a farmer might wear, if he could afford brocade. Their cut was plain, the color the same as his hair.

The heat between them began to rise as it always did when they were alone. Anthony stayed silent, and she wondered if he had some new infraction of his rules of correct behavior to charge her with. But as they stood together, the silence lengthening, she began to see there was only the warmth of desire and a slow-growing affection between them. For one night, at least, they might declare a truce.

Caroline waited without moving, so he might make the first move toward peace. Anthony smiled as if he knew what she was thinking, as if he knew she meant to challenge him with her stillness. He did not rise to the bait but pushed a strand of her long hair behind her ear.

Caroline stayed where she was and let him come to her. Anthony leaned down and pressed his lips to hers.

He tasted as sweet as he always did, like a spice she had longed for all her life. She savored the taste of him and his scent, letting both fill her senses like an incoming tide.

His mouth opened over hers as he drew her against him, against the hard planes of his body beneath the softness of his loose shirt and brocade waistcoat. His tongue plunged into her mouth, teasing her, coming into her and then withdrawing, mimicking the act of love.

Caroline pulled away from him, for she had no interest in being toyed with.

"Dinner has been served, Husband, if you would eat it with me."

Anthony drew back. She saw that though he had sought to tease her, he had drawn himself into his own web of lust. His eyes were black with desire.

"There is a delicacy here that I would sample first," he said.

He did not kiss her again but lifted her in his arms as he had when bringing her into his house that afternoon. Caroline's passion filled her, and she relished the taste of it.

Anthony did not carry her to the bed but sat with her in a deep armchair drawn close to the table where their meal was laid out. Caroline took in the scent of the spices from the food that steamed in china dishes on the mahogany table. Anthony held her in his lap, leaning back against the cushions of her chair.

Caroline sighed and turned her head so he could take her lips with his. She did not kiss him back at first but made him court her.

She felt him smile under her mouth before he turned to the work of wooing her, coaxing her with his lips and teeth and tongue. When her mouth fell open, he devoured her, his mouth slanting over hers as if he would take all of her in. The heat of his passion beckoned her to join him, but still she did not touch him. Instead, she let him feast on her lips until that no longer satisfied him.

Caroline still had not forgiven him for leaving her alone the night before the way he would have left a whore. She had too much pride to rail at him like a fishwife or a jealous mistress. Instead, she did not touch him as she longed to but kept her fingers light on his shoulders. His hands began to move over her body, slipping beneath her night rail to glide his fingertips over the curves of her breasts. Her nipples tightened against his palm as he ran his tongue along her throat, taking her ear in his teeth and tugging gently until she sighed again.

That concession made him bolder. Anthony began to draw her long shawl away from her slowly, dropping it onto the floor.

He then raised her up, and she thought he would finally carry her to the bed, but he did not. Instead, he set her back down on the cushions of her chair and knelt at her feet, burrowing under her gown with his hands.

She watched as his fingers ran along her legs, caressing the silken smoothness of her thighs where the ribbons of her stockings were tied. She had left them on, remembering how he liked to strip them from her himself. Anthony unlaced her stockings slowly, one ribbon at a time, and still she did not move to touch him.

Thoughts of retribution began to fade from her mind as he went to work on her in earnest, feathering kisses along the silk of her stocking as he brought first one and then the other down over her foot. Anthony cast each aside. He kissed one bare foot and then the other, scraping his teeth along the line of her instep.

She had never known her feet could feel such pleasure. Warmth pooled between her thighs as if a fire had been lit there. Still he did not take her to the bed but raised her gown even higher, parting her thighs so he could nestle himself between them.

Caroline gasped when his tongue touched her. She almost came out of the chair when he began to kiss her there as he had on their wedding night. He held her down, and she could do nothing but let the pleasure wash over her, one stroke of his tongue at a time, until it crested and broke over her head, washing her up on a foreign shore.

She lay back in the chair, her nightgown bunched about her waist, her hair trailing behind her. She found she could not move. He had to scoop her up and carry her to bed with no help from her at all.

Anthony laid her down and drew her gown off at last. But he left his clothes on, so when he climbed on top of her, she could feel the weft of his brocade waistcoat and the roughness of his trousers as he ran one leg over hers. He had unfastened them, his manhood pressing against her thigh.

He was inside her then, and she moaned as she expanded to take him in. He gave her pleasure with his first thrust, and that pleasure built as he moved over her, his body close to hers, his waistcoat rubbing against her breasts. She cried out under him, the pleasure building more quickly than it ever had, and taking her over the edge not once but twice as he worked over her, watching her face. As she lay limp beneath him, he reveled in his own pleasure, and with a few more thrusts emptied himself into her.

They lay together in the soft bedclothes and feathered mattress of their marriage bed. Anthony regained his strength first and raised himself on one elbow. He grinned down at her, well satisfied. Caroline looked into the dark beauty of his eyes and could not help but smile back.

"Am I forgiven then?" he asked.

She sighed and stretched beneath him, pressing her body against his as if to remind him that whatever pleasure he gave her, she still belonged to herself.

"You are forgiven, Husband. But don't leave me like a thief in the night again."

He laughed and kissed her, pressing his lips to her collarbone, running his tongue along the softness of her skin. She did not soften beneath him, and he met her eyes. "I will not leave you, unless I must."

Caroline looked into his eyes and saw that was all the concession she would get. She accepted it with a hope for better things to come. Her mother had taught her never to be cloying, for no husband would tolerate it. So she let all thoughts of the future go and stretched once more, this time her eyes half-open so she could watch Anthony as he stared down at her naked body in the firelight.

"I am hungry, Husband."

She spoke low, her voice throaty, still half-breathless from the pleasure he had given her. As she watched, Anthony swallowed hard and licked his lips, bending down once more to run his tongue along her shoulder.

"I find that I, too, have an appetite."

"For food, Husband? There are beef tips braised in butter on the table."

Anthony laughed, kissing her lips, drawing her up to lean against him as he sat on the edge of their bed. He was still fully dressed but for his unfastened trousers. Caroline felt the urge to reach down and fondle him, but she fought it. He had not given her the concession she had asked for. Instead of drawing him back into love play, she would eat.

Caroline tried to pull away, but her husband held her tight against him. She thought he might draw her down onto the bed and cover her, for he was hard once more. But he did not. Instead, he stroked her hair where it fell in long waves down her back. At first, Caroline leaned against him, wondering when he might let her go. But soon the feel of his hand on her hair soothed her, and she leaned against him, letting him support all of her weight.

The silence stretched between them, and Caroline began to forget the food on the table, as well as the pleasure he had given her. She found her mind drifting as she sat moored safely in his arms. She would have slept but for the sound of his voice in her ears.

"There is food, Wife. Come, let us eat it."

Anthony took her hand and helped her rise from their bed. She leaned against him for a moment before she knelt down and swept her nightgown up from the floor. She stepped away from him and drew the soft confection over her head in one smooth motion, so Anthony was left staring after her.

Caroline caught him watching her, and she smiled a sleepy smile, still well sated from their lovemaking. She rose on her toes and kissed him, but when he reached for her, she slipped out of his grasp and went to sit at the table where their evening meal was set.

He laughed under his breath as he fastened his clothes. No woman had ever walked away from him. Anthony found himself dismissed for the first time in his life by the only woman on earth sworn to obey him.

He was surprised that instead of irritation or a rising temper, he felt only pride. For some inexplicable reason, he was proud of the tilt of Caroline's head as she walked away from him, of the clear strength in her brown eyes. He had never known a woman strong enough to match him on his own ground in bed or anywhere else. The more he came to know her, the more fascinating his wife became. He began to think it would be many years before he came to know this woman well, if he ever did.

He drew his armchair close to hers as they began to eat. He watched as his young wife devoured the beef tips braised in butter, and the rich white bread baked that afternoon from wheat grown on his land.

He almost did not recognize himself as they sat together. Anthony took in every bite she swallowed, staring all the while into her eyes. He would have worried he was acting too much like a moon-sick boy, except his wife did not seem to notice.

To claim her attention, Anthony fed her bites from his own hand. Caroline laughed, offering morsels to him, as well, until they left the food unfinished on the table and fell on each other once more.

This time Anthony lay back against the softness of their bedclothes and let her draw his waistcoat and trousers off him slowly, along with his billowing shirt, one piece of clothing at a time. Her eyes seemed to linger over the sight of his body in the firelight. He ached with the need to have her beneath him, but he was a man in control of himself, so he did nothing.

Anthony drew his hands behind his head and cradled them there so he would not touch her. Caroline saw the challenge he offered her, and she smiled a long, slow smile as she dragged her night-gown over her head.

Her hair spilled around her in a curtain of gold. She smiled at him between the strands, crawling on her hands and knees to where he lay in the center of their bed. She straddled him but did not mount him. Instead, she lay across him, keeping her eyes on his, waiting to see if he would move to take her. Though his breathing became labored, Anthony did not touch her.

His wife set herself to enjoying him as he had so often savored her. She ran her hands over the hard length of his chest, trailing her palms down to his waist and over his thighs, leaving his manhood untouched, but barely.

He shuddered under her hands; his smile faded. It would be only a matter of time before he rolled over, pinning her beneath him. Anthony held himself still and called on all his powers of self-control. But this woman seemed set on challenging that control, as she challenged him in everything. She followed the path her hands had taken with her lips and teeth, until her tongue grazed his inner thigh.

Caroline raised her head then and gave him a wicked smile. Anthony laughed under his breath, but he did not move to touch her. So she lowered her mouth to his manhood, taking him between her lips, running her tongue and teeth over him.

Anthony's control broke. He dragged her up the length of his body, turning in the same fluid motion to trap her beneath him. Without even testing her for warmth and wetness, Anthony plunged into her as into a river, as if he was on fire. She gasped under the onslaught, but soon she was moaning beneath him.

Anthony remembered himself and worked over her more carefully, trying to contain his lust, trying not to hurt her. But it seemed Caroline would have all of him or nothing. She moved under him, drawing him deeper into herself, clutching him hard so he gave himself up and took her blindly, without caution or care.

Caroline trembled beneath him, moaning in inarticulate supplication even as Anthony gasped her name. They lay together when they were through, clinging to each other as if the body beside them was the only stability they knew.

Anthony's laugh rumbled in his chest before he gave it voice. His wife, her face flushed from their exertions, moved slowly, as if she could barely find the will to rise. Still, her voice was tart when she spoke to him.

"Do I amuse you, Husband?"

She seemed to gather her strength with great effort, enough to raise her head so she might look him in the eye.

"No, my love. I amuse myself."

She did not seem satisfied with this answer, but she lay down again, pillowing her head on his chest. Little time passed before she was breathing deeply, her sweet limbs heavy against him.

This time, Anthony did not move to pull away. She lay draped over him for the rest of the night as he reveled in the memory of her beneath him on their marriage bed. He was amazed by the pleasure he had found in her arms, as well as the joy. These things he had not looked for when he first went to Yorkshire. He had gotten far more in this marriage than he had bargained for.

Chapter 17

London

TWO HOURS BEFORE DAWN, ANTHONY WOKE CAROLINE. He pressed his lips to her cheek, trailing down to the softness of her mouth. She smiled at his touch and turned to him, reaching to draw him down into bed with her. Then she woke fully and saw he was dressed to leave for London already.

"I must go. But I wanted to see you first."

"When will you be home?" she asked, her voice thick with sleep.

Anthony wanted nothing more in that moment than to crawl back into bed with her, his work with the Prince Regent's supporters be damned. Her warm body, naked beneath the bedclothes, beckoned him.

"As soon as I am able. I will send word before I come."

"Just come home soon, Anthony."

Her tousled hair and soft breath on his cheek almost weakened him past bearing, but he pulled away from her in spite of his desire. He found he had begun not just to desire her body but her company. He pushed that thought from his mind as he took the road to London on Achilles's back.

Once in the city, he went about his affairs just as he had before he met Caroline, but he could not forget her. His valet came to shave him each morning while his steward went over the day's work that lay before him. As Gerald pressed the hot towel to his face before drawing a sharpened razor across his chin, Anthony found himself wishing it was Caroline whose hands were touching him.

Anthony knew his duty, and he followed it to the letter. He saw to his shipping interests and his business with the East India Company. He attended sessions in the Parliament building to prepare for the opening of the House of Lords. And all the while, he thought of Caroline and how her golden hair looked against the silk of his pillow.

He was thinking this pleasant thought as he strode out of Parliament, nodding to friends and acquaintances as he passed. It was then he saw Victor lurking in a doorway, speaking with one of his faction.

Almost as if he could sense his presence, Victor turned to meet Anthony's gaze. The rest of the men in the room stopped to stare, to see what might come of this. The eyes of the others were on Anthony, a weight he could not shake off.

"Well met, Ravensbrook."

Victor's tone was as calm and oily as ever. At no time in all the years he had known him had Anthony ever heard a different cadence of his voice. Victor always spoke to him with the same even calmness, and his blue eyes always held the same mild gaze. He had

looked just the same on the day they had met with
Prinny to settle Anne's fate.

"I thought I'd heard you were in Edinburgh,"
Anthony said, trying to keep his own tone as even and
cool. He knew he failed.

"These rumors get started, but we never know from
where," Victor answered. "And how is your lovely wife?"

A sea of red rose from the ground at Anthony's
feet. That this man had sat beside his wife at a dinner
laid out for whores was bad enough. That he would
mention her so casually made Anthony's fury rise so
fast he almost could not stop himself from reaching for
the dagger in his boot.

He knew his temper bordered on madness. One
man might ask after the health of a wife or a sister or
a mother. He always seemed to lose his grip on both
his sanity and his temper where Victor was concerned.

"My wife is well." The words stuck in Anthony's throat.

"Well protected, I hope. Women can get into
mischief when our backs are turned." Carlyle smiled.
If they had not been surrounded by their peers,
Anthony would have killed him. He thought of Anne
and stayed still.

"My wife is being looked after." The tension
mounted between them, and neither moved or backed
down. The men stared at each other until a footman
dressed in the royal livery came to Anthony's side.

"My lord, the Prince Regent sends for you."

Anthony stood silent, still taking the measure of
his enemy.

"Indeed, Anthony. If Prinny calls, do not let me
keep you."

Victor's voice was mild, but for the first time Anthony saw a gleam of anger behind his gaze. Victor was a member of the opposing faction in Parliament, one of the few lords of the realm who spoke out against the Prince Regent and his policies, both at home and abroad. Though he was out of royal favor, though he thwarted the Prince Regent at every turn, Victor still hungered for his regard.

Anthony bowed, then turned to follow the footman out of the main hall to the plush carriage that waited to take him to Carlton House. He signaled to his man, who nodded from a distance. His barouche would be waiting outside the prince's residence to take him home.

∝⌑

Anthony was led through the anteroom of the Prince Regent's chambers, through the hall of audience, and into the Prince Regent's personal apartments. Carlyle would hear that not only had he been called alone into the presence of the Prince Regent, but he had been received as a guest and an equal. Let Victor chew on that.

The Prince Regent sat in a comfortable chair drawn close to the fire where sandalwood burned, making the whole room smell sweet.

Anthony bowed low, careful not to presume on old acquaintance. But the Prince Regent rose when he came in, taking him in his arms as he had since Anthony was a little boy.

"Anthony, you must not let Victor back you into a corner. What would you have done if my men had not been watching over you?"

Anthony knew that no matter how much he loved this man, he would not draw him any deeper into the old conflict between his family and Victor's. The Prince Regent had enough troubles of his own.

"Do not fear for me, Your Highness."

The prince laughed. "I do not. I only chide you, as your father would if he were here."

The two men did not speak for a long moment, both thinking of the great man who had died five years before. Anthony had been his only living son and had worked hard to learn the family interests and to keep them strong, as his father had left them. In the last two years, he had even been able to increase their income, making his ships that sailed with the East India Company an even greater prize for Victor to feed on.

"I thank you," Anthony said.

The Prince Regent waved his words away. "You have a wife."

"Yes, Your Highness."

"And you do not bring her to London?"

"No."

"What, are we not good enough for your Yorkshire girl?"

Anthony smiled. "I have not tamed her yet."

The Prince Regent laughed, one short bark that set him coughing, so Anthony moved to bring him water. But before Anthony could step away, a footman came forward and served his prince. The Prince Regent drank, gasping until he had caught his breath. Anthony knew that, in spite of his wild living, or perhaps because of it, the prince was not always well. He vowed that, tamed or not, he would bring his wife to meet the man who had been his father's best friend.

"Bring her," the Prince Regent said, echoing his thoughts. "I would look on her and see if she is as great a beauty as is rumored in the scandal sheets."

"I will, my lord."

"Is she as beautiful as they say?"

Anthony's smile widened in spite of his efforts to quell it. "More so."

"Bring her to my Christmas ball. Let all of London look on her. You cannot keep her all to yourself."

Anthony bowed, a smile still playing on his lips as he thought of Caroline and her long golden hair. "I will, Your Highness."

Once the Prince Regent had given him tea and sent him on his way, Anthony returned to his town house on Grosvenor Square, where a jeweler waited.

"My lord, I brought the merchandise you asked for."

Anthony looked down at the velvet palate, where pearls were laid out in a hundred different sizes and a dozen different colors. He selected one large black pearl from the distant Indian Ocean and ordered it strung through with a chain of fine silver. Next, he selected a second pearl the size of a robin's egg, one of lustrous cream to be strung on a chain of gold.

He held that one pearl between his fingers for a long time, lingering over the feel of it, letting his touch warm it. His mind turned to Caroline and the sight of her skin in the candlelight, her head thrown back as she lay sated on his bed.

The jeweler, Levi, a man of the same family who had served the earls of Ravensbrook for generations, discreetly cleared his throat. Anthony knew Levi had more business to transact before sundown, when he must return home, for it was the eve of his people's Sabbath.

"I am drawn by the beauty of what you offer me. It leads me down the path of memory."

"Pleasant memory, I hope, my lord."

"The best."

Anthony waved his steward over. Barnabas paid the jeweler in gold and made arrangements for the pearls to be drilled and for chains to be woven through them.

"This one is for Angelique Beauchamp, the Countess of Devonshire," Levi said, holding the black pearl. He tried for an air of discretion, but his fair skin colored beneath his beard as he mentioned Anthony's long-acknowledged mistress. He was young and had just taken over the business from his father the year before.

"Yes."

"And this one?"

Levi raised the creamy pearl so that it caught the light from the high windows. Anthony found himself transfixed by it and knew that soon he must go home to Shropshire.

"That one is for my wife."

His voice was harsh in his own ears, filled with barely suppressed longing. Levi blushed again, turning an even deeper shade of crimson. "So you will take it with you when you leave London?"

"Yes, Levi. I will deliver both pearls myself."

The necklaces arrived Monday next just after dawn and were waiting for Anthony when he came in from his morning ride. He was shaved and barbered, and after settling the last items with his steward, he called for his barouche to be brought around to take him to the home of his mistress.

He enjoyed coming upon Angelique unawares. Though they had an exclusive understanding, he was always vigilant, making certain she had no other lovers but him. Angelique was a wealthy widow and a countess in her own right. Though she was always gratified to receive remembrances from him, there was never any mention of money between them.

Her servants greeted him as a matter of course, as they would have greeted the master of the house had he still been alive. They took his greatcoat, for the mornings had grown chill. They brought him not into her breakfast room but to her bedroom on the floor above.

He arrived unannounced and found Angelique as beautiful as she always was. As he stood looking at her in the early morning light, he wondered idly if she was a witch. Or if perhaps she paid a servant in his household to warn of her such unannounced visits. Anthony stood, thinking these thoughts, looking at her as he would a painting.

Her dressing gown was of the finest silk, a deep blue to match the blue of her eyes. Her curling dark hair fell around her shoulders, an invitation to mystery, a cloud of midnight that had more than once drawn him in.

Angelique greeted him with a smile but did not approach. Instead, she held out one hand and let him come to her. She made it clear without saying so that she had heard of his marriage.

"You honor us, my lord."

Without being told, her servants set breakfast on a

table inlaid with mother-of-pearl. They brought fresh bread baked that morning, jam from the country, honey from her estate in Shropshire, eggs, and a rasher of bacon. Anthony bowed over her hand and took in the fragrance of orchids that she always wore whenever he was with her.

Angelique allowed him to kiss her hand, but when he moved to kiss her mouth, she turned away so his lips grazed her cheek. He almost smiled at the silent set down but knew that to do so would escalate hostilities. He had come to make peace.

Anthony sat in the chair her footman drew out for him and allowed himself to be served all his favorite dishes in the order he enjoyed them most. As always, he was impressed by her ability to run her household. He wondered idly if she might work with Caroline, who most certainly knew nothing of such matters, but he banished the thought almost as soon as he had it.

He looked into his mistress's eyes and saw that, while she was silent, her mind was working even as she watched him.

"I understand I am to congratulate you, my lord, on your upcoming nuptials."

Anthony finished chewing his bit of bread, then reached for a mug of fragrant coffee. "I am married already. As you know, Angelique."

Her elegant brow arched in mock surprise, but she showed no other sign of emotion. She raised one hand, and footmen sprang forward to offer two more dishes, one of eggs and another of roasted pears. Anthony nodded, and they served him some of both before stepping away.

"I wanted to tell you myself," he began, when Angelique pierced him with a look, a smile lighting her lovely face.

"Except you were too busy signing the papers and bedding your new bride to send a message," she said.

Her voice was calm, her tone even, but Anthony began to wonder if the king's ransom he had brought would be enough to purchase her goodwill. They had never had a scene, and he did not expect to have one now. Angelique was a woman who ruled herself and her emotions, only one of the reasons she had been his mistress for almost a decade. Though she would never raise her voice to him, she might have him turned out of her house and order her doors barred to him for the rest of his life.

But then he remembered the way she cried out under him when he rode her. If she had not thrown him out yet, she was not going to.

"An oversight for which I apologize," he said.

They finished their breakfast in silence. Or he finished his while she watched, her food untouched before her.

They stood, her footmen drawing their chairs out behind them so they might step away unencumbered. Anthony wondered how to broach the subject of the present he had brought her.

"So you have something for me, I take it."

He blinked, wondering if she did indeed have a spy in his household.

"When I saw it, it made me think of you."

He brought out the drawstring bag from his coat pocket and placed the velvet in her hand. She opened the sack, and the pearl and silver chain fell out into her palm. He was not certain, but he thought he saw the beginning of tears in her eyes before she blinked them away. When she met his gaze, her eyes were the calm, cool blue they had always been. For the first time since he had known her, he saw her strength. It was so obvious he did not know how he had never seen it before.

"It is beautiful. I thank you."

He thought she would call her lady's maid to hang it about her neck. Instead, she turned, stepping toward him so he could take in the scent of orchids on her skin. She tossed the drawstring bag down onto the breakfast table with one contemptuous flick of her wrist. She raised the long, trailing mass of her hair, the darkness he had lost himself in more times than he could count.

Anthony stood close behind her, breathing in the scent of her, suppressing the desire to kiss the curve of her throat. He took up the necklace from where she had dropped it and hung it around her neck, fastening the clasp himself.

The scent of her beckoned him as ripe pomegranate on a silver tray. Angelique turned and fastened her eyes on him, letting her hair fall so it swirled past her shoulders in one long curtain of darkness.

"Will you not stay, my lord?" Angelique asked. She did not incline her head toward her bed, for she did not have to. They both knew what she meant.

They waited together in silence for his answer. Anthony was not sure which of them was more surprised.

"No," he said. "I must go. There is business that needs tending, and I am already late."

"You are going back to her," Angelique said. "To your little Yorkshire girl, with her long blond hair, soft young body, and eyes like pools to drown in."

Anthony did not flinch from her anger. He knew he deserved it.

"Yes."

Angelique smiled then, a smile that reflected her name. All evidence of her ire melted away like snow in sunlight. "Of course you will go to her," she said. "But no matter how long it takes you to get your heir and to have your fill of her, you will always come back to me."

Anthony gestured for his greatcoat to be brought. Her footman opened the door for him, and her butler waited to show him out. He meant to leave without speaking but found he could not. He was an honest man. He had always been honest with her.

At the door, Anthony turned back and met her eyes.

"No doubt you are right."

Chapter 18

Ravensbrook, Shropshire
October 1816

CAROLINE WAITED FOR HER HUSBAND'S RETURN AS SHE
had once waited for her father to come home from
war. She looked out every evening over the road
that led to their house, hoping to see his horse in the
distance somewhere along the rolling hills. She did not
question her motives for her hope that Anthony might
soon return. Her feelings for her husband were a dark
morass she did not wish to bring into the light.

After a week, she took a firm grip on herself and on
her own affairs. Her husband's house already ran like
a clock, but she took it in hand, using her time alone
to learn the workings of the staff: who was married to
whom, who had children and how many, who was
good at their job and who was not. She found his
country steward was a good man, and the kitchen was
well in order under the discerning eye of the cook. By
the end of her second week of marriage, her husband's
household had taken to Caroline as a bear to honey.

They loved her lilting accent and her easy way with them. They brought fresh flowers to her rooms every day without prompting, just as they had for Anthony's mother years before.

The house ran well, and the staff grew happier under her watchful eye. Tabby ran about as always, selecting the best gowns for each occasion and dressing Caroline's hair. The young maid took in the new household with wide eyes, listening to all Mrs. Brown's instructions.

As Caroline began her second week without her husband, she rode out over his lands, seeing to the people who lived there. The tenants were all well fed and well cared for, the village curate honest. When her husband was not home for Michaelmas, Caroline arranged a small festival for the tenants on the Ravensbrook estate so they all might meet her and take a day off from their labors.

So on the third week, Caroline was able to ride out for the sheer pleasure of it, taking in the golden beauty of that country as the harvest was brought in.

One evening as she turned toward home, the sun had begun to slant to the west, and she rode over the fields on her way back to Ravensbrook. She heard a rustling in the barley less than a mile from her husband's house. She stopped her mount, a delicate mare Anthony had given her for a wedding present in an effort to encourage her to ride like a lady.

Hercules was being reshod, so for the first time, Caroline had ridden out on Bonnie. The horse was gentle and sweet but too skittish for Caroline's taste. It was Bonnie shying at the movement in the high grass that made Caroline stop and look again, only to see a blond woman rise from the barley, gasping for air. Caroline heard the woman shriek, then saw a man come up from the grasses behind her.

At first, she thought she had caught a girl and her man at love play. But then the woman thrashed violently, trying to escape. She could not scream again, for the man's hand was on her throat.

Caroline wheeled Bonnie around and leaped down from her back without a thought for a mounting block, without a thought for caution. The ground under her boots jolted her hard as she landed, but she caught herself and stood firm. Bonnie needed no more motivation to flee. She ran as if a lion were at her heels, leaving Caroline alone in the barley, facing a man almost twice as large as she was.

"Let her go!"

Caroline watched as the girl surfaced from the high grass. The girl was crying, but she could breathe. The man had let go of her throat and had turned to see who approached him. As soon as his grip loosened, the girl ran away.

He was much larger than Anthony. Wide across the shoulders and broad across his paunch, he was one of the men who had come to work the land during the harvest. Such drifters came and went at harvest time, and no one remembered them once they were gone.

The lessons of her childhood whispered to her as if her father's trainer still stood beside her. She cursed the long skirt of her riding habit, hitching it up to keep it out of her way. She wore old breeches beneath her gown, as she always had at home.

She watched as the anger in the man's eyes turned to a gleam of lust.

She reached into her sleeve where her dagger lay sheathed. She had never drawn it before in combat but had used it only in practice with her father's men at home.

The blade shone in the fading light as she raised it, testing its weight in her palm.

She faced the man who would have raped one of her tenants and anger shook her to her core, the anger her father's men had taught her to cherish, the fury that made every warrior strong. It was a cold, clean rage that rose from her feet and into her arms, meeting the dagger still clutched in her palm. Her throwing dagger still rested in her boot, but she did not reach for it.

The man's eyes gleamed as he came to her. They met halfway into the barley, which grew high enough to block Caroline's path. She knew she had been a fool to step forward. She should have fought the man on the clear roadside, where her husband's ripe crop would not hinder her.

Caroline had no more time to think then, for he was on her.

She felt the man's heavy breath on her cheek as she raised her dagger to strike at his throat. She was quick and did not let him keep his grip on her. Once she had drawn blood from along his jaw and left cheek, she dodged back again, trampling the barley well underfoot so she would have clear ground to work in when he made his next move.

He was toying with her, she knew, for a man his

size should already have taken her under him. She had expected this and waited for it so she could drive her dagger up and into him from behind. That killing blow was one her father's men had drilled into her over and over on the practice field. It was a blow she knew she could deliver, even in her sleep.

Elation rose to balance her anger as she drew back, watching her enemy's blood slide down his cheek and into the collar of his shirt. His eyes were hot with fury, the fury of a fool, the anger of a man who would soon make a mistake.

He reached for her, and she sliced at his arm, cutting into the tendon all the way to the bone. He went into a killing rage and grabbed her hair, dragging her down onto the barley she had already trampled. Caroline saw his surprise as she smiled at him and embraced him.

She lifted her legs around him, as she would have around Anthony in their bed. She used his body as purchase, even as he held her down. She raised her dagger, waiting, but he did not lean down far enough for her to wield her knife still clutched behind him. In that moment, she saw his fury turn to fear. She raised her knife once more, this time to cut his throat, since she could not reach the proper spot on his back to force her blade beneath his ribs, that it might pierce his heart.

He did not scramble to take her knife from her as he had every pass before. He got to his knees and then ran from her, faster than she would have thought possible for a man of his bulk.

Caroline was on her feet in the next moment, intent on her prey, when she was lifted off the ground from behind, her knife wrenched out of her hand.

Caroline could not see who her attacker was. She went immediately limp in his arms. Just as she had hoped, her attacker loosened his hold long enough for her to kick her leg up, drawing her throwing dagger from her boot. In the next moment, her hand moved in a flash to her second attacker's throat, but he caught and held her hand in his. She stopped moving then, for she saw his face.

"Let me go," she said.

Anthony dropped her at once, as though she were a sack of meal. She saw that the girl stood behind him, holding the reins of his horse as well as her mare's. She must have kept her head long enough to run and fetch him. Caroline had no notion Anthony was even due to return that day, for he had not bothered to send word.

She moved toward the girl to see if she was all right. Caroline stopped when her husband's hand came down hard on her shoulder.

"Did he harm you?" Caroline asked.

"No, my lady."

"We will see you home then."

"No, we will not," Anthony said. "Get home quickly, Betty. Your father will wonder where you are."

The girl dropped a frightened curtsy, then ran without looking back.

"We should see her safe home. She has been through a horrible ordeal," Caroline said.

"So have I," he said. "She is her father's problem. You are mine."

Anthony lifted her in his arms, and for the first time, she realized the strength had drained out of her legs.

Caroline sagged against him, taking in the spicy-sweet scent of him, the scent she had missed so much over the three weeks of his absence.

He did not put her on her horse, as she had expected him to. Instead, he placed her on his saddle and rose behind her onto Achilles's back, pulling her close so her bottom nestled against his thighs. "Be still," Anthony said. She could hear behind the anger in his voice that he was weary. She wondered what he had been doing in the city to make himself so tired.

Caroline said not a word but felt her hunger for her husband rising along with the hunger for food. She had tasted death as well as victory in her enemy's blood, and now she shook with it—and with the need to prove to herself that she was still alive.

When they rode into the stable, she saw Bernard, the head of Anthony's stables, standing at attention. The grooms waited for their master's orders, bracing themselves for his temper. The master of the stables stood ready to take whatever punishment the earl would hand out.

Anthony slid down from his stallion, handing his reins to a waiting groom. Before he brought Caroline down, he faced Bernard.

"Never let my wife ride out alone. Two men go with her at all times. And they must go armed."

"Aye, my lord."

"Anthony, that is ridiculous," Caroline said, leaping down from Achilles with no help from her husband. "I do not need a keeper."

He faced her then, and she saw his anger with no

lust to blunt the edge of it. "We will not speak of it here. You will do as I tell you."

"Not when what you tell me is so unreasonable."

"You were almost killed."

"No. The intruder was almost killed. I had my knife at his throat. It was you who let him go."

She saw the looks of horror on the faces of the grooms at her cutting words. Anthony did not speak to her again but took her by the arm and began to drag her toward the house.

She took a deep breath and set her face in calm lines, working to keep her temper. Clearly, she was not done fighting yet.

❧

Anthony strode into the house past the servants without a word even to Billings. He slowed his steps so Caroline could take the staircase with him. He was tempted to sweep her into his arms and carry her, but he was afraid of his anger.

He kicked open the door to her bedroom. Tabby dropped the soap she had been carrying along with its basket, so both rolled across the polished floor in different directions.

"Your tub is full already, my lady," Tabby said. The girl was less used to the wild swings of a man's emotions, for she simply ignored Anthony's anger and spoke to Caroline as if he were not there. "I've sprinkled in jasmine scent and rose petals, just as you like."

"Thank you," Caroline answered.

Anthony took in the rumpled gown his wife wore and the blood on her green velvet riding habit. His eyes fell a second time on the men's breeches beneath the trussed-up dress, and he turned away so he would not have to look at her again until the room was cleared.

She continued to issue orders in a calm, clear voice, as if it were any other night in the country. "Send food up, Tabby. We will take our evening meal in here," Caroline said.

"Yes, my lady."

Tabby cast one fearful glance back at them, and then left.

Anthony took a deep breath and turned back to his wife. "Take those breeches off."

His wife ignored his words as if he had not spoken. "You let him escape," Caroline said.

Anthony's black rage consumed him. He closed his eyes against it, reaching for the edges of his control even as he felt it slipping away. His wife had almost died. She had brandished a weapon at a man who very easily might have killed her, and she still labored under the delusion she could have won the fight.

"My men are even now searching the countryside. They will not find him in the dark."

"I could have killed him," Caroline said.

Anthony fought to see Caroline through the black haze of his anger. It took him several heartbeats, but he was finally able to see his young wife, a woman little more than half his age, a woman who barely reached his shoulder. He saw the barley strands still caught in the golden beauty of her hair. He saw the blood on her face, on her hand, and on the sleeve of her gown. In his mind's eye, he watched again as that man dragged her beneath him.

His anger began to shift into fear. He had felt this same horror and helplessness the entire week Anne had been missing. He had thought her dead or worse as he scoured the countryside, looking for her. He had almost collapsed as his mother had when Anne returned home, safe if not unharmed. Carlyle, villain though he was, had never drawn a weapon against her. Anne's life had not been threatened; she had merely been ruined then abandoned. Caroline had been a hairsbreadth away from losing her life, and she was too foolish to know it.

Anthony clutched her, desperation consuming him as his anger began to fade. He almost shook with the need to embrace her, but he held back. He still feared his own temper.

"I should beat your disobedience out of you."

"You might try, my lord. You saw what I did to the last man who attacked me." Her gaze remained steady on his.

"I saw you wrap your legs around him like a common whore."

"I had to. Let me show you the hold. I would have killed him, I swear. He would never have harmed me."

"I do not want you to show me that 'hold,' as you call it, or any other. Caroline, you don't seem to grasp the salient point here. He would have killed you had I not been there," Anthony said.

"No," Caroline said. "I would not have allowed it."

"He was a man more than twice your size and weight. If he had wanted you dead, you would be dead."

"Anthony, I am trained to fight. I tell you, I would have been the death of him."

The last of his anger drained from him, along with the strength it had given him. He let her go, stepping away from her. He knew of no way to make this woman see reason. He had been told all his life that women were incapable of it, and Caroline seemed bent on proving the theory right.

"And how would you have lived with that? With a man's lifeblood on your hands?"

Caroline looked as if his words had struck her at last. Something seemed to have penetrated her mistaken certainty in her own invincibility. "He was a bad man," she said. "He tried to rape that girl. He attacked me."

"I do not disagree with you, Caroline. But if you had killed him, as you say you wished to, it would have changed you for the rest of your life, and not for the better."

She did not speak but stared at him as if she were truly listening to him for the first time.

"I have spent years at war. I know what I am talking about."

"You have killed many men," she said, looking at him as if she had never seen him before.

His friendship with her father stemmed from the campaigns against Bonaparte. His life on the Continent, his time at war, was something he would never speak of with her, that evening or ever.

"Even if you have no respect for me, you must have a care for your own safety." Anthony spoke calmly, his voice low. Caroline tilted her head as if to hear him better, a look of surprise on her face.

"I do respect you, Anthony. But I also respect myself. I am used to listening to my own judgment."

She faced him without bending, as fearless and foolish as she had been in the barley grass. Anthony moved across the room and sank into the armchair by the fireplace, his head in his hands.

"If he had killed you, it would have been the death of me."

Chapter 19

THAT CONCESSION FROM HER HUSBAND'S LIPS TOOK HER breath away. Caroline stood a room apart from him, staring at the slump of his shoulders. For the first time in their marriage, her husband almost looked defeated.

She set aside her own exhaustion, which was beginning to make her joints feel like lead. Her struggle with the man in the field had taken more of a toll than she had thought it would. She had not kept up her training in more than a month, and she could feel that neglect in the muscles of her arms.

No matter what Anthony said, she would have to find a teacher in Shropshire and continue to practice, or it would be too dangerous for her to carry a knife at all. She had worked too many years, and she was too proud of her abilities to give up her blades now. Those skills had been the only link to her father all the years he was away at war. Now that she was gone from his house forever, she cherished her talent to wield a blade even more.

"I am sorry I spoke so harshly in front of the grooms in the stable. I am sorry to have pained you."

He raised his head at her apology. Caroline swallowed

her pride and let her anger go. Anthony stood and crossed the room to her. He did not touch her but searched her face as he spoke. "I will let you keep your horse. I will ride out with you when my schedule permits. And when it does not, you will ride out with two armed men or not at all."

"Keep my horse? Anthony, of course I will keep Hercules. I would sooner cut off my own arm than give him up." She swallowed the anger that threatened to rise again at his high-handedness. "And why must two men ride with me?"

"I have enemies, Caroline. You must be cautious."

She was too tired to question him about who those enemies might be. She would tell him what he wished to hear today and do as she pleased tomorrow. She would find a way around his men in the stables. She felt a niggling sense of guilt at the lie, but she found she was too tired to fight him anymore that day.

"All right, Anthony."

His arms came around her, and his touch was almost tender as he raised her up and carried her behind the bathing screen.

Anthony drew her riding habit from her, unfastening her gown with care as if afraid to hurt her. He let the dress fall so it pooled at her feet, then lifted her out of it. He moved her closer to the light from the window so he might see her skin.

He ran his hands over the bruises along her side where she had fallen beneath the man who had held her in his grip. Anthony caressed each injury as if it pained him. He drew her shift over her head until she was standing only in the breeches she had taken from a stable hand.

Her husband drew her close. "I am the only one to wear breeches in this family, Caroline."

"But they are so much more sensible for riding," she said.

"And for knife fighting, which you must promise me you will never do again."

Caroline said nothing to that. Anthony lifted her into the tub of cooling water, her breeches left behind on the thick carpet. He stripped down and climbed into the tub with her. As always, his nakedness made her throat go dry. Caroline took in his beauty and was distracted from her irritation. It seemed she could not stay angry with him whenever his clothes came off.

Her hunger for him smoldered beneath her skin. She leaned back against him and luxuriated in his warmth.

"We need more water," she said, trying to distract herself from the potent heat of his nearness. She tried desperately to remember what she had meant to say before his trousers fell to the carpet.

"We have enough."

Her husband lathered his hands and washed her, and she softened under his touch. He soaped her hair and breasts, her thighs and stomach, each curve heating as his hands ran over it.

With all the blood and dirt washed from her body and from his, Anthony rose from the tub. Caroline murmured in protest, too languid to do anything else. He helped her to her feet, then took up a pitcher of warm water and rinsed the last of the soap from her skin. Anthony kissed her as he lowered the empty pitcher to the floor.

He helped her climb out of the bath, handling her carefully, as if she might break between his hands. Caroline stood dripping on the soft rug, and Anthony began to rub her dry. As his hands lingered on her breasts, she moaned, pressing herself against him.

She raised herself on her toes to kiss him, leaning into his strength. She would think about the things that irritated her about her husband tomorrow.

❧

Anthony carried her to their marriage bed and laid her down, her wet hair gleaming gold in the firelight. He wondered why he had gone to his mistress at all, when such bounty was his. He pushed away the memory of her reckless disobedience, of her defiance before his men in the stable. He would deal with that tomorrow. For now, Anthony bent to kiss her, drinking in her sigh of pleasure, his lips warm over hers.

Caroline met his mouth with hers as if to devour him, and he let her push him back onto the silk sheets. Her long hair fell over one shoulder, hiding her body from him. She pushed her wet hair out of her way, her lips and tongue and teeth moving over him. She rose over Anthony in their bed and sheathed him in her body. She began to move without his prompting, riding him as she would her stallion.

Anthony was shocked, even as his sudden pleasure consumed him. He had never taught her such bold-ness. But in the candlelight, her face showed only innocence and her desire for him.

He gave himself over to her, then to the feel of her body on his. His hands slid over her breasts, kneading them, until she gasped and leaned down, closer to his touch, riding him still.

He moved toward the peak of pleasure, and he tried desperately to hold himself back. His wife rode him harder when she felt his resistance, and for the first time since he was a green boy, Anthony came against his will, unable to control himself.

Caroline joined him at his peak, falling against him as the last of his seed shuddered into her. She lay across his chest as if slain. Anthony took in the scent of her skin.

"Where did you learn to fight like that?" he asked.

Caroline smiled, her voice low, her tone deep with satisfaction. She writhed against him, and he saw that in her languor she could barely lift her head.

"Why, you taught me, my lord. I never fought with a soul before I met and married you."

A rumble of laughter came from deep in his chest. He stroked her back, the damp flesh that was still warmed by his own. "No, Wife. Where did you learn to wield a knife?"

"My father's veterans taught me. He wanted me to learn, in case I was ever alone and in need."

"Fencing, archery, daggers. Is there no end to your womanly accomplishments?"

Caroline did not rise to that bait but swatted him half-heartedly, her hand lingering on his chest, the gesture turning into a sleepy caress. Anthony laughed again but knew he must use that moment to teach her, whether she wanted to listen to him or not.

"You can put your knives away, Caroline. You will never be alone and in need for as long as I live."

"That remains to be seen, Anthony. But let's not argue anymore tonight. I find I am too weary." She raised her head and pressed her lips to his temple.

He meant to chide her again, to speak with her once more about the need for her to obey him in all things, but the need did not seem as pressing as the softness of her body against his, and as the sweet sleep that dragged at his limbs. He wrapped his arms around her and took her with him into it.

They slept until past midnight. Anthony woke to find Caroline's head on his chest, the light from the fire beginning to burn down. He took in the jasmine scent of her and kissed her hair.

"I have something for you, Caroline."

His wife gave him a wicked smile and boldly ran her hand over his body. She cupped him in her palm. "Indeed, my lord. And I have something for you."

Guilt gnawed at the edges of his pleasure, and he wondered at it. He never felt guilt. It was not in his nature.

But then he remembered the pearl he had given his mistress. That black pearl pressed on his mind like a boulder. Try as he might, he could not push aside the thought of it.

His wife had not yet seen his gift to her. The sudden memory of Caroline's pearl, the creamy purity of it, was like a balm on his soul. He would give her that pearl, and his guilt would fade into nothing.

Anthony drew away, kissing her one last time, his lips lingering on hers. "Stay here," he commanded as he rose from their bed.

"Am I your dog, to fetch and heel as well?" she asked.

He ignored her gibe to retrieve the pearl from his coat pocket. She reached for him as he returned.

He wanted to lose himself in her flesh again, to forget London and his mistress, the man who had attacked his wife, and Carlyle altogether, but he knew he could not put those things aside. He pressed his lips not to her mouth but to her temple. When he did that, she sighed in defeat.

"What do you bring me, Husband?"

"This," he said, handing her a velvet bag tied with a strand of silk.

She looked puzzled. Anthony laughed as she drew the bag open.

His wife was still smiling at him when the jewel fell into the palm of her hand. Tears filled her eyes, and he opened his mouth to apologize, to say he would bring her diamonds instead. But when she smiled, he saw they were tears of joy.

"For me?" she asked.

Anthony thought his heart would break as he looked at his wife holding the alabaster pearl as if it was a gift from God. He would have bought every pearl the jeweler had and laid them all at Caroline's feet if he had known she would look at him like that.

"For you," he said, his voice rough with emotion.

She launched herself at him and clung to him as though he had saved her from drowning. He kissed her golden hair and listened as she sniffled and dried her eyes on the skin of his chest. The same woman in his arms, weeping over his gift, just the day before had stood alone to face an enemy twice her size, undaunted. How many facets lived behind the eyes of this one woman?

"I love it. Put it on me. Please."

The gold and pearl were warm from her hand as he clasped the chain around her throat. As he watched the pearl fall between her breasts, he knew he would buy her many more pearls to wear with that one.

The color matched her skin exactly. He kissed her between her breasts, just above where his pearl rested. She lay back on the bed and drew him down with her, taking him into her body almost without any help from him. He gasped over her as her hips moved against his, bringing him closer and closer to climax. For the second time that night, he did not take control back from his lover but let her undulate beneath him, holding himself just above her so she had room to move.

His breath became ragged as she moved against him, until she moaned under him and shuddered in her own release. Anthony lunged against her then, driving into her with three quick thrusts that left him spiraling into his own chasm of pleasure. He lay against her afterwards, breathing hard, the pearl on its golden chain wedged against her heart, a small bond between them.

Chapter 20

ANTHONY LEFT FOR LONDON AGAIN BEFORE THE MONTH was out. Parliament would open officially in November, and he had work to do both for his own interests and for the Prince Regent's. This time he told Caroline when he was going and left just after dawn so she could rise from her bed to wave him off.

With Anthony gone, Caroline always wore the pearl he had given her, hidden beneath the bodice of her gown. She did not want the servants carrying tales to him that she displayed his gift openly, pining for him.

Caroline continued her life much as she had intended, in spite of the fact that Anthony was certain that she would give up her knives. Though he had asked for such a concession, she had never agreed to it. She began the search for an instructor who might help her drill her fighting skills and perhaps teach her new ones. Despite all Anthony said, he and his men could not be everywhere at once. Her father had taught her to look to her own safety.

She instructed the grooms to set up an archery

range just beyond the stables, far enough away that
the horses would not be bothered, but close enough
that she could run indoors if a sudden rain came up.
She practiced with her bow and arrows until her
fingers bled beneath the soft leather of her gloves,
until she was sure that skill, at least, would not
be lost.

The sound of the myrtle shaft striking its target was
satisfying, but she knew a bow and arrow were worth-
less against an attacker. Unlike the goddess Athena,
she could not walk about wearing her bow and quiver
with her day gowns.

During the second week Anthony was in London,
Caroline went to the village of Ravensbrook, osten-
sibly to buy material for a new gown, when truly she
hoped to find a teacher. She looked in windows along
the village high street, but though she found pretty
ribbons and lovely bonnets, no one she spoke to led
her to believe a fencing master lurked in the depths of
Shropshire. She had almost resolved to simply practice
her knife fighting on her own in secret, when she took
tea at the local inn and public house.

The Wick and Candle stood on the edge of town
where travelers might easily stop, break their journey,
and have a meal. The food was fine and the propri-
etress friendly. Caroline had struck up an acquaintance
with her as soon as she moved to Ravensbrook, when
she was first becoming known to the village and the
tenants on her husband's estate.

Mrs. Bellows always welcomed Caroline with a
smile and a fresh-baked scone. She seemed to keep
the steaming confections in the oven at all times, for

never once had Caroline called without a pile of hot scones being offered on a china plate with fresh butter and hot black tea. That day was no exception, though for the first time, Mrs. Bellows did not lead Caroline directly into the private parlor.

"My lady, a gentleman traveling to London has stopped here for a day and a night. He has taken the parlor at the moment. Would you mind sharing it with him if I kept one of my girls present?"

Caroline knew that it went against all propriety, but with her husband gone and her mother far away in Yorkshire, she was confident she might do as she pleased. "For one of your scones, I would brave a wild lion. Lead me to the parlor, and I will introduce myself."

Mrs. Bellows smiled, her relief evident. She waved to a girl bringing food to the taproom. After Molly had delivered her wares to the occupants of the main room, Caroline followed Mrs. Bellows and her would-be protector to meet the stranger. Caroline knew her reputation must be guarded always, especially since Anthony was protective to the point of madness. The villagers seemed to know of her husband's tendencies, and respected them as she herself did not.

Mrs. Bellows opened the door to the parlor and curtsied to the gentleman inside. "My lady, if I may present Mr. Carstairs. He is a traveler on his way to London and is happy to share the parlor with you. Her ladyship, the Countess of Ravensbrook."

Viscount Carlyle stood as the women entered the room and bowed. "Your servant, ma'am."

His blue eyes gleamed with mischief, as if he knew a great joke and would share it with her as soon as they were alone. Caroline nodded to him and let the lie of his false name pass.

She sank onto the settle by the fire as Mrs. Bellows brought scones and cream, as well as the strawberry jam she had made that spring, then left them. Hot tea was placed at Caroline's elbow, and she poured in silence while Molly stood by, poking the fire to make it burn brighter.

"Molly, would you be so kind as to fetch me more clotted cream? This is lovely, but I don't think we have quite enough for Mr. Carstairs and myself."

"Of course, my lady." Molly bobbed a quick curtsy, leaving Caroline alone with the viscount..

"You turn up in the most unlikely places, my lord. I never know when I will see you next."

Carlyle laughed. "I might say the same of you, my lady. Marriage seems to suit you."

"Tolerably well." Caroline dismissed any further niceties with the wave of one hand. "We have little time to talk openly. What are you playing at?"

"Well, my lady, your husband, as you may recollect, is not overly fond of me."

"No, he is not. But then he does not seem overly fond of anyone, save Pembroke."

"And yourself, of course," Carlyle said.

Caroline did not acknowledge that statement one way or another, and Victor continued to speak. "Suffice it to say that your husband and I do not always see eye to eye, in business or in anything else. Though this grieves me, there is little I can do about it at this late date. I find that when I pass through towns near his properties, if I expect decent service, I must offer a name other than my own."

"So you are famous among my husband's people then?"

"Infamous, one might even say, my lady."

Caroline shrugged one shoulder. She sipped at her tea, warming her hands against the thin china cup. "I suppose I will leave your business between my husband and yourself. God knows I have enough of my own concerns without troubling myself with yours."

"Indeed." Viscount Carlyle smiled. "Always a sound policy."

Molly returned then with a heaping dish of cream. "Here you are, my lady."

"Thank you, Molly."

Caroline spread the confection over her still-warm scone and watched it melt for a moment before she bit into it. She sighed in delight.

"Well, Mr. Carstairs, if I might ask you a personal question in regards your own wife?"

"Of course, my lady. I am your servant."

Caroline hid her smile behind her teacup. His false servility sounded a bit over the top to her own ears, but Molly did not notice it at all.

She wondered for a moment if she could trust a man so glib with the truth, but there was always the knife in her reticule.

"Does your wife look at all to her own safety?"

"Forgive me, my lady. I am not certain what you mean."

"It occurs to me that a lady, while well protected,

might also want to learn how to protect herself. My father always thought so."

"Indeed, Lady Ravensbrook. The teachings of our fathers are surely to be adhered to. How did the illustrious gentleman instruct you?"

"In fencing and in the use of a short blade." Caroline was not certain she should say such a thing openly, but she knew if she did not find an instructor soon, she would begin to forget all she had learned, and her hard-won skill would be gone.

"I see."

Carlyle did not look shocked, nor did he condemn her. "Mrs. Carstairs does not feel the need to defend herself in that way, but I can certainly understand why a woman might. She might fall in with unsavory characters without realizing it, perhaps."

"I suppose she might," Caroline said. "Do you know of anyone who might instruct a lady in such a pastime?"

Carlyle glanced at Molly, but the girl seemed to be lost in her own thoughts. He turned back to Caroline.

"As a matter of fact, I do. I am acquainted with a distant neighbor of yours, Angelique Beauchamp, the Countess of Devonshire. She has in her employ a gentleman who also works for me."

Caroline's gaze sharpened. "What man would work for both you and your countess friend?"

"A man I have asked to spy on her."

"How unsavory," Caroline said.

"Indeed. But information has its uses, Lady Ravensbrook."

"And you want information about her. Is she your mistress then?"

"My word, you are impertinent. I am surprised your husband has not cured you of that."

Caroline smiled sweetly. "He has tried. But as you can see, he has failed."

Victor smiled back, and she saw a hint of challenge in his look. "So far. Your marriage is young."

"Indeed. As with all things, time will tell the tale."

Caroline met his eyes without flinching until he smiled at her, raising his hands in surrender. "So true, my lady, so true. But whatever the case, my man can certainly help you."

"What would he be able to do?"

"Ralph Higgins is his name. He would be happy to ride to your estate and instruct you on the use of a blade."

"We cannot meet there. My husband does not approve of this endeavor."

"Ah," Victor said, leaning back in his chair. "That does make things more difficult."

"But not impossible," Caroline said.

Victor smiled. "No. Not impossible." He sat in silence for a moment while she watched him.

"There is a house to let not two miles from here. If you can get away from your duties once every two weeks or so, Ralph could meet you there."

"What assurances do I have that he will not try to take advantage of the situation?" Caroline asked.

"None," Victor said, smiling. "You had best bring your own man with you, as well as your blades, until you are sure of him. He has always served me well, but he is a slippery character, taking money both from myself and from Countess Devonshire."

"Men like that can never be trusted," Caroline said.

"No." Carlyle took a sip of his tea. "But from time to time, they can be useful."

Anthony did not spend all of the autumn in London, though Caroline came to miss him more and more when he was away. She began to enjoy his presence when he was home, not just for the pleasure she found in their bed, but for his company.

Every few weeks, when Anthony was away, Caroline spent an afternoon of her free time working with Ralph Higgins. He was a quiet man who opened his mouth only to correct her. His advice was always welcome, for as a small man, he knew some of the disadvantages she faced when fighting. But they worked together only every few weeks. When she was not scheduled for a lesson, she hungered for physical activity that went beyond her rides on Hercules, with a groom trailing behind her.

Anthony came home for a week toward the end of October. One morning, he woke to find Caroline gone from their bed. When she did not return within a half hour, he dressed and went to look for her in the breakfast room but did not find her there either. He did not ask the staff where his wife had gone, for he did not wish to look like a fool. Instead, he walked down to the stables to see if she had ridden out on Hercules without telling him.

He found her, not in the stables, but in the meadow

directly behind it. She stood facing an archery target, just as she had the first time he had ever seen her.

No gentlemen of the *ton* looked on this time. Indeed, the stable lads ignored her as they went about their business inside. No one seemed to think it odd that the lady of the house had a lethal weapon in her hands.

She had not bothered to dress her hair, and the golden mass fell braided down her back, all the way to her waist. She wore a day gown of pale blue trimmed in white, and looked for all the world like a lady who might sit and take tea, save for the wild fall of hair and the weapon she held.

Anthony held his breath as she drew back on the bow. Her arrow flew straight and far, burying itself just left of the center of the makeshift target. She smiled and drew again, making each successive shot better than the last. When she had emptied her quiver and strode toward the target to pick up her arrows, Anthony fell into step beside her.

"You are a fine shot, Caroline. I have never seen a woman shoot so well or so far."

She blinked, clearly surprised to see him there. She did not stammer or mutter an excuse but continued to draw her arrows from the target. He helped her pull them out and replace them in the quiver on her back.

"I shoot better than most men, my lord, save for on horseback. I have not had enough practice hunting with a bow while riding Hercules."

"That would be a savage practice indeed, my lady. I for one am glad you contain your archery to the range."

She smiled at him then, her soft mouth rising in a

sensuous curve. His loins tightened at the sight of that smile, one he rarely saw, save when they were alone in their bedroom.

"Do you fear I will ride after you, wailing like an Amazon, my bow at the ready?"

Anthony laughed. "I am much more used to you whole and alive."

She leaned close and pressed a kiss to his lips before deftly stepping out of his reach. "That is true, my lord."

She went back to her place, and Anthony followed. She drew back on her bow, but Anthony interrupted her. "Might I make a suggestion?"

She lowered her bow. "What suggestion would that be?"

"Perhaps if you raised your grip very slightly toward the fletching, the arrow might fly farther."

He watched her process this unsolicited bit of advice, but she did not dismiss it. Her brow furrowed with thought, and Anthony suppressed the desire to kiss the frown that appeared between her eyes.

"I do not see how that would help," she said. "I shoot well now."

"Yes, Caroline. But one may always improve."

She shrugged one shoulder. "Show me."

Anthony stepped close, but instead of taking the bow she offered, he wrapped his arms around her. He stood behind her, one hand on the bow, the other on her arrow. His breath came fast as he took in the scent of roses on her skin and jasmine under that. His desire for her rose though they had been together only hours before. He found himself transfixed by the heat of her slight body, by the softness of her curves as she stood close. She noticed his arousal against the small of her back, and she pressed against him harder.

"Caroline, focus, please."

He saw her smile, her gloved hands tightening their grip on the bow. "As you say, my lord. You are the instructor here."

Anthony thought for one heated moment he would toss the bow aside and take her on the damp ground then and there. But anyone might step out from the stables. Though she drove him mad with desire, he did not have to let all of his stable hands know it.

He placed his hand over hers and helped her draw back on the bow. Once she was in place, he moved her fingers an inch back on the arrow, closer to the fletching.

"This is uncomfortable, Anthony. My hand is too far back."

"It feels that way only because you haven't done it before." He pressed his lips to her ear, his breath hot on the pearl-pink shell hidden behind her hair. "Trust me."

Caroline let her arrow fly then, and she missed her mark.

"That one does not count," she said. "You distracted me."

"Indeed, I did. Let us try again."

Anthony kept his hands on her hips this time, holding her against his growing erection. He knew she wanted him as much as he wanted her, for her breathing had quickened far too much for archery. It was his nearness and the heat of his body that distracted her, and he knew it.

Her second and third shots went wide.

"Anthony, I cannot think with you standing so close. Please step back."

"I thought you were a master archer who could hit her target no matter what distractions she might encounter."

Caroline did not answer but fitted another arrow onto her bow. She squared her shoulders as he leaned close and ran his tongue along her ear. She breathed deeply, her hand trembling once before she took her shot. This time, she did not miss.

She threw her bow down and dropped her quiver into the mud, turning on him like a lioness. Anthony braced himself for a tirade but instead found his arms full of willing woman, her tongue slipping past his lips, lingering in the heat of his mouth.

He moaned without thinking, pulling her close for a heated kiss. She did not lead for long, for his own desire rose to the fore, his hands moving from her hips to her bottom, pressing her hard against him. She spoke his name, the sweetest sound he had heard all that day.

"Anthony, come inside."

"We'll frighten the horses."

"They'll get over it."

"We'll frighten the stable boys."

"They've seen it before."

Caroline pressed herself hard against him until he could no longer resist her. The Earl of Ravensbrook lifted his countess in his arms and carried her into the stable. The saddle room was empty. Anthony pushed the door closed with one booted foot, and the heavy wood slammed in its frame.

"I'm sure they all heard that," he said. "No doubt, they'll stay away."

"No doubt they'll hear more. They had better take themselves out of the stables altogether for the next fifteen minutes or so," Caroline said, her fingers moving with skill against his breeches.

She had his clothes unfastened in a trice, but any thought he had harbored of finding a nice bed of sweet-smelling straw in which to ravish her was banished as soon as her fingers touched him. He swelled in her tiny palm, and she ran her hand over him even as he lifted her skirts.

"There is no blanket here," Anthony said.

"We don't need one," she gasped. "This wall is sound and will serve."

Anthony laughed under his breath, and then she squeezed him in both hands. He shuddered, his laughter dying even as his tongue sought hers, his lips ravishing hers.

She moaned as his hand trailed up her thigh, past her garters to the soft inner flesh above them. Anthony fought his body and hers, trying not to rush headlong into oblivion. He wanted to linger over her, to draw out their pleasure. He feared he might hurt her in his desperate need.

She clutched his shoulder with one hand as she milked his manhood with the other. He drew her hands away, raising them above her head as he pressed her back against the wall. She moaned in protest, but his lips sealed hers, silencing her with his tongue.

"I am the one wearing trousers here," he said. "I am the one in control of this encounter."

"Are you really?" she asked, raising an eyebrow.

She lifted one leg and wrapped it around his waist, pressing the heat of her core against him. He moaned, and she wriggled against him, swirling her hips to show him he was not in charge after all.

Anthony raised her other leg then, both hands on her bottom. When he entered her, she stopped circling her hips and moaned long and loud. She seemed to forget who was challenging whom as pleasure began to consume her.

Anthony lost himself in the warm, tight feel of her flesh as she clasped him. He raised her higher and thrust into her again, unable to speak, able only to focus on what he was doing. The pleasure filled him like a flash tide, swelling higher and higher as he moved.

Caroline gasped beneath his lips, her hands caught in his hair. She clutched him close, all thought of control gone. Anthony saw her eyes glaze over with passion, and he began to move harder, faster, watching her face all the while. When he saw her eyes close and felt her center tighten around him like a vise, he held her still, letting her convulsions rise before driving himself into her again, making her pleasure last.

Caroline sobbed his name at the last, and that was what finally broke his control. He thrust one last time and lost himself in her, shuddering with his own release. He breathed her name, his lips in her hair. He felt the ground shake and realized it was his legs that were trembling. He withdrew from her and drew her down onto a bench with him, holding her on his lap as his limbs slowly began to stop shaking.

ACT III

"A woman may be made a fool,
if she has not a spirit to resist."

The Taming of the Shrew
Act 3, Scene 2

Chapter 21

"SHE IS A TIGRESS," ANTHONY SAID. "IT HAPPENED three months ago, but I cannot get the image out of my mind. I have never known another woman like her."

He finished relating the story of Caroline's fight with the attacker in the barley field as he sat in his study with Pembroke, smoking cigarillos. December had arrived, and soon Anthony's friends would flock to London for the Prince Regent's Twelfth Night ball. The time had come for Anthony to decide whether to take his wife into the city or stay at home with her.

He had not left her often in the last few months. They had ridden out together the times his schedule would permit it, though they never visited the saddle room, after scandalizing the head groom with their last visit. Caroline rode out with a young groom when Anthony could not go with her.

They had shared time on her archery range. Anthony had bought his own bow, and neither was able to best the other in their ongoing contest of wills. Caroline no longer seemed to feel the need to resist his strictures set up to protect her. Anthony was not certain he truly knew her in spite of the relative peace of the last months, in spite of the pleasure he found in her arms. Her brown eyes were as fathomless as they had been on the day they first met.

His wife had introduced him to his tenants, some of whom he had never before bothered to meet, though he had lived at Ravensbrook for almost all his youth. Anthony had not realized that, while he was abroad fighting for the king off and on for more than a decade, life in Shropshire had gone on, babies being born and old folks dying. Caroline bridged the gap between him and his tenants, reintroducing him to each family in turn, making certain each tenant knew their value. She had arranged a festival at harvest time, with dancing and feasting and cider for all from the extra pressings from the apple orchard.

She ran his household with such calm skill, with such unflappable coolness, he almost did not recognize the fiery woman who came to his bed in the dark reaches of the night. She was a tigress there, learning every trick he taught her and coming up with more. He had sampled women in London and on the Continent, but no woman had ever fascinated him as much as his lovely wife.

Pembroke blew smoke in rings to the ceiling as his friend watched him from his perch beside the window. "I have never known a woman who could fight with a knife."

"Neither have I," Anthony said.

Both men sat in silence, contemplating the smoke above their heads. Anthony found his thoughts drifting to the supple length of his wife's arm and the deceptive appearance of her frailty until she drew her dagger. "I have forbidden her to do it again," Anthony said. "But she is an incredible woman."

"And she obeys you in this?" Pembroke asked, his eyebrow rising.

Anthony's dark eyes grew hard. "She does," he answered. "She has learned obedience."

Anthony saw the speculative gleam in his friend's gaze, but he did not answer it. He knew as well as Pembroke that three months was too short a time to be certain his errant wife had been tamed of her wild ways. He had not taken her knives from her, but they had disappeared as if they had never been. He had even searched her trunks for evidence of them and found only the pressed rose petals and jasmine soap she favored in her baths.

"That is good news," Pembroke said, a circle of smoke rising above his head. "Not all men would sleep well, knowing a knife lay just steps from the pillow."

"She has no need of knives. She has me to protect her."

"But who will protect you?"

Anthony gave his friend a wry smile. "In spite of her newfound calm, I hesitate to bring her to London."

Anthony was hoping his friend would offer his opinion. Pembroke did not speak at once but put out his cigarillo, as if giving the matter some thought.

"Carlyle will be there," Anthony said. "And so will my aunt."

Pembroke knew the elderly Lady Westwood was

still a favorite of Anthony's. As one of his last living
relatives, the old lady got on rather well with Anthony.
It was Victor who concerned him.

"You are afraid Victor will see how much you value
her," Pembroke said. He was careful not use the word *love*.
"You're afraid he will interfere with her in some way."

Anthony's mouth grew tight and grim. "He might try."

"Did the Prince Regent specifically request her
presence?" Pembroke asked.

"I had a messenger from him today, inviting us to
his Twelfth Night ball."

Pembroke leaned back against the cushions of his
chair and faced his friend. "Then you have no choice.
You must bring her."

"There is always a choice."

❧

Caroline raised the knife she had just taken from
her opponent.

"You must learn to wield any blade as an extension
of your arm," Ralph Higgins said. "You will use it to
extend the reach of your hand."

She had been working with Ralph for two months,
and each day as they began her training, he always said
the same thing. He taught her even greater speed than
she learned from her father's men. Ralph was small,
barely taller than she was, and almost as slight. He lived
by speed and his wits, as her father's men had taught
her to do.

Ralph worked with her with rapiers, as well, so
her fencing skills would not leave her completely.
Though Ralph was not as deft with a rapier as she

was, his skill with a short blade was unmatched. He taught her tricks a small person could use easily against a larger opponent, and how to win a fight as quickly as possible. He reminded her that it was her wits that would serve her best in any fight, so long as she kept hold of her temper.

Caroline wondered if she would finally get the chance to use her wits among the *ton* of London. She would not enter into combat in the city, but she had no doubt there were many among the nobility who would challenge her right to be there. Though she was a baron's daughter, her family never spent time in the capital. As an outsider, she would need to keep her cool when surrounded by the aristocratic elite.

She had met some of those people at her father's house party and had little desire to see them again. But the thought of seeing London, where ships from all over the world brought people and goods to the heart of the empire, thrilled her as almost nothing else had. She knew Anthony was considering whether or not he should bring her to the city, though he had not yet brought up the subject.

Since a journey to London was what she wanted above all things, she knew better than to ask for it. She would make Anthony believe such a trip to be his own idea, so he would not fight her every step of the way on the road to town.

She cursed herself for her idle thoughts, for Ralph pressed her hard, with no quarter given for the fact that she was his employer, with no intention of shielding her or making her way an easy one. She thanked him silently even as she gained her footing and pressed back against him, blade to blade. If he was soft with her, a real opponent would not be.

They fought, and for once he could not regain his advantage. Though he weighed more and had faced men in hand-to-hand combat, he could not move faster than she did. That day, in the dim lamp light of Viscount Carlyle's rented cottage, he gave way before her. Caroline smiled but did not lower her guard until she heard the stamping of booted feet and a shrill whistle pierced the air.

Ralph nodded to her and stepped back, no longer her opponent but her teacher. Caroline saluted him and lowered her weapon, turning toward the noise by the door.

Her groom, Jonathan, clapped enthusiastically. He followed her everywhere, when she went into the gardens at home and whenever she rode out on horseback.

Anthony had relented and let this one youth accompany her instead of two grooms. Her husband knew the seventeen-year-old boy was devoted to her. She confided in Jonathan that she worked with a blade as a surprise for her husband, that one day she hoped to thrill the earl with her prowess.

Caroline felt a sting of remorse at that fiction, but she wished it was true. In her deepest heart, she hoped that someday Anthony would accept her as she was. Until that day, if it ever came, it was not her fault she had to sneak around to protect herself. Anthony had brought her to that.

She sheathed her blade and nodded to Ralph as he put his away. Jonathan left to saddle the horses, but someone else watched her from the doorway.

"Is there no end to your talents, Lady Ravensbrook?"

She smiled, straightening the skirt of her riding habit. She no longer fought in breeches since the day Ralph pointed out that if she were truly under attack, she would very likely be wearing a riding habit or a gown.

"You flatter me, my lord Carlyle."

"Indeed, I do not. You are highly skilled."

"That may be, but my skills remain a secret. My husband would not approve."

"Perhaps he has not seen your prowess with a blade. If he did, surely he would be proud of you."

Caroline frowned. "No," she said. "My husband is not proud of me."

Victor's blue gaze was steady on hers. "Then he is a fool."

Caroline thanked Ralph for his work, handing him a gold sovereign. He bowed to her and pocketed the coin. "And now I leave you to speak with your other employer," Caroline said.

"One of them," Victor remarked.

She mounted Hercules unassisted, drawing the reins tight so her mount danced in a circle as she waited for Jonathan to join her. She and her horse were both impatient to be gone.

"Was that Viscount Carlyle, my lady?"

"It was."

Jonathan did not mount his horse. "Lord Ravensbrook loathes that man, my lady, though I have never been told why."

"Neither have I, Jonathan."

"You should not speak to him, my lady. I think Lord Carlyle is a bad man."

Caroline smiled. "I am sure I have known better, but there seems little harm in him."

"I think he is a bad man," Jonathan said again.

Caroline saw in the implacable expression in his eyes. From the set of his jaw, she was suddenly certain he would tell someone of her outings if she did not concede now. She had learned much in the two months she'd been working with Ralph Higgins. That would have to do for now. In future, she would find another way to practice.

"Do not trouble yourself, Jonathan. We will not come here again."

The boy looked relieved. "Very good, my lady."

Jonathan mounted then, and Victor bowed to her from where he was standing in the cottage door. If he had heard it all, he did not look surprised. Caroline still did not know why Anthony loathed that man, and she no longer cared. She knew only that Victor had helped her when her own husband would not.

Caroline rode home in time to greet Anthony and Pembroke over tea in her sitting room. The sun had long since set, and the fire was warm in the hearth. She poured tea for both the gentlemen first, preparing Anthony's as he liked it, with a touch of cream and no sugar. Pembroke prepared his own, his eyes on her. Anthony sat on the settee beside her, content as always to sip his tea and leave most of the talking to his friend.

Watching Caroline, Pembroke turned to Anthony. "There is no way you cannot bring this woman to meet the prince. He will love her on sight."

Perhaps this was the moment she might press her suit. She hungered to see London the way she hungered for her husband's body.

As much as Anthony irritated her and as much as she wished her husband would communicate with her in some way other than issuing orders, she still wanted him. And a delicate tenderness had grown between them, a bit like a hothouse flower. Something lovely and very fragile. As she sat staring at her beautiful husband, she wished it was enough.

Had she asked to go to London, Anthony might have refused outright, stating yet again how he wanted only to keep her safe. Perhaps if he thought the journey Pembroke's idea, he might give his consent.

She kept her eyes on Anthony. "Yes, Husband. Will you take me to London for the holidays?"

She leaned close to him as if to offer more tea, but as she poured and pressed one breast against his arm, Anthony stirred next to her restlessly. Caroline saw the smile in his eyes and reveled in the desire that simmered between them. Had they been alone, he would have reached for her. As it was, Anthony kept his hands on his cup and saucer.

"The Prince Regent has asked to meet you, Caroline. Of course, we will go."

Chapter 22

London

THEY CAME TO LONDON ALMOST THREE WEEKS BEFORE the holidays, and Caroline began to realize there was more to her husband than the autocratic man she had come to know over the past months.

While he tried to keep a close watch on her in Shropshire, he did not keep her from the excitement of London. On hearing that Caroline had never seen a play, Anthony took her at once to Drury Lane. She loved it so much they returned each night for a new production.

They watched plays by Shakespeare and Marlowe and a modern farce neither of them liked. Caroline even found herself enjoying a production of *The Taming of the Shrew*. The actress who played Katherine, a woman named Titania, breathed life into the old language, as did her fellow players.

At the end of the play, when Katherine admonished wives to obedience, tamed at last, Anthony seemed to miss the heavy irony with which Titania infused the scene. He leaned close and whispered in Caroline's ear, "An example to live by, Wife."

Caroline laughed under her breath and turned her head to whisper back, "Husband, you are mistaken. It is I who will tame you."

He took her hand and led her out of the theatre. He did not wait until they got home that night but had her in the closed carriage on the short ride back to their town house.

On most days, Anthony went out on business with his colleagues in Parliament and to care for his shipping interests with the East India Company. On one of those days, Caroline took advantage of his absence to go out and buy herself a sword.

It was a fencing rapier meant for a boy, but it had a decent weight for her arm, and its hilt was coated in a layer of fine leather. She purchased it and the box it came in as Tabby looked on in consternation.

"What his lordship does not know will hurt no one," Caroline said. She had a rapier already, but she had been forced to leave it behind in Shropshire after her lessons with Ralph Higgins had ended. Though it was winter, she saw no reason why she could not practice her fencing alone indoors. She would drill herself in the motions, though of course she could not spar.

She took herself home to Ravensbrook House and skipped luncheon, climbing instead straight to the ballroom on the third floor of the house, where she drew her new rapier from its box. The blade gleamed in the sunlight from the high windows, and she waved the blade with a flourish, not minding that its edges and tip were blunted. It was useless in combat, but that made it no less a work of art.

She had removed her cloak already, so she stood in the ballroom in her day gown, its brown wool shot through with gold. She put herself though her paces one position at a time and soon lost herself in the joy of motion, feeling her heart pump and her legs and arms respond as if there were an opponent present.

She felt the joy she found only on the fencing floor, on the archery range, or on horseback. Here she could be her true self, and it did not matter if that self would have been shunned by society at large, especially the London *ton*. There was freedom in motion and in the sweet feel of a blade slicing through thin air. She turned as if to parry a thrust that was not there, only to find her blade stopped in midair by her husband's hand on her wrist.

"Caroline, did I not tell you that knife play is unacceptable in my house?"

She stepped back, freeing her hand as well as her blade. "You did indeed, my lord. But this is not knife play. This is fencing."

"So I see."

He held out one hand, and she reluctantly placed her new sword into it. He hefted the blade, testing its weight. "This is a decent sword. Where did you find the money for such a thing?"

"My pin money, if you must know, my lord. My needs are few. I have been saving for a blade since August."

"Before you ever met me?"

"That's so. I knew I would marry and get to London eventually."

Anthony's bark of laughter filled the room and made her smile. He did not keep her blade as she had feared he might, but turned it around so the hilt faced her. "This blade is not fine enough for you," he said.

"It is blunted," she answered. "And the weight is sound."

He did not answer but watched as she wiped it down with a cloth and put it back in its wooden case.

"Will you take it from me?" she asked.

"No," Anthony said. "If you prefer blunted blades to ribbons and bonnets, that is your prerogative."

Caroline stared at him for a long moment. "You may be learning my ways, my lord. It is still too soon to tell, but you might become civilized yet."

He laughed again, drawing her close so she could take in the scent of his skin. She rubbed her fingers on the black velvet of his coat, enjoying the softness of the cloth and the strength of his arm.

"I think I must learn more of your ways, for you seem to have no intention of learning mine."

"Giving up so easily, my lord? I would not have thought it."

"I concede nothing, Caroline. I intend only to humor you, so when I strike next, you will not expect it."

Caroline raised herself on her toes so she might run her lips over the edge of his jaw. He crushed her to his chest, their banter forgotten, lowering his mouth to cover hers. She did not savor her triumph, for she was too busy savoring him.

∽

Caroline was not certain if it was the cold of winter that drove him indoors to her side or simply something about the city that made her husband relax, but Caroline found for the first time in their marriage that she and Anthony could talk to each other.

One night, as they sat alone in her bedroom, she told him of her childhood in York, growing up with her father gone.

"Yorkshire is beautiful, but a lonely place when all the men are off to war. I had trouble sometimes remembering the sound of my father's voice. I had a miniature of him, but it did not truly look like him. Papa was never still, for one thing. He taught me to ride before he went away."

Anthony swirled the brandy in its glass, watching the play of the amber liquid. "It is like that with those we love. No matter how long we are apart, we carry them with us."

"I wish I had carried a clearer image of him," Caroline said.

"I felt the same way when I was off fighting and had to leave my sister behind. Anne was a beauty. I had a miniature painted of her too, but I lost it in the war."

"I am so sorry. Did she die young?"

Anthony met her eyes, coming back from a far distance. He tried to smile but failed. "No. She lives still."

"Why have I never met her? Where is she?"

Anthony swallowed hard. He did not speak for a long moment, so she went to him, taking his brandy from him, sitting on his lap so he could not look away from her. She pressed herself against him, offering the only comfort she knew.

In spite of the relative peace they had reached since coming to London, there was a gulf between them, a gulf she did not know how to bridge. He wanted her, and she him. Their mutual desire was a slender thread, but it was all she had. She offered her body to him silently, and for the first time in their marriage, he did not take her.

Instead, he drew her close, burying his face in the softness of her hair. There was no lust in his touch but a different kind of desperation. She thought for one horrible moment he might weep, but he did not. He drew back to look into her eyes, pushing her hair back from her forehead.

"Anne lives still, but she is a recluse. She had a shock and does not like to go out in company."

"Will we see her for Christmas?" Caroline asked.

His voice was rough when he answered her. "No. She prefers to be alone."

He did not say what had happened to Anne, and Caroline did not press him. Whatever had occurred, it was a tragedy that still touched his heart. She would not give up on his sister, though she let the subject alone. She would find a way to meet Anne after the New Year and see if she might bring Anthony and his sister back together in spite of whatever had driven them apart.

❧

They spent Christmas day with Anthony's only other living relative, Lady Lucy Westwood, who had spoken to Caroline so plainly in Yorkshire the day she and Anthony had become engaged. She arrived for dinner promptly at seven, the early hour set by Lady

Westwood's specifications. Dressed in gray bomba-
zine, the gray silk turban on her head fastened with
a diamond brooch, Lady Westwood had raised her
quizzing glass and inspected Caroline's arrangements
down to the place settings in the dining room.

Lady Westwood made polite conversation all
evening as she very impolitely inspected every morsel
of food and every servant who crossed her path.
Anthony glowered, but Caroline pressed his hand, so
he said nothing. She smiled at his elderly aunt, waiting
for the moment when she would speak her mind. She
was not disappointed.

At the end of the evening, as Lady Westwood stood
in the front hall, waiting for her carriage to be brought
around, she met Caroline's eyes. "You have taken this
one in hand. I was not sure you were the woman to
do it, but I see now that you are."

Anthony opened his mouth to protest, but Caroline
laid her hand on his arm, and he stayed silent.

"Anthony is a good man," she said. "I am fortunate."

Lady Westwood harrumphed and turned her eagle
gaze on her nephew. "See that you remain a model
husband, Anthony. Keep her happy, young man, or
you'll answer to me."

Anthony forced a smile. "As you say, Aunt."

Lady Westwood laughed out loud at that answer
and let Anthony escort her down the marble stairs of
the town house and hand her into her carriage.

❦

That night, in the shadows of their bed, Anthony asked,
"Am I a model husband, Caroline?" He loomed over

her, drawing out her pleasure. Caroline gasped beneath him, moaning his name and writhing, but he would not let her pleasure peak until she answered him.

"Yes, Anthony. Yes."

He moved within her, and she shattered. He did not wait long for his own pleasure but went over that edge with her. They lay entangled on their bed and slept, her hand on his chest, his lips on her hair.

After Boxing Day, Anthony took Caroline to the most fashionable modiste who served the *ton*, Madame Delacroix. Caroline suspected the lady was not originally from France but from Cheapside, though she was too polite to say so.

Whatever her origins, Madame Delacroix was a master seamstress. Her designs in sprigged muslin for the daytime and damask and silk for the evening flattered Caroline's figure, with their high waists and low-necked bodices.

For the first time in her life, Caroline was able to choose her own fabrics and styles, all a great deal more sedate than anything her mother would have preferred. She thought at first Anthony would try to control the very clothes she wore, but after he saw the shades of peach and cream she wanted for her day dresses, and robin's-egg-blue and shell-pink gowns she desired for their evenings at home, he relinquished the field of her wardrobe to her without complaint.

The only design with which he insisted on being involved was the gown for her debut at court. During the Twelfth Night ball she would be presented to the Prince Regent, and Anthony had very specific ideas about how he wanted her to look. Caroline stared at the gown of soft, pearlescent white in the full-length looking glass of the modiste's salon. When Caroline moved, the fabric shifted in color from opal to pink to gold to cream, depending on the way the gown caught the light. It was lovely but not something she would ever have chosen for herself.

"I fear you spent too many years on the Continent, my lord. You have too much of a care for women's fashions."

"I was too busy fighting to notice what women were wearing in France, Italy, and Belgium, Caroline."

"Unless you were stripping their gowns off them," she said.

Anthony did not laugh, but he did not contradict her either. She was suddenly miserable, surprised to find herself jealous of all those unknown women who had once lain beneath her husband as she now did every night.

Anthony seemed to notice a shadow cross her face, for he nodded to Madame Delacroix, who drew back but did not leave the room. He stepped close, his lips brushing Caroline's temple, the heat of his breath moving the curls next to her cheek.

"I will take great pleasure in stripping this gown off you, when the time comes," Anthony said. "I told you once before, there are no other women between us."

She looked at her reflection, struggling to control the strange emotions that had risen in her breast. She found she could not answer Anthony so she spoke to the seamstress instead.

"Madame Delacroix, I have never worn a gown so fine in my life."

She caught her husband's gaze in the glass, and

they shared a moment's affinity. For once, they were thinking the same thing.

She knew he was thinking of the beautiful blue silk gown he had brought for her to wear on the day she married him.

"Well, only once," Caroline said.

Anthony wrapped her in a protective embrace that was as tender as it was filled with desire. He held her close, and Caroline could see nothing but him. In that moment, she felt as if the rest of the world simply did not exist.

Caroline was transfixed by the dark fire in his eyes. He kissed her in front of the seamstress and her staff as if he cared nothing for propriety or fashion. It was not fashionable among the *ton* for a husband to desire his wife. In this, her husband was unique.

The night before the Prince Regent's ball, Anthony took a private supper with Caroline in their bedroom. His wife had covered the room in roses and dahlias, all bought at great expense. White petals drifted across the blue damask bed linens, the snowy sheets peeking from beneath.

That night they did not speak much but sat close together at her marble-topped table, sharing one great armchair. They feasted on oysters and caviar, eaten with soft, warm bread from the ovens downstairs.

As they finished their meal, before Anthony's thoughts turned inexorably to making love to his wife, he wondered idly if he should tell her of his mistress.

Anthony knew they would see Angelique at Carlton

House the next night. He also knew the Countess of Devonshire would not simply retreat, leaving the field of war to her younger rival, even though her rival was his wife. Caroline would eventually hear of her existence, if not from Angelique's own lips, then from someone else.

He thought of the dagger Caroline had once carried in her reticule. He was glad he had made her give up her weapons. If he had not, she might have drawn a blade in the Prince Regent's presence as soon as his mistress provoked her.

Perversely, though he had forbidden her to touch a knife again, the thought of a blade in his wife's hand made him harden with desire. Though he knew he should tell Caroline the full truth, he did not want to break the truce between them.

The memory of his mistress faded until there was no one in the world in that moment but Caroline. He looked at his wife, wrapped in the sable he had given her for Christmas. She had taken to wearing it and nothing else when they were alone in her room.

Caroline leaned back against him with a sated sigh, drawing the fur close about her. The fine china plate they shared sat clean before her, and Anthony held up the serving ladle, offering her more braised beef, a spark of laughter in his eyes.

"Will you have more, my lady?"

"Two servings of each dish are enough for one night, I thank you," she said, unabashed. She had been eating more lately, but her newfound roundness only served to stoke his lust for her. His wife let her sable slip off one shoulder.

"My lady, you are not decent."

"Nor do I mean to be, until morning," she said.

Caroline took the serving ladle from his hand and laid it back on its tray. He watched her, the hunger rising in his eyes as she let her fur slip down a second shoulder. He could see her body in the candlelight then, her breasts glowing peaks, her rosy nipples beckoning.

"Wife, you might catch your death of cold, even this close to the fire."

Caroline straddled him, the large chair they sat in cradling them both as she wrapped her fur around them. "I can think of no better way to die. Can you, my lord?"

Her fingers moved beneath the sable, hunting him, and it was not long before she found what she sought.

Caroline's deft fingers unfastened his trousers until they were loose enough to push aside. He was ready for her, and when her hand brushed him, Anthony took an involuntary breath. Caroline smiled like a cat that had just found the cream.

He did not move but let her lead, keeping his hands still on the arms of his chair.

"Well, my lord, it seems I have found something of interest here."

Anthony's breath came short as she raised herself a little higher, her hand still on him. He did not know how she managed it, but she freed his manhood all on her own while they were both covered in her fur mantle.

The fire touched her golden hair with sparks of light. Her flushed face leaned close to his as she kissed him, running her tongue along his lips. His wife raised herself once more and guided him home.

Anthony clutched her hips but did not move. He let her set the pace, keeping his control, but only barely, as she rose and fell over him. She let the mantle slip, and her breasts were revealed to him in the light of the candles they had dined by, the soft, round peaks raised in the chill of the evening air, her soft hair coming down over them, one curl covering her heart.

He moaned as she moved on him, the sight and smell and feel of her all coming together at once to break like a wave against the wall of his self-control. He faltered but did not fail.

Caroline dropped the sable altogether and rode him as she would her horse, rising and falling with her own breath, quickening the pace as she would for a gallop. Her tight flesh combined with the motion of her body threatened to bring his release too quickly. Still he held firm and watched her rise and fall over him again and again. She had no thought for his pleasure now, but only for her own as she rode after it, hunting it down.

Anthony did not move until she gasped and fell against him, sated. He laid her down on the carpet next to the fireplace, knowing he did not have the strength to make it to their curtained bed.

He was on her then and in her, thrusting blindly time and again, finally letting himself go, letting the hounds of his lust slip their leash and take her down, and him with her. She gasped in pleasure for a second time beneath him. He lay still, his passion spent, his heart and hers thundering in his ears.

"My lord, it is better when you do it."

"When I do what?"

He could barely form the words, much less hear her answer.

"I like it best with you on top."

Anthony laughed and kissed her. Her lips tasted of honey, of bread and butter, of oysters and wine. He drew back and looked down at her, where the laughter still lingered in her eyes, even after his kisses.

"We will have to remedy that, my lady. But in a while. I am an old man and must conserve my resources."

Caroline laughed at him, rolling with him until she was on top of him, her hair spilling over them like a gossamer curtain. "By all means, Husband, take care of yourself. For there will be more for you to do tonight."

"Vixen," he said, his breath still catching in his throat.

Caroline laughed again and pressed against him so his manhood rose against her thigh, unable to help itself. "You see, my lord. You are not as old as you think."

Anthony laughed as he rolled her beneath him. This time he stayed on top. He carried her once more up and over the barrier between reason and pleasure. He followed her over that barrier himself again before they finally slept.

As they lay together on her bed in the firelight, Caroline heavy with sleep beside him, Anthony felt a shadow fall over him, a chill that had nothing to do with the cold of winter. He suddenly remembered his mistress would not be the only one in attendance at the Prince Regent's ball. Viscount Carlyle would be there, as well. And as always, Victor would be hunting for ways to bring him down.

Anthony drew Caroline close, pressing a kiss to her temple. She did not wake but burrowed closer to him under the covers. He thought of Carlyle, of the damage he inflicted on everything he touched. It was a long time before Anthony slept. He held his wife against him, as if she might somehow slip away.

Chapter 23

CAROLINE DRESSED SLOWLY IN THE GOWN HER HUSBAND had ordered for her. Tabby stood by, ready with her sable wrap. That night everything had to be perfect. That night, Caroline would be presented to the Prince Regent and to the London *ton*.

Caroline wondered idly if she should be nervous. The people of Yorkshire thought little of the prince ever since he had usurped the old king's place. They thought even less of the London elite. A bunch of fops and women of light virtue, her mother had said. No place for a real lady.

Caroline smiled at herself in the silvered mirror above her dressing table. It was a good thing she was no lady herself. No woman who rode a stallion on the moors, who fought with a dagger, who bested men at archery, could ever be considered a lady. And Caroline was glad of it.

She touched the reticule on her arm, a confection of gold and silver silk that closed with a drawstring. She was supposed to carry smelling salts in it and a handkerchief. Instead, her smallest dagger lay sheathed within. Caroline touched the bag, feeling for the smooth lines of her knife as if it were a talisman. Anthony claimed to have enemies among the men they would meet that night. If one tried to malign her, she would be ready.

Though no doubt Anthony would never let her out of his sight long enough for anyone to offer insult, much less injury. Caroline watched as Tabby wove a strand of diamonds through the curls of her golden hair. She had worn the same rope of diamonds to bed the two nights before, and nothing else.

She would be presented tonight as his wife, the Countess of Ravensbrook. The Season was about to begin. She would have to receive callers and make social calls of her own.

Anthony had put it about that their reticence to join Society had been because they were still honeymooning. Caroline gazed at her reflection in the full-length mirror. As of this night, their honeymoon was over.

The night of the Prince Regent's ball found Anthony waiting for his wife at the foot of the staircase in his front hall. The clock on the landing chimed, reminding him of how late they were. One could never be late to a party thrown by the Prince Regent. Once again, Caroline refused to conform to convention.

He seemed unable to impress upon her the importance of this evening, of what it meant to her career in Society, of what it meant to him. She seemed completely uncaring of the *ton* and its expectations, even of the prince himself.

Another half hour crept by. Just as Anthony thought he would have to send someone to fetch her, Caroline appeared at the top of the stairs.

Her gossamer gown caught the light, throwing a sheen around her as she moved. Caroline's hair was drawn up in a mass of curls, for she refused to cut one strand of it, fashion be damned. The rope of diamonds he had given her two nights before shone in the soft gold of her hair. She wore no other jewels, save for the alabaster pearl between her breasts.

Anthony fell back on the language of his youth, on what he had said to the first woman who had had him, an old duchess and friend of his mother's, who had initiated him into the act of love when he was fifteen.

"You are the most beautiful thing I have ever seen."

Anthony's voice was hoarse and low, and at first he feared she would not hear him. Her eyes met his, their gazes catching with a sudden warmth that made him burn. Caroline gave him a slow, haunting smile he knew he would never forget, not if he lived forever.

"I thank you, my lord."

She did not kiss him as she would have done on any other day but let him lead her by the hand out into the night. His lacquered coach waited for them, the closed carriage he used in town. His crest shone silver against the black, the knight's helm and plumes catching the light of the lamps.

For the first time, his wife seemed to take notice of it. She stopped before the door of the carriage and stayed still even after the footman had opened it. She looked first at his crest and then at him. "I will make you proud, my lord."

Anthony almost could not find his voice. For the second time that night, his throat seized, clenching as if he might never speak again. He swallowed hard, his emotions under control, but barely. "I am proud of you already."

Caroline allowed him to help her into the carriage. As they left Grosvenor Square, headed for Carlton House, she did not let go of his hand. The leather of his glove met the kidskin of hers. She did not touch him in any other way, and he was grateful, for he knew he could not trust himself to touch her again until they returned home that night.

He wanted her, more than any other woman he had ever known. But Victor would be at the ball that night, lying in wait to do Anthony harm. And the Prince Regent would be there, waiting to be introduced to Caroline.

Anthony knew his duty and shouldered it easily, as he had all his life. But as the carriage turned onto The Mall, he wished fervently he might turn his back on his duty and keep Caroline only for himself.

Chapter 24

Carlton House, London

THE PRINCE REGENT'S PALACE WAS BATHED IN LIGHT. It glowed with torches and candles, its white magnificence shining like a beacon on the world. Caroline had never seen such a lovely place. The white portico rose far above her as she climbed out of the carriage, her husband's hand on hers. For the first time she realized the *beau monde* was a place of beauty as well as debauchery. People who valued beauty surely could not be all bad.

Anthony's hand stayed on hers, almost as if he would protect her from the very place he had brought her to. His gloves were leather and matched the black of his evening clothes and the deep black of his hair. His silver cross of the Order of the Garter gleamed in the torchlight. He stood proud, his shoulders back, and moved to lead her into the palace with the unconscious grace of a warrior. Caroline took in the sight of her beautiful husband, and smiled, grateful he was hers.

As if he could read her thoughts, Anthony kissed her. He pressed his lips to hers as he would have had they been alone in their bedroom, letting all the world know she was his. She was breathless when he pulled away.

Caroline would ask him to keep those leather gloves on once they were home again, with their bedroom door locked behind them.

They stepped into the entrance hall, and once more Caroline was moved by the beauty of the palace. The hall was bare almost to plainness, but its white walls stretched far above her head, the ceiling held high by gilded columns.

She had no more time to time to look around, for his friends surrounded them. Introduced to one member of Parliament after another, she barely took in each silk gown as a dozen ladies of the Carlton House set were presented to her, or she to them.

The women eyed her warily, some with condescension, a few with jealousy, but none with kindness. She knew then that the people of the *ton* looked down on her; they considered her a country girl from the wilds of the North and beneath them. It meant nothing to them that her father was a baron in his own right who had served the crown for years in the war against Bonaparte.

She almost laughed in their faces at the absurdity of it, that lecherous and weak-minded people would have the audacity to look down on her. But she held her tongue for Anthony's sake and kept her contempt hidden behind a benign smile, the very smile her mother had drilled into her.

She allowed her husband to lead her deeper into the palace, their way long and slow. For he knew many people, and it seemed every person he knew stopped him so they might greet him and be introduced to his wife. There was one man who did not approach, who stayed back in the doorway, surrounded by women.

Viscount Carlyle did not come near, and her husband did not acknowledge him. Victor caught her glance as she passed and gave her a wry smile, the first smile she had received that did not contain lust or veiled scorn. Caroline nodded to him, offering him a genuine smile in return.

Pembroke appeared at her side, blocking Carlyle from view. She let the thought of Victor pass, for no doubt she would have a chance to say hello to him inside. Lord Pembroke's boisterous voice buoyed her up as he drew her up the grand staircase, Anthony at her other side.

The marble of the staircase, smooth under the soft leather of her slippers, gleamed like the pearl she wore between her breasts. Candles lit every surface, and the high ceilings shone with light from the chandeliers. Caroline caught her breath as she glanced up. Never had she seen anything so beautiful as the glass creations reflecting the candlelight.

She did not look long, though, for she was conscious of being watched. She would not show these people she was from deep in the country, that she had never before been in a palace like this one. Pembroke turned from her husband and kissed her hand, her kid glove slippery in his palm.

"My lady, I have never seen you look so beautiful."

Anthony's hand tightened on her arm, and she wondered if he was jealous of the dearest friend he had in the world. As they entered the grand ballroom, Anthony did not look at her or at Pembroke but froze in place as if a witch had cast a spell on him.

There was no witch present, but perhaps he had been enchanted. For Caroline caught him staring at a beautiful woman with curling hair of midnight black. The woman's brocade gown shone black and silver in the candlelight. If Caroline had not known better, she would have sworn the gown had been made to match Anthony's dark evening dress and the silver Star of the Garter he wore on his left breast.

Anthony bowed stiffly as the woman passed, his face a blank mask. Caroline felt a sharp prick of jealousy, and when she pressed her hand to his arm, he would not meet her gaze. He simply led her farther into the ballroom, his eyes scanning the crowd.

Caroline allowed herself to be soothed by her husband's hand on her arm. Before she could ask Anthony who that woman was, Pembroke pressed a glass of wine into her hand, spinning some long tale of how his mare had foaled and almost lost the stripling before it was barely an hour old.

Caroline listened with half an ear, searching for the mysterious woman in the crowd. But the lady in silver and black had disappeared into the crush of nobles in their silk gowns and glittering jewels. So Caroline swallowed her unease and the jealousy that had left a sour taste in her mouth. There were beautiful women everywhere. She could not be jealous of every one of them. She turned back to Pembroke and his talk of horses.

Pembroke soon had Anthony laughing, but she could still feel her husband coiled like a spring, his arm tense under her hand. Now that the woman was out of her sight, she wondered what the lady might have done to offend him.

Though she watched him closely, she saw no evidence of disquiet on his face as Anthony smiled down on her, leading her out among the dancers. Then Caroline was in her husband's arms as he guided her through the steps of the waltz.

The black-and-white parquet floor seemed to melt away under her feet as they danced. As always, when Anthony touched her, the rest of the world fell away. Viscount Carlyle, Lord Pembroke, the rude gentlemen and their ladies, even the woman in black and silver faded from her mind like mirages in a desert. There was only Anthony, holding her too close for propriety as they danced. The velvet of his sleeve was soft beneath her gloved fingers. His dark hair was tossed back from his face, his chestnut eyes on hers as they moved among the dancers. She let herself forget everything but his beauty and the way it felt to move in his arms.

The music stopped much sooner than Caroline would have wished. Anthony took her hand in his and led her from the dance floor. People moved out of their way as a matter of course, their eyes devouring her and her husband, the women whispering behind their fans.

Caroline thought the members of the *beau monde* odd, but did not any longer feel dislike as they stared at her. The people of Society now seemed more curious than anything else, as if she were a captured beast in a menagerie.

Caroline kept a benign smile on her face, revealing nothing of her true self. She pressed her hand to the reticule at her wrist. Her knife was still sheathed there, ready if she were to need it. The touch of that blade, even through silk and leather, made her feel more at ease.

The dinner gong sounded, and the *beau monde* paired off to find their places in the dining room. Caroline moved to follow them but was detained by Anthony's hand on her arm.

"Before we dine, my love, I must present you to the Prince Regent. I would have done so before now, but I found I did not want to share you."

Caroline spoke low, so he had to lean down to hear her. "I do not want to share you, either, my lord."

She thought in that moment that Anthony might kiss her again. He must have felt the weight of the eyes of the company on them, for he did not. Instead, he pressed one hand over hers where it rested on his arm and led her to the dais where the Prince Regent stood.

The prince looked to be at least ten years older than Anthony, his great jowls trapped on either side by a high, starched collar. He was dressed in fine black evening clothes, his silver star over his left breast, along with a midnight-blue sash that covered his paunch. His hair was raised with pomade in the most fashionable style, a style her husband avoided.

The prince stood with one foot forward, taking in the sight of her face and form as they approached. She saw the light of lust in his eyes, but for some reason, she was not offended. There was an easiness to the prince's manner, a warmth that reminded her at once of Pembroke.

She curtsied low, as her mother had taught her, knowing full well the prince was taking that opportunity to look down the bodice of her dress. She met his eyes as she stood, and the intelligence behind his light brown gaze made her smile. Her husband loved this man, and as she looked into his face, she began to see why.

"Anthony, you bring us your beautiful wife."

"I do, Your Royal Highness. She is honored to be in your presence."

The prince beckoned her closer, that he might take her gloved hand in his. He did not release her at once but kept her in his grasp.

"Is that true, Lady Ravensbrook? Are you honored?"

Caroline heard the clumsy trap set to spring and felt all eyes on her. She did not shrink from the prince but smiled directly into his face.

"I am new to London, Your Highness. You honor me with your invitation, and by accepting me as one of your own."

"You became one of us when you married, my lady."

"I became a Ravensbrook, Your Highness. I think I must serve longer and serve well in order to become a true member of your court." She curtsied again, conscious of the fact that all the hangers-on around the prince had stopped to listen to her words. They watched her with interest, no longer dismissing her completely.

"Well said, Lady Ravensbrook. Well said."

The Prince Regent raised one hand and helped her rise to the applause of those surrounding them. Caroline could feel jealous daggers in her back as the Prince Regent led the company into dinner.

The room buzzed with speculation as the *ton* followed in his wake, everyone wondering if perhaps the prince sought to make this new woman from Yorkshire his mistress. Caroline almost laughed when she caught wind of that. She turned to her left to share the ridiculousness of the idea with Anthony, only to find Pembroke at her side, offering his arm to lead her to the table. He sat with her, for it seemed the *beau monde* preferred not to sit with their spouses. She looked behind her, but she could not find Anthony anywhere.

Pembroke smiled at her, but for once she was not charmed. "Where is Anthony?" she asked under her breath.

"Smile, Lady Ravensbrook, or they will think we have quarreled."

"Where is he?" she asked again, careful not to let her anxiety show. She began to unbutton the wrists of her gloves so she might draw them back in order to eat.

"Not to worry, my lady. He was called away to discuss an upcoming vote in the House of Lords, business that would not wait."

Caroline did not believe him, but the first course had been served, and she began to eat. She enjoyed the meal because it was delicious and varied, as one might expect when dining at the Prince Regent's table.

She kept her eye on the door to the ballroom, but

she did not see Anthony emerge. She sat surrounded by the *ton*, their eyes glittering as they laughed, their teeth sharp and gleaming in the candlelight. Even with Pembroke beside her, on the back of her neck Caroline felt an unwelcome chill.

Chapter 25

"WHY ARE YOU WEARING THAT GOWN?"

Anthony's voice was a hiss as he drew Angelique out of the ballroom. The Blue Velvet room lay on the same corridor, empty until he brought his mistress into it. He knew he was adding grist to the rumor mill by slipping away with Angelique, but he had to deal with her now. He had let this loose strand of his past dangle too long already.

"Why? Do you not like it, Anthony? You always love it when I wear your family crest, your mistress wearing your livery."

Anthony stared into her eyes, this woman who was the last vestige of his old life.

"I always wear clothes to match your own at the Prince Regent's ball. I saw no reason why this year should be any different," Angelique said.

"I have a wife."

"And I have a new maid. What does that matter, after ten years between us?"

"It matters," Anthony said. "It matters to me."

They stood together in the soft light of the Blue

Velvet room. The beauty of the setting seemed to enhance Angelique's loveliness without eclipsing it, the way a mahogany case might hold a single, brilliant jewel.

"You love that girl," Angelique said.

Her voice held no self-pity. As he looked at Angelique in the candlelight, her strength was as clear as the sorrow in the deep blue of her eyes. He did not answer her.

Angelique bowed her head, her long curls falling like a veil before her face, a curtain of darkness he had so often sought to hide himself in. When she raised her head, her eyes were clear but for a sheen of tears that might have been a trick of the light.

"I won't take you back. If you leave me tonight, we are done with each other."

Her gaze pierced him as a sword would on a battlefield.

"I understand."

Angelique did not speak again. Anthony did not move to touch her, not even to press her hand in parting, because he knew he had lost the right.

He walked away from her. He looked back only once. Angelique kept her back to him, her shoulders straight, her eyes turned to a candle that burned on a low table beside her.

Anthony missed the midnight supper. The footmen were serving the fruit when he came back, and a sweet wine from Germany. Pembroke gave up his place beside Caroline as the women of the *ton* raised their eyebrows in reproach and as the gentlemen shook their heads to see Anthony brought so low as to play court to his wife. Anthony saw none of them, and neither did Caroline. He ignored his own seat farther down the table and sat down beside her. He took hold of her hand as if he had lost her and she had just now been found.

"What is wrong, Anthony? Where have you been?"

He spoke low, his lips against her ear, caressing her with the warmth of his breath. Caroline shivered.

"Later, love. I will tell you later."

Caroline did not ask again but drew out a tiny, gold-rimmed plate holding a broiled quail. She had hidden it under her napkin and had waved the footman away when he tried to take it from her. Anthony laughed, the low sound making her insides quake. She wondered how much longer they would have to stay in this place, surrounded by these people. She did not ask, for she had agreed to come, had even wanted to see his world and the people he honored. After only a few hours, Caroline could see very little to value among the Carlton House set, save perhaps the Prince Regent himself.

Anthony ate the quail with a gold knife and fork. Caroline took pleasure in watching him eat, as if she had cooked the bird herself.

The meal ended soon enough. The Prince Regent rose first and announced that the gentlemen would return with the ladies, forgoing port and cigars. He led the company back into the ballroom. Caroline moved forward in the press, confident her husband was behind her, but when she turned, she did not find him. Anthony had been stopped by a friend of his from the House of Lords, Baron Fitzgibbons, who no doubt wanted to discuss something endlessly tedious.

Caroline did not wait for Anthony but stepped into the ballroom.

As she passed through the doors, she saw Viscount Carlyle. He smiled and bowed, his blue eyes full of mischief as always. Besides Pembroke, she was certain Victor was the only man present who possessed a sense of humor.

He was still surrounded by women, but by different women than she had seen with him earlier in the evening. No doubt he was popular with the fairer sex, and for more than just his money. He tossed a blond lock of his hair back from his forehead and adjusted his red and gold waistcoat. The black superfine of his jacket seem to absorb the light all around him, leaving him in shadow.

Caroline blinked, certain this must be a trick of the light. Most of the gentlemen wore black that evening, but no other man seemed shadowed. Her mind must be playing tricks on her. She had been too long among the *ton*, surrounded by people she did not like. Her dislike had started to become fanciful, making her imagine things that were not there.

Viscount Carlyle, while not overly friendly with the truth, seemed relatively harmless, especially when taken in the same dose as the rest of the company that evening. But even as she turned away from Victor to look for her husband, a chill of foreboding ran along her skin. Victor smiled and stepped away from the women who flocked around him. He crossed the distance between them without a backward glance at the ladies he left in midsentence.

"Good evening, Countess Ravensbrook."

"Good evening, my lord."

"You have forgotten my name, I see."

Caroline laughed. Surely she was wrong to feel uncomfortable in this man's presence. It must be the glare of the *beau monde*, their brittle laughter and their contempt for her that made this man suddenly appear sinister.

"Don't be absurd, my lord Carlyle."

"I am always absurd, my lady. One of my great failings, I fear."

Caroline laughed again, beginning to relax. She noticed then a strange silence in the ballroom. Music still played from the dais, but for one long moment, no one spoke. There were a few whispered conversations near the edges of the room, but beyond that, there was no sound. The musicians played harder, the swell of violins rising to cover the quiet. As Caroline looked across the ballroom, she saw all eyes on her.

"What is wrong, my lord? Why do they stare?"

"You are too beautiful for their peace," Victor said. Caroline smiled wryly at his foolish flattery, and he laughed.

"There is nothing for it," Victor said, "but that we dance."

Caroline felt the silence of the hall like a weight on her back, but she lifted her chin and did not falter. She took the hand Victor extended and stepped with him into the set that was forming.

❧

Anthony watched his wife move onto the dance floor with the man he hated most in the world.

For one mad moment, Anthony wondered if they had been meeting behind his back all during their marriage, ever since he had last seen Carlyle at Pembroke's house in Derbyshire. Perhaps Victor had taken Caroline in some dark corner, or worse, had made love to her at Ravensbrook House while Anthony was out on business.

He felt the bile rise in his throat, and he swallowed it. Anthony knew he was mad with jealousy, that his reason had been broken by Victor's presence, as it always was. Caroline had never made love to his enemy, but Anthony found himself as angry as if she had.

The Carlton House set, the crème de la crème of the *ton*, all stood with their heads together, murmuring poison into one another's ears, casting their eyes on him to see what he might do. He felt the weight of the Prince Regent's stare.

As he watched his wife dance, her hand in Carlyle's grip, Anthony knew he should do nothing, say nothing, and pretend as if it did not matter to him. But as always with Victor, fury overrode his reason. All Anthony knew was he could not endure the sight of that man's hands on his wife for one moment longer.

Chapter 26

"I THANK YOU, LADY, FOR THE FAVOR OF YOUR COMPANY."

The music had ended, and Victor bowed low to her. For a moment, Caroline thought he was going to leave her alone on the dance floor. But then she saw her husband bearing down on them, his face black with anger.

Victor melted into the crowd, leaving Caroline to face her husband alone. Anthony took her arm, his grip bruising. He drew her forcibly out of the path of the dancers, for a new quadrille had begun.

"Come away from here."

"Anthony, what is wrong with you?"

His eyes were so dark she could not see anything in their depths but a hatred she knew was not directed at her.

"Come with me now."

She lowered her voice, mindful of the others standing by. Though the dancing continued, everyone was watching them. "Have you lost your mind?"

"Have you?"

Anthony did not speak again but dragged her by the

arm behind a screen set up to keep the draft from the door away from the dancers.

"How dare you dance with him."

"With whom, my lord? Lord Carlyle? Why would I not dance with him? He asked me."

She watched as Anthony worked to keep his temper. He breathed deeply, his grip flexing on her arm.

"I told you in Pembroke's house never to speak to him, much less dance with him. How dare you disobey me."

"Anthony, this is the prince's ball, and Viscount Carlyle is his guest, as we are. I do not understand you."

"I do not ask you to understand. I ask you to do as I say."

"You *ask* nothing. You give orders with no explanation. How many times must I tell you I am not a hound to come to heel."

"You are my wife, Caroline. You will obey me."

"Round we go again, and we go nowhere, Anthony."

Anthony did not answer, but his grip tightened on her arm.

"You are hurting me," she said.

"Caroline, never dance with a stranger. Never. Not even in the Prince Regent's house."

"I met Viscount Carlyle twice before with you standing by. I know your city ways are different, but it was only one dance."

He raised his voice in spite of himself, and she heard pain as well as anger in it. "You do not know who he is to me."

"Tell me then. Why do you hate him so much?"

They stared each other, opponents once more on

their old battlefield, his face a mask of fury. She could not see beyond that mask to find the man she had begun to know. That man was gone. Anthony did not speak but stared at her as if she had killed his last hope.

"I cannot look at you. Pembroke will take you home."

"I will not go. You must talk to me." Caroline tried to pull away, but Anthony caught her arm once more in his grip. She winced, her arm bruised, but he did not release her.

"You will do as you are told. You are my wife."

"I am not your whore, to be ordered about as you please."

"You are my wife, and you will obey me."

After the last few weeks, she had been lulled into complacency. Surely they had come to understand each other better. Surely with the time they had spent talking of their past and of their loved ones, they knew each other better than they had on their wedding day. But now he was ordering her about as if she were his valet, as if those weeks had never happened.

Caroline was so angry she could not see a foot beyond her. She tore her arm from his grip, this time moving fast enough that he could not catch her.

She left him behind the screen, striding back into the glare of the ballroom. She stopped in her tracks not five feet into the room, for she could feel the eyes of everyone on her. Sinuous whispers swelled like a hiss over the music as those few who had not heard her argument with Anthony had the couple's angry words repeated to them.

Caroline raised her head and straightened her back as her mother had taught her. She walked slowly toward the grand door that led to the staircase beyond, not knowing where she would go, thinking only that she must escape the weight of those eyes.

Before she reached her goal, a woman moved to stand beside her.

It was the mysterious woman who had captivated Anthony's attention earlier. This close, Caroline could see the silver trim on her dress looked much like the silver on Anthony's waistcoat.

She was the most beautiful woman Caroline had ever seen. She had ignored convention, ignored fashion, and had left her long midnight hair to curl past her shoulders. Her blue eyes were as dark as fine sapphires.

This woman knew how her husband had shamed her in front of the *ton*. And from the look on her face, Caroline could see the woman thought Anthony was right. Her own pain seemed to fade as she stood before that woman's censure.

Why dancing with one man would offend an entire ballroom full of people, Caroline could not fathom. There was some essential point that was eluding her, but as her pain faded, her temper began to rise. These southerners with their dissolute ways had a great deal of nerve to look down on her. She held her temper, barely, as she waited for the woman to speak.

"Good evening, Countess Ravensbrook."

"Good evening."

"Allow me to introduce myself, since Anthony was too rude to do so. I am Angelique Beauchamp, Countess of Devonshire."

Caroline kept her voice even as her mother had taught her to do. This was the woman Viscount

Carlyle had mentioned, the woman who employed Ralph Higgins in Shropshire. "It is my pleasure to meet you, Lady Devonshire."

Angelique smiled. "The pleasure is all mine."

Caroline noticed for the first time silver gleaming at the woman's left shoulder, a knight's helm flanked by two plumes, worked in diamonds. The jewels caught the light and winked slyly at Caroline. Her mouth went dry, and the air in her lungs dissolved in her chest like fire.

She gasped for breath but could not draw one, almost as if her stays were too tight and she had tried to run in them. This woman wore Anthony's family crest as if it belonged to her.

Angelique saw Caroline's gaze fall on the jeweled crest. She smiled, the indigo beauty of her eyes mocking. "Ah, yes. Anthony's crest. I often wear it to affairs such as these."

The woman with the midnight hair gestured with one elegant gloved hand, the motion of her arm graceful as it took in the ballroom and the *beau monde*. Caroline watched her as a snake might watch its charmer.

"I see he gave you a pearl to match mine," Angelique said.

Caroline's hand moved reflexively to her alabaster pearl, her fingers covering it protectively. Angelique drew a black pearl on a silver chain from the hollow between her breasts.

"I beg your pardon?" Caroline's voice was tinny in her ears, distant, as if she were hearing someone else speak.

"Your husband. My lover. Anthony Carrington, the Earl of Ravensbrook. I see he gave you a pearl as well. I wonder if he bought them on the same day."

Caroline stood blinking in the false light of those candles, the romantic strains of the music rising as if to mock her.

She remembered the times Anthony had gone to the city without her during the fall. She remembered the day he had brought her the pearl she wore around her neck. Though it had been the most important gift of her life, in her memory it seemed as if he had handed it to her almost as an afterthought.

As she looked into Angelique's eyes, she knew with unwavering certainty Anthony had given his beautiful mistress that black pearl first, less than a month after they had been wed.

Caroline took a reflexive step back, away from Angelique, as if she might run from the truth, as if she might flee from the pain lodged above her heart. She thought of the last few weeks, when she and Anthony had seemed to reach a new place with each other, when the distance that divided them had seemed to be bridged, not just by lust, but by growing affection. Those shared moments looked different to her as she saw them through the prism of his mistress's sardonic smile.

The ground opened up like a chasm at her feet, waiting for her to fall in. She saw her future stretching out before her, a worse future than she would have thought possible, even on her wedding day.

She would bear his children and keep his house in Shropshire while he sported with mistresses and doxies in town. Her marriage was what it had always been, what it had been intended to be. Anthony was a man who hoped to control her every move, their marriage a business arrangement for the getting of his heirs. That and nothing more.

Only as she felt the sharp pain squeezing her heart like a vise, taking her breath, did she realize the truth. She had begun to love her obstinate husband more than a little. Somewhere during the last few weeks, she had found a friend buried in the eyes of the man who had bought her from her father.

Anthony was an honorable man, and often kind. He was domineering and infuriating and mad with jealousy and the need for control, but she found, as she stood looking into the blue of his mistress's eyes, she had loved him in spite of all that, because of it. Anthony was uniquely himself, a man of power, a man who stood up to her and faced her as no one else could.

A man who kept a mistress. A man who did not love her, and who never would.

Caroline took one more step back and stumbled. She almost faltered, but then she remembered herself and whose daughter she was. It was as if her mother stood beside her, her tiny hand on her arm, offering her strength. It was as if her father's strength flowed into her all the way from the wilds of Yorkshire. Just as Caroline had not been raised to be a fool, she had not been raised to make a fool of herself. She would not disgrace herself before an enemy and before all her husband's peers.

Caroline nodded to her husband's mistress and

walked away. She could not bring herself to speak. Her breath came shallow, and her voice caught in her throat, like something she had choked on.

She could see her husband coming through the crowd to follow her, his friend Pembroke hurrying to her side. Caroline moved as swiftly as she ever had, grateful for all the exercise she had done that fall, for she was fast as well as strong. Lifting her silken skirts, she dodged through the crowded ballroom and managed to elude them both.

Caroline slipped through the grand entrance and stopped in her tracks. If she fled to the entrance hall below, to freedom, Anthony would catch her. She looked around frantically for someplace to hide, but she did not know where. She hoped never to lay eyes on Carlton House again. She knew she must get away, and quickly, but her mind was one large bruise.

Then she felt a hand on her arm.

Nearby, liveried footmen looked neither left nor right but stood impassive as stone.

Caroline met Viscount Carlyle's eyes. He took her hand. "Come with me."

Chapter 27

VICTOR DREW HER INTO AN OPULENT ROOM OFF THE corridor done in blue velvet. She felt dwarfed by the grandeur of the soaring, gilded columns, and more alone than she had ever been in her life.

The door was half-open, and she peered into the hallway beyond, hidden behind the door hangings. Pembroke and Anthony burst from the ballroom, hurling themselves toward the grand staircase in pursuit of her. Neither man saw her in the shadows; neither so much as glanced in her direction. Caroline felt suddenly bereft, abandoned, even though it was she who had fled, she who had hidden from them.

There was a fire in the marble grate. Caroline crossed the great room to warm herself by it, stretching out her gloved hands. The fire did little to warm the room and little to comfort her. Now that she was away from the press of the overheated ballroom, the cold crept close, chilling her. She raised her hands and rubbed her upper arms. She did not know if she would ever feel warm again.

She pressed her forehead against the cool marble of the mantel, which was high enough for her to lean against. She knew she should not stand so close to the blaze, that she might easily singe her fine gown, the gown her husband loved so much and had longed to see her wear only for him. Her stomach roiled, the taste of the pheasant she had eaten at dinner rising in her mouth.

The beauty of her husband's mistress seemed to have followed her into that velvet room. Even now, she could smell the woman's orchid perfume and hear Angelique's voice—low, sultry music that promised much. Caroline thought of the way that woman's hair would fall across a silken pillow. She thought of her husband rising over that woman and entering her. She wondered if he made the same sounds with his mistress as he made with her. She wondered if in his release he called out that woman's name.

Caroline took a deep, cleansing breath so she would not be sick. Victor put his hands on her arms and drew her back from the fire. "You will take in too much smoke," he said.

She leaned against that marble mantel once more, this time pressing her hand to the cool stone. Empty of all but pain, she fought the rising need to weep. Then she heard Victor move close behind her.

She had forgotten for a moment the man who had rescued her from detection, the man her husband seemed to hate so much, and for no apparent reason. When she turned, she saw Victor looking at her, standing only a few feet away. She did not feel he was taking a liberty, only that he wanted to be close in case she collapsed. Though he had always greeted her with a smile before, he was not smiling now.

He did not ask foolish questions or offer idiotic platitudes when he saw the tears on her cheeks. He simply handed her his handkerchief, his family's crest embroidered on it, and his initials, VGC. She took the soft linen and wiped her eyes with it.

"I will have it laundered, my lord, and sent back to you."

"No need. I am pleased to offer it in service of a beautiful lady. Take it with my compliments."

She turned from him then, for she had no strength to make polite conversation. No matter how deeply she breathed in the scent of coal smoke, Caroline could not get the perfume of her husband's mistress out of her nose. She feared she might be haunted by that scent for the rest of her life.

"It is hard, the first time you are betrayed. You will find it gets easier."

Caroline's anger replaced her tears. "What do you know about it?"

"I know your husband has shamed you before the London *ton*. I know that even now people speculate as to whether you are too young and too countrified in your ways to accept that, in this city, men take mistresses and do not ask their wives' leave. They say you are weak and too much of a child to have married into so noble a house."

Caroline's rage washed over her, a rising tide she could not fight. She did not fight but swam, keeping her head above the water of her fury. Finally, it receded, and she was left alone on an empty shore.

"These people do not know me," she said.

Victor stepped forward, and she noticed for the first time that he was handsome. Not like her husband was, not like a hawk who had lit on her as his prey. This man had a friendly, open face and clear blue eyes that seemed to hide nothing.

"No," he said. "They are fools, and they are beneath you."

She felt cold without her anger, empty, like a wine cask that had long since been drained. She knew she would have to go back into the corridor. She would have to pass through the entrance hall and call for a hackney carriage to take her home.

But as she thought of Anthony's mistress with her sapphire eyes, Caroline knew she could not do it.

"Have you a carriage?" she asked.

Victor smiled, and for the first time in their acquaintance she saw lust behind his eyes before he masked it. She wondered if he would try to seduce her somewhere between St. James's Park and Grosvenor Square. As she stood looking at him, the warmth of the fire seeping past the silk of her gown, she found she did not care. If he only got her away from that place, she would take her chances.

He did not lead her back toward the corridor but pressed a panel in the wall beside the fireplace. A door opened into a chasm of darkness.

"This way, Lady Ravensbrook."

She did not touch him but followed him through the hidden door. The narrow passage led down a set of wooden stairs. Caroline wondered where they were going. She was grateful not to have to face the ballroom again, to feel those eyes on her, measuring, judging, condemning, even as they laughed at her behind their hands.

The dark passageway opened directly onto a hidden courtyard. There was no crush of carriages as there always was at the main entrance to Carlton House. Only one barouche waited, the one that belonged to Viscount Carlyle.

"I always take a different route from the masses," Victor said. "One never knows when one might need to flee a place, even Carlton House."

Caroline did not comment on the intimacy Victor seemed to have with the palace of the Prince Regent. Clearly, this man was enmeshed deeper in court politics than she had thought. She did not care for politics one way or another. She wanted only to go home and pretend this night had never happened.

Victor handed off a coin to a royal footman who had been standing guard by the outer door. No entrance to the palace could be left unlocked and unattended, no matter how hidden. With a bow, the Prince Regent's servant disappeared into the palace, closing the door behind him. The hidden entrance vanished once more into the white walls, the building's façade unbroken save for a faint line between the bricks.

Caroline took the hand Victor offered and allowed him to help her into his barouche. She arranged her gown against the cushions of his well-sprung coach. The night air was cold, and she shivered in spite of the lap blankets and the warm bricks at her feet. She had left her sable in the palace. One more gift from her husband that now meant nothing. Perhaps the prince would give it to his latest mistress. The unknown woman could have the fur, and welcome.

Victor smiled, his blond hair falling over one blue eye. He cast it back in a way she once might have found charming. Now she could only look at him and wonder when she would ever be able to feel anything other than pain again.

"Thank you for getting me out of that place."

"I fear your husband will be angry that you have come away with me," he said, watching her, some calculation lurking behind his blue eyes that had nothing to do with lust.

Caroline thought of how her husband had shamed her in front of all those people, as if she had done something unforgivable by dancing with another man. All the while, his mistress and all who knew of her, laughed at Caroline behind her back.

"It is my own anger I'm afraid of."

"You are passionate."

Victor caught her chin in his hand so she could not look away from him. He searched her eyes for something he could not find.

He let her go, but not before his fingers lingered on her cheek. He had never taken such a liberty before. Caroline knew she should chastise him, but she felt too tired to fight a man for whom she cared nothing. She leaned as far away from him as she could and loosened the ties of her reticule.

"It must be your Yorkshire blood," Victor said. "The women of our city are insipid compared to you."

Caroline knew this to be a lie as she thought of her husband's mistress. Angelique was anything but insipid. Caroline saw before her eyes the black pearl nestled between that woman's magnificent breasts, set there like a prize of war. It was a war Caroline had lost before she had ever come to London, a war she could not fight, because it was not her place to do so. Men took mistresses, and women accepted it. Husbands bedded whom they pleased, and wives looked the other way. She had been raised on this truth.

But now that she was faced with it, she found she could not accept it. No matter how Anthony plagued her, even at the worst times of their marriage, he never gave her any indication he had been unfaithful. He had always been ardent for her body, always ready to take her, no matter how badly they had been fighting or what the cause had been.

Caroline knew she had been a fool, and she looked back on the months of her marriage with new eyes. She heard every soft word her husband had given her again in her mind, every look of warmth, every touch of his hands and lips. She felt them all again, as if they were happening for the first time, only now she knew them to be tainted with that lie.

For every kiss he had given her, he had given Angelique a thousand more. For every sweet word murmured in the dark of the night, in the shadows of their bed, all the while Anthony had been giving words like that, along with his body, to the woman who wore his crest so proudly on her midnight damask gown.

Caroline leaned against the side of the carriage. As she stared out of the window, they drew up in front of Ravensbrook House. It was a short journey from

Carlton House to Grosvenor Square, from one world to another.

She turned to Victor. "I will bid you good evening, Lord Carlyle. Thank you for your kindness."

"My lady, I live to serve."

Victor had barely touched her for the entire journey. He had helped her escape, asking for no price. But now he reached for her, as if to draw her against him. She smelled the wine on his breath and saw by the gleam in his eye he was in earnest. For the first time since she had known him, he moved close to kiss her.

She dodged his lips, reaching for the carriage door. She managed to open it, but Victor caught her in his arms, drawing her back.

"Release me, my lord."

"One kiss is all I ask."

"You ask too much."

She pushed her elbow into his side, to no effect. He simply held her tighter.

She gave up on politeness. Her hand slipped into her reticule, and her knife was in her palm in the next moment. The edge of the blade gleamed in the lamps lit outside her husband's house as she raised it in one swift arc to Victor's throat.

His eyes widened in surprise, but he made no move against her. Admiration for her soon took the place of his shock, and he laughed, his warm voice filling the carriage and spilling out into the night. He released her and raised his arms in surrender, the gleam of his eyes turning from lust to mirth.

"Touché, Lady Ravensbrook. I see that your time working with my man was not wasted."

Victor would have said more, but Caroline backed away, stepping carefully out of the carriage, her eyes and her knife still trained on Carlyle. He did not move to follow her but leaned back against the velvet squabs.

In the next moment, she felt herself propelled from behind, drawn onto the stairs of Ravensbrook House. Anthony's hand closed over hers and took the knife from her.

She let her husband disarm her, her grip suddenly nerveless. She watched as he slid her blade into an interior pocket of his coat, heedless of the damage it might do to the dark, expensive cloth.

"Do not come near my wife again."

Victor smiled, his contempt clear. "If I had such a wife, I would not let her stray so far."

Chapter 28

CAROLINE SAID NOTHING TO HER HUSBAND AS HE pulled her into the house. But she struggled in his grasp, trying to get away. For the first time, his touch was cold, indifferent, like the hands of a stranger. Anthony would not look at her, and he would not let her go. He simply dragged her up the formal staircase. Jarvis, the butler, closed the front door behind them, a look of horror on his face.

He slammed the door to their bedroom. He said nothing but tossed Caroline away from him as if he could not bear her close to him for a moment longer. She caught herself on the marble-topped table where they so often shared their evening meals.

"How long have you been deceiving me with him?"

She looked into his eyes and saw how deadly his fury was, his hand raised as if to strike her.

Caroline swallowed her guilt. She had done nothing to be ashamed of.

"I have not been meeting him in secret. Carlyle helped me find a teacher to practice my knife work."

"Viscount Carlyle helped you. The one man I told

you never to speak to. The man I loathe above all others. Where did you meet him?"

"I met him by chance at the Wick and Candle. I worked with Ralph Higgins, my instructor, in a rented house."

"You've been meeting not just one man, but two?"

"For God's sake, Anthony, I did nothing wrong. Ralph Higgins was my hired man, and Lord Carlyle introduced us. That is all. I never went unarmed to any of these lessons, and I always brought Jonathan with me."

"I will question him when I return to Shropshire. If Jonathan says you were ever alone, even for the space of a minute, with either man, I will lock you away in the country. You'll never see London again."

"And will you go to your mistress, then? That woman you've been flaunting in front of your friends all evening behind my back? Why didn't you just marry her to begin with and leave me in peace?"

Anthony was on her before she could take her next breath. He did not strike her, though she expected him to. Caroline did not retreat but pressed close to him, reaching into his coat.

"I want my knife back. She can have you, she can have the diamonds in my hair, but I'll be damned if either of you keep my favorite knife."

Her fingers touched on the handle, and she drew the blade out of his pocket.

Anthony wrested the dagger from her grip and threw it down. She listened as its steel blade rang against wainscoting of the far wall.

He clutched her close, but his touch lacked all

tenderness. He no longer moved as if to do her violence, but the coldness in his eyes made her shake with fury.

"Angelique Beauchamp is not your concern. What I do when I am away from you is none of your business. You cannot sit in judgment on me. You've been meeting Carlyle in secret," Anthony said. "Did he have you?"

"Would you care?"

Caroline watched as his jaw clenched.

"Answer my question."

"You answer mine."

His eyes were black with fury that had begun to heat. He pushed her back until she felt the cold of the marble table behind her. He bent her over that table, her arms above her head, one of his hands holding her wrists fast in his grip.

For one moment, his ire was so complete she was sure he would wring her neck. Instead, his grip only tightened painfully on her wrist and arm. The marble tabletop was cold on her back. He had made love to her there only a few nights before. The marble had been cold then, too. She felt tears rise, but she held firm. She would not let him see her weep.

"If you let him have you, then any child you may be carrying could be his. I would divorce you, and I would marry again."

The knife of her humiliation twisted in her heart. She held her tongue and glared up at him, defiant.

Anthony raised her up, gripping her shoulders in both hands. He lifted her in his arms and carried her into the shadows until he pressed her hard against the far wall in the alcove next to their bed. She could smell the rosemary the housemaids pressed into the bedclothes and feel the cold plaster of the wall behind her back. She thought for half a moment he would take her there against that wall as he had on the day after their wedding, as he had in the stables, but that night all she saw in his eyes was contempt.

"Did he have you?"

Each word was pronounced clearly, with a loathing she had never thought to hear in his voice. Caroline's sorrow choked her as her own fury drained away. In a moment of strange clarity, she wondered how they had come to this, when just hours before they had both been so happy.

Then she remembered. She had been alone in that, too.

"No, my lord. I say again, I did not arrange to meet Carlyle, but I paid his hired man to give me lessons in fighting with a knife. Viscount Carlyle did not have me."

Anthony walked away from her, pacing the room like a tiger in a cage. Still, he did not leave her and lock her in her room alone.

"Can you believe me, my lord? Or do you think me a liar as well as a whore?"

When he flinched and turned to face her, she saw enough pain in his eyes to mirror her own, and she felt a bolt of triumph. If she could wound him even a little, it was more than she had hoped for.

"You are no liar."

"I spent years working with my father's veterans to be able to defend myself with a knife. I did not want to give up those skills. I wanted to keep them. But those lessons are over now. I stopped my practice before we came to London."

Caroline faced him, walking toward him, her anger mounting her again. Her pain stayed behind its wall of stone.

"I do not know what lies between you and Viscount Carlyle, and I no longer care. But I am not a coward. I gave my word before a man of God to be your wife, and I will keep it. I am bound to you for the rest of my life. I will bear your children. But I will never wear your gifts again."

Caroline ripped the pearl and its chain from her throat and tossed it onto the marble table in front of her. It lay there, glinting in the candlelight, alabaster against cream, a fragment of her lost hope.

"Give it to your mistress, for I will have none of it."

The look on his face drove a stake into her heart. As angry as she was at his betrayal, she wished her words back.

Anthony blinked, staring down at the pearl he had given her with its broken chain, the pearl she had not taken off since she had received it from his hands.

Caroline watched as her husband breathed deeply, trying to gain control of himself. Her words had hurt him, as she had meant them to. But instead of feeling triumph, Caroline felt only shame. His pain did not assuage hers but compounded it.

She wanted to go to him; she wanted to hold him whether he loved her or not. In spite of the bleeding wound in her own chest, she wanted to comfort him. But she knew she could not.

Anthony walked toward her. In the first moment, hope filled her breast to vie with her pain. She thought he would touch her. He would make love to her to clear away the hurt between them, as he always had before. But this time, with Viscount Carlyle and the Countess of Devonshire standing between them, she was not sure she would even be able to feel desire for him anymore.

Though she knew she was a fool, a surge of hope and longing consumed her. It seemed as if she had not felt his arms around her in weeks, though it had been only hours. She hoped his touch might heal her, and hers might heal him.

He did not touch her. Instead, he stopped by the marble table and scooped up the necklace she had thrown down.

Caroline's heart seized. She bit her lip until blood came, so she would not cry out in pain and falter. He would give that pearl to his mistress or to some other lover she had not yet seen, some woman she did not even know about.

Anthony walked away from her without a backward glance. He stopped by the door long enough to open it, and spoke to her over his shoulder, as if he had resolved not to look at her again.

"The man you danced with, the man who brought you home in a closed carriage, the man you've seen behind my back for God knows how long, is the most contemptible man I have ever known. His pirates burn my ships on the open sea and sink my cargo into the drink if they cannot steal it. He has done all that and worse, so much worse I cannot name it to you. That is who you danced with, not once, but twice, in front of all your betters."

Caroline was shocked at his words. Viscount Carlyle, the man who always seemed to appear when she needed him, the man who always offered her a way to circumvent her husband's strictures. That coincidence no longer seemed an easy one. Might Victor simply have been lying in wait for her all that time, making himself available to her simply to thwart Anthony?

Caroline thought it ridiculous, and she dismissed the idea. Victor was nothing compared to the Countess of Devonshire, no matter how many ships he supposedly had burned. What Angelique had done was sink her marriage, not just for that day, but for all the days to come.

"How was I to know he burns your ships? You never told me that. You never told me anything."

"If you had obeyed me, you would not have needed to know."

They stared at each other across the cavern of their bedroom. She saw nothing in his eyes but coldness. Caroline's sorrow threatened to overwhelm her, her anger feeding her pain until she thought she would lose her breath.

"You will leave for my sister's home in Richmond tomorrow," he said.

In spite of the gaping hole in her heart, in spite of her fury, she wanted to ask him to come with her. Caroline was tempted to throw herself at his feet, to beg him to love her, even if only a little. She felt an overwhelming urge to tell him she would accept any humiliation he served her, she would overlook every mistress he tossed in her face, if only he would touch her again.

Caroline did none of those things. She stayed still and silent, listening as the door closed and locked behind him.

❧

She did not sleep that night. She could not bring herself to lie down on their bed. She wrapped a cashmere blanket around her shoulders and sat in the center of her window seat. The window looked out over the garden behind their townhouse. There were a few winter flowers blooming, but the trees had lost their leaves, standing as forlorn in the cold as she felt. She stayed at the window until the sun came up. That was where Tabby found her.

"My lady, you will catch your death."

Caroline tried to smile, and failed. "I am not so fortunate."

She saw the pity on Tabby's face, and she remembered her pride. She let her lady's maid help her up from where she huddled so far from the fire. Tabby wrapped her in flannel, bringing Caroline close to the hearth. She drank the tea Tabby brought, but she could not bring herself to eat the fruit offered on a silver tray.

For once in her life, Tabby said not a word. She simply untangled the strand of diamonds from Caroline's hair. They glinted in the light of morning, as bright and untarnished as they had been the night before, as if all the horrors at Carlton House and after had never happened.

Tabby helped her dress and packed a portmanteau.

Within the hour, she stood by her husband's traveling chaise. She stood beside the carriage, her hand on the door that bore her husband's crest. She remembered the same crest drawn in diamonds, catching the light against the darkness of Angelique Beauchamp's gown.

Caroline breathed deeply and climbed inside without looking back. She would go to his sister's house until Anthony decided what to do with her. She wondered if Anthony would go to Angelique as soon as his wife was on the road to Richmond, or if he had gone to his mistress already.

Caroline sat quietly in her husband's lacquered carriage as Tabby fussed over her. Her maid arranged the lap robe around Caroline again and again, as if by finding the right way to warm her, she might actually save her mistress from disgrace. But of course, she could not. The damage had been done.

❧

Anthony stood at a window on the third floor of Ravensbrook House and watched her go. He did not move from his place for hours, long after her golden head had disappeared beneath the shelter of the traveling coach, long after the sound of her voice speaking low to give instructions to her maid had faded.

Still, Anthony stood at the window as if she might come back to him, as if somehow he might find a way to make it right. Whatever Victor was, whatever he had done, Anthony blamed himself. He should have found a way to guard her better. He should have told her from the first all of who Carlyle was, to him and to his family.

She had betrayed him as no other woman had ever done, and yet he still wanted her. He sent her away because he could not bear the sight of her face. In a few weeks' time, he might relent and go to her. If not, he might send her back to Shropshire while he stayed in town.

But the fragile peace they had built together, the knowledge they had shared of each other, was gone. He had taken the coward's road because he could not face her or himself. Even now, at the end, he had not told her the truth of what Carlyle had done to him, what that villain had done to his sister. Once more, he had stood on his pride and held his tongue. His pride would make a cold bedfellow.

Chapter 29

Lovers' Knot Cottage, Richmond

CAROLINE ARRIVED AT ANTHONY'S SISTER'S COTTAGE just after noon. The cold had stopped snapping at her fingers in her fur-lined muff, but when she stepped out of the traveling chaise, her breath rose from her lips in clouds of steam.

The cottage was small and snug, with plaster walls trimmed in oak. The oak beams had darkened with age, but the interior of the cottage was whitewashed and perfectly proportioned.

Anne seemed to fit the house as if it had been built for her. Anthony's sister waited for Caroline in the entrance hall, dressed in a bright blue gown covered in a long white apron. She had clearly been in the kitchen before Caroline's arrival and had forgotten to take the apron off. Or perhaps she did not feel the need to stand on formality with family, even family she had not yet met.

Caroline had expected to find some regal Society miss, but Anne was nothing like the creatures Caroline had met the night before at the Prince Regent's ball.

The girl was quiet and so young as to be almost child-like in her slenderness, unlike Anthony in every way save for the black sheen of her hair and the chestnut-brown of her eyes. Those eyes, so fierce and fiery in Anthony, were modest and quiet in the face of his sister. Anne seemed to have a great deal of dignity for a girl of eighteen.

"Good afternoon, Sister." Anne embraced Caroline gently, not as if she were afraid of startling Caroline, but as if she were afraid of being startled herself.

The elderly housekeeper took Caroline's thick traveling cloak, and Anne led her into a tiny sitting room. Tabby went to unpack her trunk while Caroline sat down for the first time with her husband's sister.

"I am sorry I could not come to the wedding," Anne said, her voice so soft and gentle Caroline actually had to lean close to hear the girl at all.

"Oh, think nothing of that," Caroline said, pouring tea from the pot when Anne seemed too flustered to do it herself. "It was a sudden thing. I met Anthony, then married him two days later."

"Indeed," Anne said, taking a meditative sip of her tea. She added neither cream nor sugar but drank it as it was. She seemed fortified by the first taste, for her voice got slightly stronger. "Anthony has always known his own mind."

Caroline did not trust herself to speak of Anthony with even a hint of civility, so she said nothing to that. Her bruised heart responded to his name with a dull ache, which she tried to ignore.

"We missed you at Christmas," Caroline said. "I am sorry you were too ill to come to visit us."

Anne blushed, then turned pale, looking down into her half-empty teacup. "Yes. I was ill. I suppose that is the word for it. My child died in December, you see, December a year ago. I am never able to go anywhere on most occasions, but Christmas is especially difficult for me."

Caroline almost dropped the teapot. This was the first she had ever heard of a child. She wondered who this slip of a girl might have married at such a young age, and how she had managed to get out from under Anthony's thumb long enough to marry at all.

"I am sorry for your loss," Caroline said, the manners her mother spent years drilling into her head coming to her rescue. "I hope your husband at least was able to attend you."

Anne's pallor became even more pronounced. "Did Anthony not tell you?" she asked in a tone so low it was almost a whisper.

Caroline sighed, and after pouring her sister-in-law a second cup, set the teapot aside. "Anthony tells me almost nothing. I am sorry to grieve you by asking foolish questions."

Anne forced herself to face her. Caroline could see the effort it cost her in the line of her jaw, in the tension in her graceful neck. For a long moment, the girl could not speak at all. Caroline abandoned her own teacup and took Anne's hand in her own. "Please, you need not speak of it. I will ask Anthony when next I see him."

If I see him, Caroline thought to herself. But she pushed such thoughts aside, along with the pain lodged above her heart as she held her sister-in-law's hand.

"No," Anne said, gathering her strength. "Anthony has sent you here for a reason. He did not tell me what the reason was in his letter, only that you fell in with bad company, as I once did, and were obliged to come here."

"I fell in with the company he chose for me." Caroline pushed aside her anger which had come to couple with her pain. She forced herself to focus on Anne's face. "My husband and I do not agree on many things."

Anne did not look at her, but she did not grow any paler, either. She took a shaky breath, and all the while Caroline held tight to her hand.

"I was sent here in disgrace," Caroline said. "I would never judge you. Did your husband run away?"

Anne raised her eyes. "I was never married."

The room seemed to tilt beneath her before righting itself. She had heard of such things as a child. Her mother had warned her about such folly throughout her girlhood, though Caroline had rarely heeded her. She had never understood how a girl could be foolish enough to give up so much for so little, her entire life and future, for one moment's pleasure.

Now that she was a woman, now that each night without her husband she woke hungering for his touch, she had a much better idea of how a girl could fall into such a trap and never climb out of it. There were unscrupulous men in the world, and one of them had been Anne's undoing.

"I am so sorry. Forgive me for pressing you. I never know when to hold my tongue." Caroline held tight to Anne's hand when her sister-in-law tried to pull away.

"I tell you I had a child out of wedlock, and you apologize to me?" Anne was so stunned her face went from pale to bright pink in a moment.

"I apologize because I was rude. Forgive me. Let us speak of something else. The state of the roads, perhaps. I found them very dry between here and London. Is that usual for this time of year?"

Anne stared at Caroline for one long moment before covering her face. Caroline leaped to her feet, wringing her hands, though as far as she remembered, she had never wrung her hands in her life. She stood helpless over Anthony's sister, wondering if she should not call for smelling salts. Never having been a weeper herself, she had no idea of what to do with this woman's grief.

Then Anne raised her head from her hands, wiping her eyes, and Caroline saw she was not weeping but laughing.

"Oh merciful, gracious Lord, I cannot remember the last time I laughed like that. No wonder Anthony loves you."

It was Caroline's turn to be shocked. She sat down on the settle, her mind whirling. She caught herself before hope could vanquish her. "No," she said. "Anthony does not love me."

"Of course he does," Anne said. "He sent you here to keep you safe from foul men. He has kept me safe ever since it happened. I know he will keep me safe for the rest of my life."

"You live here, alone, by choice?"

Anne met her eyes, and for once she did not look away. "I do. I am not fit for Society. Here I can be alone and search for peace."

Caroline took her sister-in-law's hand. "I am sorry for the loss of your child."

Anne took a breath to steady herself. Her eyes were dry but for the tears of laughter that still stood in them. She blinked them away. "Thank you. I grieve, but so do many others. I am learning not to feel sorry for myself. I am learning to forgive."

"Forgive whom? The blackguard who abandoned you?"

"Yes," Anne said. "I must forgive Viscount Carlyle, or I will never find peace."

For the second time in less than an hour, Caroline was as dizzy as if she had been caught in a whirlpool. She thought that she might have drowned, if Anne had not caught her hand.

"Viscount Carlyle," Caroline said. "He was your seducer?"

"I thought you knew," Anne said. "That is why Anthony sent you here, to keep you safe from him in the only place he would never look for you: my home."

"Victor is not looking for me," Caroline said.

The haunted look in Anne's eyes made Caroline hold her hand tighter. "I fear him still," she said. "It is good that you are here. Anthony will keep us safe from him. I promise you."

Caroline spent only one night in her sister-in-law's house. Though the cottage was cozy, the food good, and the staff well trained, she could not bear to sit in that house and to think of Victor making love to Anne, only to leave her without marriage, and pregnant, too.

Try as she might to reconcile the man she thought she knew to the man Anne had spoken of, she could not do it. Only one of them could be the true Victor. Caroline thought of Anthony's face when he saw her dancing with that man. She thought of the months Anthony had spent trying in his own clumsy way to keep her safe.

He was a controlling man who wanted power over every aspect of her life. Even a saint like Anne could not have tolerated it. But now that she knew the true reason for it, Caroline felt sick. Why had Anthony never told her? He had treated her as if she were a fool, or worse, his dog that came to heel when he called, a dumb beast that need know nothing.

The worst of it was that he would never forgive her. Whatever Anne said, whatever good intentions Anthony might harbor, the fact remained that she had met secretly with the man he hated most in the world. Now that she knew the depths of Carlyle's perfidy, she also knew Anthony would never forgive her for her association with him. She could not stay in his sister's house and wait for a visit from him that would never come. Anthony would cast her off, he would divorce her, and she could not bear it. She would leave first.

She spent a sleepless night. At dawn Caroline took some food from the kitchen and packed it into a leather saddlebag. She dressed in a pair of too-large breeches smuggled out of the stable, along with a large and dirty wool coat, and thick woolen hose. She strapped her knife to her arm and put her throwing dagger in her boot. She bound her hair into a tight knot and covered it with a cap that kept falling into her eyes.

She knew anyone with eyes in their head would see her for the woman she was. She had grown in the last month, so her breasts were even larger than they once had been. Her hips curved beneath the thick, cheap wool of her stolen breeches. She was not sure she could pass for a boy, but she knew she would try.

When she left the cottage, she snuck away, as she had done once before in her father's house, the day before the wedding. She wore her boy's clothes beneath the loosest of her gowns and slipped away from her lady's maid while Tabby was sitting with Anne, taking her first reading lesson.

Caroline rode away from her sister-in-law's estate with no groom to follow her. A mile away, she stripped off her gown. She looked back only once, down the road she had come.

In the next moment, she raised herself into the saddle and turned Hercules toward York.

Though she was rash, she was not a fool. Caroline knew that by running from his sister's house, she was driving Anthony even farther away. If he did not come for her, at best, she would end up living in her father's house, and then in a cottage on his lands after his death, maintained on a pittance once her father's estates were entailed away. At worst, after her disgrace, her father might not take her back. She would be dishonored and disowned completely, cast out in the world with nothing and no one.

After the first moment, when she turned Hercules down the road toward Yorkshire, she did not let herself think on these things again. She could not think of Anthony, of how much she loved him, of how much she missed him. She would go and see her father. She would feel her mother's arms around her, and for a moment she would pretend to be a child again. She would pretend she did not harbor a woman's pain and a woman's broken heart.

It was her father she called up before her, as he had looked on her wedding day, vital and full of hope, proud of the son-in-law he had chosen. Caroline did not allow herself to think of her father's horror when next they met, now that she had been disgraced and had compounded that disgrace by running away. A woman could not run from her fate. By doing so, she had damned herself, and she knew it.

But Caroline could not wait in Anne's house for Anthony to cast her out of it. She would not stand by while he dallied with his whores in the city, returning to her only when it pleased him, if ever.

Before long, he would come to the certainty that she had not simply been practicing knife play with a man of Viscount Carlyle's choosing, but that Victor had been making love to her for two months behind his back. Caroline shuddered at the thought of Carlyle seducing her as he had seduced Anthony's sister. Her bile rose so fast she almost had to stop Hercules by the side of the road to be sick. She controlled herself, but her breakfast that morning was hard to keep down.

She knew Anthony better now that she also knew his sister. She was sure her imagined lovemaking with the man he hated most on earth would fester in Anthony's soul until he never spoke to her again. After the love she had borne him, in honor of the love she had once hoped he would feel for her, Caroline

Chapter 30

Montague Estates, Yorkshire

CAROLINE RODE FOR THREE DAYS. SHE KEPT TO THE main roads and spoke to no one. She was fortunate, for it did not snow as she traveled. On the first day, an icy, driving rain bit into the skin of her face, but the wool of her stolen coat and scarf kept her warm even when she was wet.

She slept little, only a few hours while on the road. One night, she stopped at an inn, where the stable master took pity on her, giving her shelter for a few coins. She slept in the stall with Hercules, one hand on his bridle, the other on her dagger for fear someone might try to steal him. Hercules slept, standing guard over his mistress. His hooves were deadly and would have dispatched any thief. The grooms were all frightened of him and warned all others away.

Caroline arrived at her father's estate toward the end of the third day. The sun had not yet set, but the sky was overcast, so it was dark already.

As she rode into her father's stable, no one looked

shocked by her boy's attire. They loved her enough to ask no questions and to look the other way.

Martin met her in the stables. He did not stand on ceremony or speak but drew her down from her horse.

Hercules was to be led away for warm oats and a stall full of hay, but not before Caroline threw her arms around his neck.

The horse breathed on her golden hair, his great brown eye looking down on her as if he would speak. She would never have made it home safely if not for him. She patted his neck, feeling stronger as she pulled away.

"You must come inside, my lady, before you catch your death."

She felt faint. She had last eaten at sunset the day before. Martin lifted her in his arms and carried her through the kitchen, up the servants' staircase, as he had carried her when she was a little girl. She tried to relax against him, but his arms felt wrong. They were not Anthony's.

He left her in her old bedroom, and she knew he would send for her mother. The upstairs maid, Mary, arrived almost at once with hot water. The girl helped her to draw off her sodden breeches and coat, and helped her with her high leather boots.

Caroline was warm after her bath. She sat on her childhood bed, dressed in a gown of her mother's that had been taken in. She watched her mother's staff as they carried her old clothes away and as they adjusted her new gown. If she lived to be a hundred, she would never learn to run a household as smoothly as her mother did.

As if summoned by this thought, the baroness appeared in the doorway of Caroline's bedroom. Lady Montague raised one hand, and the servants left as quickly as they had come, not even waiting to hear her speak.

"You have come home."

Caroline wept then, throwing herself into her mother's arms. Lady Montague did not turn away; she did not rail or accuse her; she did not speak at all. Instead, she wrapped her arms around her daughter and caressed her hair.

Caroline thought she might be ill she wept so hard, but she had not eaten in a day, so she was not sick. She blew her nose loudly, telling the tale of her disgrace, of the party at Carlton House. She spoke to her mother of her husband's mistress and of her odd friendship with Viscount Carlyle. She did not speak of Anne at all, for that story was not her secret to tell.

Lady Montague listened without a word, all the while stroking her daughter's hair. When she came to the end of her tale, Caroline looked at her mother.

"He will never have me back."

The baroness waved one hand, dismissing her daughter's words, but she stayed silent. Caroline could see her mother's mind working behind the blank mask of her face, but she could not see where her thoughts were tending.

"When he found you with that man...when he found you alone together, he did not call for the magistrate?"

"No, Mother."

"Nor witnesses, though they were close at hand?"

"No, Mother. There was only him, Viscount Carlyle, and I."

"Yes. So you say."

Lady Montague was silent a while longer, and Caroline felt the first stirring of hope. For though her mother loved her, she was not a sentimental woman. If all were lost and Caroline's honor with it, she would already have called for her father. But she did not. Instead, she sat. And thought.

"You must rest," her mother said at last. "You must sleep. It is not good for the baby."

"I am not with child," Caroline said.

"Of course you are. Why else would you behave with no sense of propriety or duty? Women always run mad when they are breeding. I always did, and your father had to stay my hand."

Caroline blinked. Her mother never mentioned the other children she had lost, the ones who lay under marble headstones at the back of the parish church.

Lady Montague did not falter or notice her daughter's surprise. She went on with her interrogation. "Have you been ill recently?"

"Yes, but I was upset."

"You have been upset before, but you have never wept or been ill. I birthed you, *ma petite*, you cannot tell me otherwise."

Caroline thought back but could remember no time when she had wept or been sick, but for the last month or so.

"Do you eat more? Sleep more?"

"Yes, *Maman*, but that was brought on by my time in London. I stayed up late a good deal."

"And I suppose London made you gain half a stone, as well?"

Caroline blushed, for her stays had been laced loosely for the last month. She had thought it all the oysters she had been eating.

"No matter. You won't need me to persuade you. We will call your father's doctor from the village. He will tell you."

Lady Montague stood to go, but Caroline grabbed her hand.

"Mother, I am still ruined, whatever the doctor says."

"What nonsense! You are a Montague. You are not ruined. You are visiting your family. Your father has been ill, and your husband was kind enough to let you to attend him at his bedside. I will say as much in the letter I will write this instant."

"*Maman*, it will take at least three days for a letter to reach Anthony."

"If we sent it by courier, yes. But I will send it by carrier pigeon. We keep a man in London. He will deliver it to your husband."

Caroline had thought pigeons were used only by the army in time of war. She saw then that for all her calm, for all her certainty, her mother was well aware of the gravity of her daughter's plight. Lady Montague also had the situation in hand.

"We will invite your husband to stay, then return to the city with you both for Easter."

"He will not come," Caroline said.

Lady Montague stood to leave, looking down on her daughter with compassion, her eyes soft for the first time since she had heard Caroline's story. All calculation done, she had time to be kind.

"If he did not cast you aside that very night, if

he did not call for the magistrate then and there to witness your disgrace, he never will. He loves you, God help him."

"He does not," Caroline said. "He loves her."

Olivia dismissed Anthony's mistress with another wave of her bejeweled hand.

"Daughter, if you were in your right mind, you would see how foolish that is. If he had loved her, he would have rid himself of you when he had the chance. If he chose her over you, he would not care what you did or where you went. As it is, I have no doubt he is tearing his hair out in the city, searching for you, thinking you dead or worse. If that does not cure him of his taste for his mistress, nothing will."

Lady Montague moved to the door, ringing the bell for food to be brought. "Remember this well, Daughter, for the time when your mind returns to you and you have the wit to heed it. Marriage is about the exchange and protection of property. Mistresses come and go, but property is forever."

The baroness left then to write her letter as Mary arrived with bread and meat, and a pitcher of watered wine. Caroline sat on her childhood bed, her mother's words ringing in her ears.

She knew her mother was wrong. What had passed between her and Anthony went beyond property, beyond money for her father's debts and an heir for his estates and title. But that her mother would see her marriage so simply, as a business transaction that could be tallied on one page, made Caroline laugh for the first time in days. Tension slid from her shoulders as she ate the good hot food Mary had brought. She was in her mother's hands now. No one discounted the word of Lady Montague. Perhaps she might even make Anthony obey her.

Chapter 31

Carlyle House, London

ANTHONY DID NOT SLEEP FOR THREE DAYS. HIS
steward in Richmond sent word immediately when
his wife disappeared. The grooms found only her
gown, discarded in some weeds by the roadside. The
thought made him sick.

He did not go to the country, for he had no doubt
who had taken her. He sent his people out into the
city to find her. They sought her everywhere Carlyle
might have taken her, giving bribes out down by
the docks, combing the city itself. Anthony called in
every favor owed him and spent more gold than he
had spent on the last of his ships that had sailed out of
port. Still, for three days and nights, he found nothing.

On the third day, he went to Carlyle.

It was early morning, but the sun had risen well
above the horizon. He did not want it said that
he came upon Victor unawares, in the dark, like a
thief or a coward. He came unarmed, and the front
door opened for him. Victor's butler gave no sign of

recognition, but he did not make Anthony wait in the hall or in the drawing room.

Almost as if Victor had known he was coming, Anthony was led upstairs to the viscount's private chambers. The butler opened the door to a small sitting room. A fire burned cheerfully in the grate, giving off warmth and comfort. Victor sat in his velvet dressing gown, slippers on his feet, a basket of pastry at his elbow, a cup of coffee in his hands.

"Lost your wife, have you?"

"Where is she?" Anthony asked, working hard to keep his voice even.

"So," Victor said, "you've come to beg for her life."

Anthony did not flinch but met the cold eyes of his enemy. "I have."

Victor laughed, lifting his coffee to his lips. "I don't have her, Anthony. If I had her, we would not be talking."

"Where have you sent her then? Has she been sold?"

"Good God, man. You give me too much credit."

"Or too little."

The voice of Angelique came to Anthony's ears, low and sweet, like the sound of water on stone. He thought it was his sleeplessness that made him hear her voice. When he turned, she was standing in the doorway in her royal-blue dressing gown, the silk gown he had given her because that shade of blue went so well with her eyes.

The sting of betrayal was sharp. Angelique had taken Victor as her lover, then. After the first moment, Anthony found he did not care. All he could think of was finding Caroline.

"Where is she?" he asked.

"Leave us, Victor. Please," Angelique said.

Anthony watched Victor soften under her gaze. He did not weaken, for he kept one eye on Anthony, but he went to her and kissed her deeply, as if she were a well he would draw from, as if he could never get enough.

"My footmen are in the hall, love, if you have need of them," Victor said as he left the room.

Anthony shook with frustration. Every hour that passed made it more likely he would never see Caroline again. Every hour the sun came closer to setting once more, whoever had stolen her would have taken her that much farther from him.

He could not think of her dead, her long blond hair trailing in the water of the Thames. He would let go of everything he had, of everything he had ever known, even his deep and abiding hatred for Carlyle, if only he might see her again.

He shut off those thoughts before they consumed him. When he opened his eyes again, he saw Angelique standing by, watching him.

"You truly don't know where she is?" Angelique asked.

"She has been gone three days. I have paid out a river of gold, and there is no word of her."

"She's worth gold to you then?"

"She's worth my life."

"You would give your life for hers?"

He spoke without thought. "Gladly."

They stood in silence. Words had never been their strong suit. Always before, they had fallen into bed and afterwards talked politics over a glass of wine. But never had they spoken of deeper matters, of emotion. As they stood apart now, virtual strangers, Anthony wondered why he had never seen the difference. Why laughter and wine and sex in the dark had always been enough, until Caroline.

"I am sorry, Angelique, for the way I ended it."

"Do not be. It was I who ended it between us, and now I have taken another lover. You need no longer concern yourself over me."

Angelique reached into the pocket of her dressing gown and drew out a black pearl on a long silver chain. She handed it to him.

"I return this now. I should not have accepted it."

The pearl and chain were cold in his hand. All he could think of was the alabaster pearl his wife had cast back in his face and how different this pearl was. The alabaster pearl had lain in his hand the night he had given it to Caroline and had pierced his heart. This one was just a bit of sand with metal woven through it.

Anthony met the eyes of his mistress, and she smiled at him. "So you see how much you love her, when you compare her with me?"

"Yes."

He had always been honest with her, and he was honest still. He thought his answer would cut her, would pierce her and make her bleed so even he would be able to see it in her face.

But instead, a lightness came upon her, almost relief, though that relief was mixed with envy and pain. "You never loved me, did you?"

She had never asked that question before, in all the years they had been together. He saw now it was not her pride she had been fighting for. He felt regret come to claim him, though he had little room for it. All he could think of was his wife and of how he had failed her.

"I cared for you," he said. "But it is not the same."

Angelique laughed then, and her laughter was not bitter. He could hear the regret in her voice for the years she had wasted, throwing herself away on a man who could give her pleasure but never love. When she stopped laughing, she met his eyes. It was as if she was seeing him from a great distance, as if she was truly seeing him for the first time. He saw affection in her face and a little hope. For once, that hope had nothing to do with him.

"Anthony, your wife is still a child. She has gone home to her mother."

Chapter 32

Montague Estates, Yorkshire

CAROLINE SAT NEXT TO THE FIRE IN HER MOTHER'S sitting room, dozing on a cushioned settee, the book in her lap forgotten. She could not focus on the words.

The fire burned sweet apple wood. The sound of the flames lulled her into a sense of peace. She was tired from her visit that morning with her father's physician.

Her mother had told her the truth when she said Caroline was with child. The doctor said the baby would come in late summer, that she must eat well and rest to keep the baby safe and healthy for her husband. She did not laugh in his face, though she wanted to. She did not tell him she was in disgrace.

Her mother had stayed in the room with her during the examination. She had made certain Caroline said nothing but the politest of thanks. Caroline had listened to the doctor's words as if he spoke of someone else. She could not feel happy about the baby, but she was grateful her ride north on wintry roads had done the child no harm. She could not truly conceive of such a change in her life. She wanted to tell Anthony about it, but of course, he was not there. She missed him more than she would have thought possible even a week before. The news of the baby to come simply made her miss him more.

As she sat alone that afternoon, she longed for Tabby's chatter. Her mother's servants were well trained, but they could not replace her own lady's maid, her own little family.

A cup of tea sat beside her on a marble table, growing cold in its delicate china cup. She had promised her mother she would finish it, but she had not. It sat there, accusing her, and she felt in yet another way inadequate.

"You are unhappy."

Anthony's voice sounded like something out of a dream. At first she did not trust her ears, until she turned and saw him standing in the doorway.

Her throat closed, and any words she might have spoken were swallowed in her attempt to clear it. Caroline stared at him, taking in his beauty, the stubble of his beard where he had not shaved in days, the dark pools of his eyes, the line of his body as he leaned against the doorjamb of her mother's sitting room.

He wore a midnight-blue coat covered by his greatcoat of black. His black trousers were tight, revealing the strong muscles of his thighs. His calves were encased in black leather boots. He was covered from head to foot in the dust of the road. She knew if she were to step close to him, he would still smell of sweetness and spice.

The sight of him made her want to weep.

So she turned from him and looked once more into the fire. The sound of the crackling fire still reached her ears, but it no longer soothed her. The pain of his nearness was like a knife in her lungs, draining her breath. When she cleared her throat, she still could not speak.

Anthony closed the door quietly. He came to sit beside her on the delicate settee.

"I am glad you are safe."

"I left you," she said in almost the same instant.

She looked up and met his eyes, but she had to look away. His beauty hurt her too much.

Anthony reached out and gently took her hand, as if it were made of spun glass and might break at his touch. She looked down at her small hand in his large one, feeling the heat of his body warm her.

He had come to her, just as her mother said he would. He had come, and he had not cursed her. For the first time in over a week, she felt a little hope. It was like dawn breaking after a long winter night, a night that lasted so long it seemed light would never come again.

"I left you," she said again to test the light she saw in his eyes.

He did not look away from her. He did not try to evade the question she would not ask. He simply held her hand, and she could feel his weariness in his touch. She wondered how long it had been since he last slept.

"I have found you again."

She knew the words she was supposed to say. She knew she was to beg his forgiveness, to ask him to relent, to tell him she had been a fool and worse. She was supposed to say if he took her back she would obey him without question for the rest of her life. Now that the moment had come, Caroline saw his beauty and the warm light of affection for her in his eyes. She knew she could not abase herself then or ever, not even for him.

"I love you," she said. "I will love you all my life. But I cannot love you if you also love her."

Anthony smiled, and at first she thought he was mocking her. Caroline stood, her cashmere lap robe falling to the carpet. She shook with fury, even after a week of misery, a week of pain and remorse that should have killed her anger and buried it forever. Now her temper rose, and she wanted to strike the mockery from his face.

His smile died when he saw her anger. Anthony caught her hand in his, so she could not leave him. Still he did not speak. Instead, he pressed his head against her hand, laying his forehead in her palm.

"She is gone," he said. "I do not love her. I never loved her. I have not touched her since you and I first met."

Caroline stood staring at him, at war with herself. Hope danced in her heart like a child, shrieking for her to relent, telling her she had been a fool, that he had loved her always, that he belonged to her and to no other. Caroline listened to this hope, but she did not heed it. Not yet.

"You gave her the same pearl you gave me," she said. "How can I believe you?"

He reached into the bag at his belt and drew out the black pearl. Caroline flinched to see it, but he pressed it into her hand. "She gave it back."

"Why?" Tears burned in Caroline's eyes. Her remembered humiliation threatened to undo her, to close her heart.

Then her husband spoke once more, and at last, she heeded him. "Once she knew I did not love her, she would not keep it. But it would not have mattered if she had wanted it, if she had wanted me. You are the only woman I want."

"What about Victor?" she asked. "He never touched me."

"I know that well. I saw you draw your blade on him."

"Have you forgiven me then?"

Her husband looked into her eyes. "I should have told you who he was to me, all of it, as soon as we met him in Pembroke's house. I will not lie to you by omission again. Our lives are too short to let the likes of Carlyle stand between us."

Caroline sat down heavily on her mother's settee, letting the black pearl fall from her grasp and roll away. Anthony picked it up again, and her with it, raising her up as if she weighed nothing.

"You will take me home?"

"I will take you home, if you will have me."

He had not said he loved her. Caroline longed for those simple words the way a starving man longs for bread. But she would not pine for them. She would take what he offered and be grateful for it. She loved him enough for both of them.

She kissed him. His skin was salty-sweet under her lips. She licked at his throat, and she heard him groan.

Caroline laughed then and bit his throat gently, like a kitten. Anthony made no sound then, but he did not let her go. Instead, he set her down and held her tight against him with one arm as he opened the door to the hallway with the other.

Caroline thought he would simply take her hand as he led her upstairs to her bedroom, but he did not. He slipped his arm behind her knees again, cradled her close, and carried her up the grand staircase to her room, heedless of the housemaids and the footmen standing by.

She clung to him. She pressed her lips to his throat and then his jaw, to see if he might lose his step, but he never faltered. She pressed her breasts against him, where the fullness of pregnancy had made them softer and more sensitive. She moaned a little then, but Anthony did not hesitate. Caroline wondered for a moment if he did not notice her desire, but when her bedroom door was closed behind them, he set her on her feet and devoured her lips with his.

"Never leave me again," he said, his voice hoarse with longing, his lips like firebrands on the delicate skin of her throat. He had not spoken of love, but Caroline was sure she felt it in the desperation of his touch, that she heard it in the longing of his voice.

"I will never leave you again," she said.

"Swear it."

"I swear."

He ripped her gown then, not bothering with the hooks and ties that bound her bodice. Her stays came off next, falling away easily in his hands, for they were not tightly laced. Her shift was next. Its soft lawn gave him purchase against her heated flesh. He did not rip that layer away, but lingered over the curves of her body beneath its softness. After his hands ran over her breasts, cupping one in each palm, weighing them, he drew the shift off and over her head in one smooth motion.

Caroline was left in her stockings and shoes. Anthony drew a second pearl from his pocket, this one alabaster. The gold chain had been mended, and he clasped it around her neck, smoothing the gold until the pearl lay warm between her breasts.

Anthony picked her up again, as if he was afraid she might escape his grasp, as if he let go of her even for a moment, she might melt away into the shadows of the late afternoon. The fire burned in the grate in her bedroom, casting warmth that did not quite reach the folds of her bed. Anthony laid her down across her dark green coverlet, pressing her into the feather mattress until all she could feel was softness at her back and the hard, unyielding pressure of his body on hers.

She tasted the desperation in his kisses as Anthony pressed his lips again and again against hers. He plundered the recesses of her mouth, caressing her with his tongue, biting her lower lip gently when she tried to pull away.

He came up for breath, and Caroline said, "I love you."

Anthony did not rise to draw off his clothes but freed his erection from the tight trousers he wore. He drove himself into her, and she gasped, crying out from the suddenness of the pleasure. She had feared she might never feel his touch again. Caroline reveled in him as Anthony drew her legs up to circle his waist. He drove into her again and again until he was sated.

Her own pleasure passed, and Caroline trembled beneath him, clinging to her husband as if he was her last link to life on earth. "I love you, Anthony," she said again. She did not expect him to respond. He had just told her he loved her with his desperation, with the way he clutched her body close as if he would never let her go.

So Caroline was shocked to the core of her soul when Anthony spoke as if murmuring a prayer, his voice so soft she almost could not hear him. "I love you, Caroline. I have always loved you. I will always love you. I can never lose you again."

Tears formed in her eyes, and for once in her life she did not blink them away. Caroline smiled as tears of joy slid down her temples and into her hair.

"You did not lose me, Anthony. And you never will."

೫

Lady Montague told her husband that night at dinner that Lord Ravensbrook was exhausted from his long journey and Caroline attended him in their room. It was just as well the baroness agreed to this fiction, for once the doors were closed behind them, Anthony did not let his wife out of bed again, claiming the cold creeping along the floor would chill her bare feet. When she offered to put on slippers, he set them out of her reach, along with her dressing gown, so she had to stay in bed with only the sable he had brought to keep her warm.

"You left this behind at Carlton House," was all he said as he wrapped the fur around her naked body.

"I am sorry, Anthony. I was in a hurry."

He took her hand in his and pressed his lips to her palm. "We will never speak of it again."

He brought candles close to the bed so the room was brightened by their light and that of the fire. He warmed spiced wine for her and fed her bits of bread and mutton and cheese until she was too full to move. She lay back on the pillows, exhausted from lovemaking and from the delicious food from her mother's kitchen.

"I am homesick, my lord. When will you take me back to Shropshire?"

"We will be in London for Easter. Your mother and father are coming with us. We'll go home after that."

"I want to go to St. Paul's again, before I get too fat."

Anthony laughed and pressed his lips to her still-flat belly. "You don't eat enough to worry about getting fat, Caroline."

She smiled at him and saw he still had not guessed her secret. And she was glad, for until that moment, she had wondered if her mother had told him the news. Part of her heart had feared the child was the real reason he had taken her back. Now as he lay against her body, drowsing with his head in her lap, his breathing low and even, she saw he loved her for herself alone, and would, all the days of his life.

"Husband, I have something more to tell you."

"Can it wait until morning, my love? I rode three days to get here and then rode you for two hours after. I have told you, I am an old man, and I need my rest."

"I have waited too long already."

Caroline felt him come fully awake beside her, his body tensing as if waiting for a blow. She knew he thought she meant to speak of his mistress, or of Viscount Carlyle. But she would never mention that woman or that villain ever again.

"We're going to have a baby," she said.

At first she thought he had not heard her, for he did not move. He lay tense beside her, the lines of his beautiful body drawn up as if in pain.

But after a long moment, Anthony sat up slowly and drew her carefully toward him, pushing her long golden hair back from her face.

"You bear my child."

"The doctor says he's due in about seven months."

Anthony did not speak but looked at her, his chestnut eyes staring into hers as if he were looking for her soul. Whatever he sought, he found, for he sank down against her, his lips on hers. He did not make love to her again that night but held her close to his heart and did not release her until morning.

Caroline spent a sleepless night tucked in her husband's arms. Sleep eluded her this time because she was so happy. She lay beside her husband, watching as the fire died down, listening to his deep, even breaths. Even after her mother's servants had come into the room to stoke the fire in the morning and to set out a pot of tea, Anthony clutched her close in his sleep behind the warm, bright curtains of their bed.

ACT IV

"I will give thee a kiss. Now pray thee, love, stay."

The Taming of the Shrew
Act 5, Scene 1

Epilogue

ANTHONY FREDERICK CARRINGTON SLEPT IN THE ARMS of his nurse as the family stepped out of St. Paul's Cathedral on the day of his christening. Caroline leaned over and kissed him. Anthony Frederick, called Freddie by his mother, woke and looked up at her with his deep blue eyes. He was nine months old, with more charm than was good for his mother's heart.

It was too cool to have the baby out in the wind, so Caroline sent him home with his nurse, letting them take the carriage. John the coachman would come back for them in an hour.

She turned to Anthony, and he took her hand, sending the footmen back to his house with his son, save for two, whom he kept by them. They walked together, both wrapped in heavy cloaks, for May was cool on the sun-drenched banks of the River Thames. The sun was not warm in spite of its light, and

Caroline wondered why her husband lingered there when they had a fire at home worth tending.

Anthony took her hand and led her carefully along the path to the riverbank. He led her onto the Ravensbrook docks, where a ship was moored, ready to sail with the tide.

Caroline stood looking at the great ship, wondering which port it would see next. The lost hunger of her youth returned to her in that moment. Though she was well loved at home, and well content with her husband and her son, a part of her longed to see the great, unknown world, cities and places beyond her province. She sighed, and Anthony chuckled to hear it.

"Do you see what she is named?"

She raised one gloved hand to shield her eyes from the glare, and then she saw it written in gilded script across the bow. A beautiful mermaid rode the prow of that ship, with maple brown eyes and long golden hair.

"The *Lady Caroline*," she said.

Anthony took her hand in his and led her onto the deck, where the sailors worked overhead, preparing the ship to sail with the evening tide. Perched high, Caroline could see the great river stretch before her. She wanted to tell Anthony to cast off then, so they might go wherever the tide would take them. But she knew her duty, and she did not speak.

As if he read her thoughts, as if he knew her mind already, Anthony wrapped his arms around her and drew her back against his chest. They stood together looking out over the great seaway of London, of the

Empire and the world. Anthony spoke softly, his lips close by her ear.

"One day, when Freddie is bigger, we will sail to all the cities you dream of, Caroline. We will go to Paris and to Rome, to Athens, even to Istanbul, if you desire it."

"Won't that be dangerous?" she asked, breathless with longing for a future she could almost see.

"Yes. But when have you ever been afraid of anything?"

Caroline said nothing else but turned in his arms and pressed her lips to his. Anthony kissed her, long and deep, but soon he drew back, for the eyes of all his crew were on them. When they returned to the quayside, John the coachman was waiting to take them home.

They went upstairs together, though her parents waited for them in the drawing room. Pembroke, their son's godfather, was trying to entertain Lord and Lady Montague with his stories and was no doubt failing. Anthony and Caroline could not bear to return to their guests yet, and they went to change their clothes from the christening. As they climbed the staircase, Anthony took her by the hand and drew her to the third floor, and into the empty ballroom.

"Shall we dance, my lord? There is no music."

Anthony laughed, pulling her close, resting his hands on her hips. "There is always music when you are with me, Caroline."

He kissed her then, and she lost herself for one long, delicious moment. She was about to tell him to take her to their bedroom when he stepped back from her and led her by the hand deeper into the shadows of the grand room.

"Why are we here, my love? We have only a few hours before dinner."

"I know that, Caroline. I have another surprise for you."

"Two in one day? My lord, you are too generous. What will this one be? An orchestra to play for us alone?"

"No, love. This."

He brought her to stand before the sideboard, which was empty but for a large mahogany case. Caroline frowned, puzzled, until he opened the lid.

"Matching rapiers," she said, her reverent words a breathless whisper.

"Dueling swords, my love. From Spain."

She raised the smallest one with care, pleased to find the balance perfect. The suppleness of the blade cut the air, and the leather handle fit her palm as if it were meant to be there.

"I had them made for us. Since you are determined to continue your fencing practice, I would rather you practice with me."

"The blades are blunted," she said.

"As they should be, so we cannot draw blood, even by accident."

She laid the sword carefully in its mahogany case, running her fingers lightly over the second blade, the one Anthony would wield.

"Have I tamed you then?" she asked, her voice rough with emotion she tried to disguise. She failed. Anthony drew her close.

"I suppose we will have to live with each other as we are, Caroline."

"We will fight," she said.

"We will spar," he answered. "But I think, if we take care, we will never draw blood again."

She pressed herself against him, and finally he led her to their bedroom, where she found one last surprise waiting for her.

On their bed lay a hundred pearls of every shape and size, every color of cream she could imagine, every shade of alabaster and white and taupe. Caroline stood over them, staring, and Anthony watched her face.

"A ship and pearls and a sword. Am I dreaming, Anthony?"

"If you are dreaming, love, then so am I. And I have no desire to wake."

"Am I to choose from among them? They are so beautiful..."

She fingered the two pearls nestled between her breasts, the one he had given her when they first wed and the second he had given her on the birth of their son.

"No, Wife. You will not choose."

Before she could speak, Anthony drew her down onto the bed. The pearls rolled toward her where the mattress dipped, and scattered across her lap, against the deep russet of her gown.

"They are all yours, if you will have them."

Caroline blinked her tears away and pressed herself against him, the pearls forgotten. "I do not need jewels, Anthony. I love you for yourself."

"I know. That's why I give them to you."

They made love, slipping and sliding over the wealth

of pearls. They were late for dinner, and they missed tea altogether. For months after that, Tabby found pearls everywhere, along the floor, tucked next to the headboard, and under the mattress. Whatever Tabby found after the first month, Caroline let her keep.

Acknowledgments

I⊤ ⊤AKES MORE ⊤HAN ONE WOMAN A⊤ HER COMPU⊤ER to make a book come to life. There are many people to thank, but I have to begin with the amazing staff at Sourcebooks. From the editing to the marketing team to the cover art, they have done a stellar job. Without my fabulous editor, Leah Hultenschmidt, her patience, her sense of humor, and her eagle eye, I would be nowhere. Thank you also to Aubrey Poole, whose kind early notes helped me begin to bring this novel to the place it needed to be.

As always, my family has supported me throughout the process of writing this novel and throughout my life. Thank you to Karen and Carl English for their constant support and overwhelming love. Thank you to my brother, Barry English, who has always stayed squarely in my corner.

I must thank the many friends and early readers who have lived with my writing since day one. Thank you LaDonna Lindgren and Laura Creasy for reading this novel in early drafts. Thank you Amy and Troy Pierce for giving me a quiet place to write more times than

I can count, and moral support always. Thank you Trilby Shier, Marianne and Chris Nubel, Vena and Ron Miller, for your constant love and support. And thank you to my fantastic agent, Margaret O'Connor, who is as much a friend as she is an agent.

And I thank each one of you who has picked up this book. I hope Caroline and her Anthony thrill you half as much as they have thrilled me.